GRIM'S DELIGHT

THE NEW PROTECTORATE SYNDICATE
BOOK 1

ABIGAIL KELLY

NEW PROTECTORATE BOOK LIST

Glow - novella
Astray - novella
Weathering - novella
Consort's Glory - novel
Empire - novella
Courtship's Conquest - novel
Strike - novella
Vital - novella
Burden's Bonds - novel
Kohl - holiday novella
Faraway - novella
Sanguine - novella
Devotion's Covenant novel
Valor's Flight - novel

The United Territories and Allies

ESTABLISHED 1917

COVEN COLLECTIVE

THE DRAAKONRIIK

THE ORCLIND

THE NEUTRAL ZONE

SHIFTER ALLIANCE

ELVISH PROTECTORATE

The United Territories and Allies
Current borders (2044) established
in the 1917 Peace Charter.

Member territories share a common
currency and many laws, but
maintain individual sovereignty. Each
territory holds representation in the
UTA Congress and Court, found in
the United Neutral Zone.

VAMPIRE BASICS AND YOU

A NEW READER'S GUIDE TO VAMPIRES, PROVIDED BY SOLBOURNE GENERAL HOSPITAL FOR THE EDUCATION OF THE PUBLIC (UPDATED JULY 2048):

WHAT IS A VAMPIRE?

A vampire is a person infected with a virus that causes human beings to feed exclusively on blood. They have sharp, hollow incisors, a venom gland in the roof of their mouth, and a reflective lens in the backs of their eyes called a tapetum lucidum. Vampires are nocturnal and can die of sun exposure under extreme circumstances.

WHO CAN GET VAMPIRISM?

Only humans can carry the virus, and those without magic (arrants) are particularly susceptible. Beings like elves, dragons, and shifters cannot be infected. In rare cases, however, they can have vampiric offspring.

CAN I GET THE VIRUS?

As of a 2045 census, the United Territories and Allies Health Organization reports that 80% of new vampires are born rather than infected. Except in very rare cases, those born with it have one vampire parent and one non-vampire parent.

HOW CAN SOMEONE GET THE VIRUS?

Though the number of infections is low, they do happen. The most common causes of infection are voluntary exchange of blood, wherein a person intentionally infects themselves, and exposure via accidents. A significant infusion of infected blood is necessary to contract the virus. However, the rate of infection even under those circumstances is roughly 25%.

CAN A VAMPIRE BITE KILL?

Death or serious injury from a vampire bite is extremely uncommon. Vampire fangs are designed to inject venom and open small holes to extract blood, not tear or slice. The vampiric stomach at capacity is only able to hold less than a pint of blood at any given time, which is not enough to harm an average adult.

WHAT IS VAMPIRE VENOM?

All vampires have venom, but it's only harmful to other vampires. Their venom is adapted to soothe the discomfort of a bite, provide an anticoagulant for feeding, and create a mild stimulant effect for relaxation. It is also vital to the process of bonding with a mate and creating offspring. Regular injections of venom serve three purposes:

1. Building a mate bond
2. Changing the receiver's body chemistry to allow for procreation

3. Making a mate inaccessible to other vampires, as their blood will become toxic

IS THERE ANY RISK ASSOCIATED WITH VENOM?

Vampire venom is safe, but sudden withdrawal from regular injections can cause acute discomfort. This includes fevers, vomiting, muscle cramps, lack of appetite, insomnia, extreme irritability, elevated blood pressure, and dizziness. There's no definitive number of injections it takes to get to the point where one will experience withdrawal, but studies have suggested it is between 6 and 10.

CAN VAMPIRES FEED ON EACH OTHER?

Vampires can only feed on each other when one of them falls into the venom neutral category.

WHAT IS A VENOM NEUTRAL VAMPIRE?

While the vast majority of vampires have blood and venom toxic to each other, a very small sub-group can not only feed and be fed on, but they can carry a fellow vampire's offspring to term. This is because their venom lacks poisonous qualities. Research suggests there is a connection between blood types and venom expression, but more study is needed.

I'VE HEARD THE NAME BLOOD BRIDE BEFORE. WHAT DOES IT MEAN?

The term blood bride has historically been used to refer to venom neutral vampires before serious scientific inquiry into the phenomenon. In vampire culture, it is an extremely significant concept strongly tied to the importance of family lines and worship of the goddess Grim. However, modern institutions like Solbourne General Hospital and the UTAHO strongly prefer the use of *venom neutral,* as it does not imply that the patient's title is defined by their ability to mate and that all are female, as both ideas are untrue.

WHERE DO VAMPIRES LIVE?

Vampires can be found anywhere in the UTA, but they are most concentrated in the Neutral Zone (colloquially known as the New Zone), which encompasses most of Maryland, Virginia, Tennessee, Arkansas, and North Carolina. This strip of land was declared neutral from all territorial claims after the Great War and the Peace Charter in 1917, which established the United Territories and Allies as it is currently known. Though not officially controlled by any one faction, it is generally considered vampire territory.

WHAT GODS DO VAMPIRES WORSHIP?

Vampires can worship any god of the nine in the pantheon, but most tend to focus on Grim, the goddess of death and mercy, who they believe is their creator.

FOR MORE INFORMATION, PLEASE SEE THE GLOSSARY AT THE BACK OF THIS BOOK.

PROLOGUE

A NOTE FROM A LIBRARIAN AT THE UNITED CONGRESS LIBRARY: THE following spotlighted excerpt comes from one of the first recorded scientific studies into the subject of vampiric blood brides, who have the unique ability to mate with their own kind. It is a jewel in our collection and can be viewed upon special request by members of the public or for research purposes.

A TREATISE ON GRIM'S DELIGHT, THE GIFT AND THE BANE, GIVEN BY THE MERCIFUL ONE HERSELF TO HER MOST CHERISHED CHILDREN THROUGH THE TRANSFERENCE OF LIFESBLOOD AND ENERGY, AS UNDERSTOOD BY THIS HONORED AUTHOR, DOCTOR RAMSFIELD TURNER OF THE MOST ESTEEMED ACADEMY OF ALCHEMICAL AND MAGICAL RESEARCH OF BOSTON

First edition published 1793 by Bramson & Daughters Publishing House of Boston, bequeathed by private collector to the United Congress Library in December 1999. It is the only copy believed to have survived the Great War.

INTRODUCTION

It is a known fact among the learned of the subject that Grim, our most beloved goddess of Death and Mercy, has bestowed her favor on vampires.

This favor began when she created them from the ill and the most wretched of the world; those beings so beyond hope that only Death's cold fingers could reach their hearts. In her wisdom, the goddess did not take them to the underworld, where succor is found on the riverbank and justice in the mud, where sinners gasp for air for all eternity. Rather, she returned the wretched to life with a kiss, and so the first vampires were born, their forms renewed and their vitality forever altered by the venom that coursed through their veins.

And so the first vampires wandered, seeking a return to the lives and homes they left behind. It was the grief of many to discover doors shut and families beyond reaching. Such was their fear of vampires, their strangeness and their nocturnal lives, that they could no longer bear to accept those they had so dearly missed.

When their families refused them, believing them to be vile monsters, many turned to creating their own through the sharing of Grim's Gift. A father or mother might be made by this exchange, whereby a significant portion of blood is donated to a person's veins. These rare children are considered rightful heirs and treated with the due reverence and expectation of a natural-born child of one's body.

Though many vampires tried this method of curing loneliness, most could not endure the pain of repeated failure. When Grim saw her childrens' agony, she bestowed yet another gift: mates whose blood and companionship tether a vampire to this world. She called them *ancora vitae*, commonly shortened to *anchor*, and commanded vampires to cherish them in all ways; for without them, they would surely perish.

It was through these unions that a vampire could sire

offspring, but one of the three ways the Merciful One has allowed her children: through the sharing of lifesblood, the planting of seed with those who are not vampires, and with those rare few of their own kind born with Grim's mercy in them. Unlike the rest of their vampire kin, they possess no deadly venom and their bodies are ripe for breeding. They can feed and be fed on by a fellow vampire, and it is believed that when two vampires create offspring, the child produced of such a union is blessed with extremely powerful blood.

This author has heard them called many names. On the Old Continent, they are commonly referred to by some variation of *donum misericors*, gift of mercy, or *sang béni*, blood blessed. In the territories of the North American continent, they are simply called blood brides.

It is the joining of a vampire and his blood bride that is the concern of this book and the subject that has consumed this author's study for many years. It is the single most unique mating of any in all the world. Its very existence proves the hand of the goddess is upon us, for it cannot be explained by other means.

It is only through divine intervention that two vampires might sustain each other and so it is most appropriate that such a miracle is called Grim's Delight.

UNKNOWN NUMBER

Hello, pet

who is this

Tell me who you think it is

someone I definitely didn't give my number to

You would've. Sadly I didn't have time to convince you when we met

when was that

also, doubtful

We met at the bar

I meet a lot of people at the bar. I probably won't remember you

You'd remember me.

then why don't you jog my memory

You encounter a lot of body bags in your line of work, pretty girl?

ONE

She knew it'd be a shit night.

Dahlia McKnight didn't like to think of herself as superstitious. She much preferred the term *intuitive*. The universe moved in predictable patterns. More than once, her survival had depended on being able to read the signs all around her.

That was why, when she woke up to no message notification, a knot of dread tied itself around the base of her spine and held fast.

It wasn't an unusual occasion, necessarily. There were long stretches — weeks, months — where she heard nothing at all. But something about *this* evening felt off.

It was another bad sign when she stepped into her tiny cubicle of a shower to become the unsuspecting victim of a spray of frigid water. Her yelp was loud enough to draw the attention of her closest neighbor. Though that wasn't hard, considering their bathroom windows faced one another with only a foot gap between them.

"If you trip and die in the shower, I'll put panties on you before I call Patrol," Cecilia informed her, as chipper and helpful as always.

Dahlia danced out of the shower, her teeth clacking, and

snatched a towel off the hook. She didn't care if Cecilia saw her tits — they'd compared sizes when they were thirteen and had synced periods since the damn things started — but she needed the warmth. It didn't matter how warm the weather got. Their apartment building was always freezing.

Kneeling on the toilet, Dahlia pushed the window open a bit more and stuck her head into the strange, dark gap between their apartments. Her best friend's perfume drifted in the musty air.

"My hot water is out again," she groused.

It only took a second for Cecilia's face to appear in her open window. Holding a curling iron in one hand, she pushed up her window with the other. "You wanna use mine? Should be a little bit of warm water left." She paused to squint her dark eyes speculatively. "Wait, are you working tonight? I thought you were off."

"I swapped with Alexa. There's a VIP thing tonight, so I said yes."

"Oh, big tips." Cecilia jammed her thumb over her shoulder. "You don't have a lot of time before opening, but you wanna use my shower?"

Dahlia shook her head and was immediately annoyed by the situation all over again when she felt how only half her hair was wet. She didn't want to talk about how she'd spent half her getting ready time staring at her phone, waiting for her boogeyman to make himself known.

"It's fine. I just wanted to inform you that today is cursed. I can feel it."

Cecilia nodded solemnly. A little bit of the sincerity of the gesture was ruined when she began curling her hair again, but Dahlia could allow it. "That sucks. I have a date in a couple hours. You think I should cancel?"

"It's worth considering."

"Noted. If I get murdered, you get custody of Oyster."

Dahlia wrinkled her nose as she climbed off the toilet. The

salvage operation on her hair and makeup had to start soon or she'd really be up Shit Creek. "I so don't want your dead cat, Cece."

"It's not about what you want," she called back. "It's about familial responsibility, Dahlia! You have to take care of Oyster, discreetly dispose of my sex toys, and for the love of the gods, pick a cute picture of me for them to put on the news feeds. None of that senior photo or embarrassing selfie crap."

Yelling over the roar of her hair dryer, Dahlia complained, "I thought we both agreed I'd die first!"

"That was before you stopped going on dates. I'm on dating apps. My risk of being murdered is much higher than yours now."

"That's dark. Real, but dark." Dahlia tipped her head over and violently blew hot air through her short blonde hair. Scrubbing her fingers through it in a vain attempt to give it a little volume, she argued, "Cece, it's not like you go on dates with criminals. The last guy you had drinks with was a middle school math teacher. And we both work at a vampire bar. I think that makes our mortality risk about equal."

"Ugh, *Jason.*" The sound of hairspray being more than liberally applied came a few seconds before the scent of it drifted across the divide and into Dahlia's bathroom. "I really thought we had fun. I don't understand what happened there."

Personally, Dahlia didn't understand it either. She didn't date because she wasn't willing to risk the life and limb of some poor schmuck who worked in finance, but Cecilia was a different story.

She'd always been the sweet to Dahlia's tart. The pink to her red. The baby to her brat. They'd been thick as thieves since the first day of kindergarten, and despite having seen every single one of Cecilia's most awkward phases and catastrophic fashion choices over the years, Dahlia still thought she was the most beautiful woman in the world.

And *kind.* Fundamentally. Wholly. In all the ways Dahlia had beaten out of her before she ever got a chance to understand what she'd lost.

Cecilia deserved a gorgeous, doting nerd with obscene amounts of money and a high tolerance for pastels, not the milquetoast jerks who kept disappointing her.

Flipping her hair back, Dahlia switched off her blow dryer and scrambled to throw on a halfway decent face of makeup. Patting concealer under her eyes, she said, "I hope Jason gets hit by a bus."

"Nooo. Didn't you hear about the substitute teacher shortage in San Francisco's school district? His untimely death would put a strain on our education system. Let's hope he gets hit by an electric scooter instead. He can still go to work with a broken leg."

Dahlia reached for her eyelash curler and bit back the retort that it might be helpful if Jason did have an accident that took him fully out of commission. Her friend had recently finished her teaching certification and was jockeying for one of those open positions.

Meanwhile, Dahlia drowned in coursework as she clawed her way to the finish line of her business degree. If she could've gotten to the finish line of a better job with a well-placed shove off a curb, she would've done it.

"Face?"

"Face."

They both appeared at their respective windows. Cecilia looked as soft and sparkly as always, with her warm brown skin glowing and her hair curled into gentle waves. Glitter caught the light on her eyelids and her lip gloss was just the right shade of purple-pink. With those doe eyes and soft lips, Dahlia was almost tempted to date Cecilia herself.

"You're wasted on men," she said, nodding sagely.

"As are you, my sexy friend." Cecilia disappeared for a moment before she leaned out the window, her arm stretching to pass along a tube of lipstick. "Here. This is my lucky red. Wear it as a good luck talisman tonight."

"Thank yo— Wait, Cece, this is *my* lipstick!"

"That's why it's lucky," she replied, utterly shameless. "It was free!"

Popping the cap off, Dahlia warned her friend's retreating back, "If you die, I'm gonna leave your sex toys out on your bed for your parents to find. That glow-in-the-dark dildo is going under your pillow. Your mother will think you used it as a night light, you animal!"

"I guess you'll just have to die first after all. Have fun at work!"

There was no time to plot a more immediate revenge for the theft. Dahlia raced around her studio, pulling on her skimpy uniform, grabbing her purse, and shrugging on her coat with impressive speed. There were many serious downsides to her apartment being so close to The Lush, the vampire bar she'd worked at for five years, but she forgot every last one of them whenever she ran late.

The sun was just beginning to set when she wheeled into the back entrance, out of breath but exactly on time.

No one paid her any mind as she stuffed her belongings into her locker. Inputting her code into the lock, she resisted the urge to check her phone again. Tonight was a big night with — hopefully — big tips. Even if it wasn't, she tried very hard not to think about how reliant on her boogeyman she'd become over the years.

She didn't *miss* him. And she definitely wasn't stupid enough to worry about him. She was just used to his constant annoyances. That was all.

Dahlia tried to shove him from her mind as she scrubbed her hands and forearms in the sanitation station. Someone had already turned on the music for the night. The thumping beat bled through the thick walls. She'd never liked it much, but it was easy to tune out after so many years of practice.

Drying her hands under the UV light, she quickly donned the long white gloves they were all required to wear. All vampire bars made their staff wear gloves, but the ones the staff at The Lush wore were one part utility and three parts kink. The length added something special to their uniform, Devon said. As if the low neckline, mesh décolletage, and high hemline weren't enough.

Her lips thinned. Working VIP events meant great tips, but it also meant exposure to her boss. She'd never seen anyone as desperate to schmooze with bigwigs as Devon, which was saying something.

She hadn't known very much about vampires before she took the server position at The Lush. Dahlia would admit she was still pretty ignorant about the finer details, but it only took her a few months to pick up on the fact that there was just one thing in the world they valued more than blood.

Status.

The nebulous ideals of prestige and respect ruled the vampire underworld, all the way from the lowest of the low to the highest rung. She'd seen fights break out over the smallest of perceived infractions and heard stomach-turning rumors about what happened to servers who thought they could survive an entanglement with one or more of the deadly predators.

A week after she started, a server named Jackson got into trouble when he tried dating two different vampires at once. One of the women ended up dead, disemboweled in the restroom, and Jackson never showed up to work again.

Despite abundant cautionary tales, some servers took the job explicitly to find a wealthy vampire to attach themselves to, but it was a very dangerous game. More often than not they got used and dumped before a permanent bond was formed, leaving them to deal with venom withdrawal on their own. On the rare occasions they didn't, there was almost always another vampire in the wings, furious that someone they thought was already their property had been snapped up.

She and Cecilia had learned quickly that surviving their job meant keeping their heads down, giving good service, and never letting a vampire get attached. *Head down, tray up,* they said.

Of course, that only worked with the customers. Management was another story.

Devon hadn't always been the boss. His brother, Duke, was in charge when she was hired. He'd been thoroughly disinterested in the job and left the staff — and patrons — alone, for the most part. It was a sad day for them all when Devon took over.

His pale blue eyes found her immediately when she stepped out onto the floor, her silver tray tucked under her arm. Devon looked at all the servers like they were meat, but he reserved a special sort of intensity for her.

She'd really hoped he'd roll in fashionably late and a little drunk, like he sometimes did. But he was bright-eyed and bushy-tailed that evening, dressed in his tightest white button-down and slacks. His pale blond hair was swept behind his ears and his thin silver nose ring gleamed in the neon lights of the bar.

Dahlia really had no idea what look he was going for. The closest thing she could come up with was *boy band member meets mobster* in all the worst possible ways.

Gesturing with his claws for her and two other servers, he flashed his fangs in a way that was probably supposed to be intimidating. She sucked in a deep breath and prayed for patience.

"Good evening," he drawled, gaze taking a leisurely stroll up and down her body before flicking toward the other servers assigned to the VIP rooftop lounge. "We've got some really important guests here tonight, so I don't need to tell you what'll happen if you fuck up, do I? I want the synth flowing all night — no limit. The most expensive stuff we have."

He was somehow more wound up than usual tonight. Urgency practically oozed out of him when he ordered, "Whatever you have to do to make our guests happy, you do it. No questions asked. Clear?"

They all nodded. There were no rookies in their little VIP crew, which meant that they all knew it was best to keep their mouths shut.

Dismissing them as carelessly as he summoned them, Dahlia was relieved to be free. She didn't make it three steps in her black pumps before she felt him breathing down the back of her neck.

"Hold on a minute, Dahlia," he purred. Devon didn't touch her, but he didn't need to. She knew better than to disobey.

Gritting her teeth, she counted her blessings that he was talking to her in the main bar, where servers and bartenders ran around getting everything ready for opening. "Yes, sir?"

"Stick close to me tonight, okay? I want the prettiest woman by my side." He offered her a slow, sensual smile. It was the same one he'd been giving her for months. Why he still thought it worked on her, she had no idea.

Bracing a hand on the bar behind her, he leaned in as close as he could without touching her. Vampires, like most predators, were picky about scents. But like everything else, they took it to an extreme. A server who smelled like a vampire sold fewer drinks. They hated the scent of each other near their food. It had something to do with the fact that vampire venom was toxic to their own kind, meaning no two people could feed from the same source.

If the bar wanted to sell synth, they needed their servers to smell fresh and unclaimed, which meant Devon had to restrain himself from laying his hands on her.

How long that restraint would last, Dahlia didn't know. Devon had been slowly but surely encroaching on her life since he took over the bar. He texted her at odd hours, demanded to know who she spent her days off with, and she was pretty sure she'd seen him — or one of his men — outside her apartment building more than once.

All the signs pointed to his patience running out. She just hoped it wouldn't happen tonight.

"You know I love having you around," he breathed, too close to her ear, "but I hate seeing you work so hard. When are you going to let me take care of you, baby? If it were up to me, you'd be in my penthouse right now, wanting for nothing."

Her skin crawled. Like all the creeps who'd come before him, he made it sound like he wanted to take care of her, to save her from a life of drudgery and poverty with his sky-high credit limit and mediocre pussy petting. He didn't mention what he'd expect in return: her entire life.

If he'd just been after her blood, she *might* have been able to see the appeal in an arrangement, but when vampires fixed on someone, they never settled for something so simple.

Dahlia had seen a lot of bad relationships, but she didn't need any of their examples to know that letting Devon into her life was a terrible idea. Not that he'd get that far. There was a very real reason she'd stopped dating and it wasn't just her lack of free time.

Devon was an asshole, but she didn't want him dead. Yet.

Putting her tray between them like a shield, she slipped away from the bar. "Doors are open. I better get to the lounge."

Devon let her go with a smug half-smile. "See you there, baby."

TWO

I<small>T WAS IN HER BEST INTEREST TO TUNE OUT EVERYTHING THE</small> important guests said. If it wasn't a drink order, a request for directions to the bathroom, or a shitty compliment that might result in a fat tip, Dahlia let it wash over her in waves.

Anything she learned about the vampire underworld, crime, and politics was strictly involuntary. She'd never admit that she knew the Vance brothers had been dealing in unlisted firearms or that over half the regulars were smugglers, mercenaries, or money launderers — each of them a gristle in the meat grinder known as the vampiric syndicate.

It was important to rinse all that from her brain, or at least appear to have done so, just like she'd been doing since she was a little girl listening to her mother's friends talk about stealing cars and scamming casinos.

She'd perfected the art of the serene, subdued server. Her eyes stayed down and her expression neutral no matter what was said or done around her. Mostly no one noticed her beyond the passing hungry glance, and the really bad guys weren't stupid enough to talk about the top tier confidential stuff in front of waitstaff.

Usually.

There'd been one extremely notable exception, but she tried not to think about that night from three years ago too hard.

Unease tightened that knot in her gut again. Not because she vividly recalled the body bag on the floor and the stench of sour blood that rose from its parted zipper, but for a far more foolish reason. The itch to check her phone made her gloved fingers curl around the edge of her tray.

What's he doing tonight?

Trying to focus without appearing like she was *listening*, Dahlia locked her gaze on the back of Devon's head. A warm breeze ruffled his hair. He was several cups of alcoholic synth-blood deep and it showed. He kept trying to make toasts every few minutes, despite the fact that no one else around the table seemed to be in a particularly celebratory mood.

If anything, the atmosphere in the luxurious rooftop lounge was all business.

There were three distinct groups of vampires spread out across the roof. One was headed by a stern-looking old man she'd heard called Mr. Bowan. The other was the security — Devon's goons and the much more professional-looking people who came with Mr. Bowan.

And of course, there was Devon.

They were waiting on someone, and with every passing minute, Mr. Bowan's severe expression got darker while Devon got drunker.

She'd been ordered to stand behind Devon and be his personal server. Whenever he snapped his fingers, she ran to get him a new bottle of expensive synth. He always offered one to Mr. Bowan, but the old man hadn't touched the elegant glass bottle she'd served him when he came in.

"…so many opportunities here," Devon crowed, waving his bottle in the air. Every once in a while, between his sales pitches and his gulps of synth, he'd absently reach back as if he expected her to be there, ready to be grabbed, but she was always just half a step out of his reach.

Vampires were handsy with their companions. They liked to keep them as close as possible — preferably in their laps — and Devon was drunk enough to no longer care how many bottles she could sell if she reeked of him. It wasn't unusual for him, but every time it happened, she had to remind herself that it wasn't right to sentence a man to death. Even if he was a gross prick.

"The elves don't look down from their towers. There's nothing but money to be made out here if you— if you have the right..." Devon reached back mindlessly again, pawing the air like an animal. *"...connections."*

Dahlia tried to hide her grimace, but she suspected she failed when she accidentally caught Mr. Bowan's eye.

The old man was handsome in a sharp, old money kind of way. His skin was a deep gold, his silver hair artfully styled around his ears and nape. He wore a pinstripe suit that probably cost more than every penny she'd ever earned.

And he looked completely fed up.

"Girl," he snapped, striking the floor with his cane, "come here."

Happy to have an excuse to no longer be in Devon's range, she stood beside his chair and asked, "Can I get you something, sir?"

"No. Stay there," he grunted. He pulled out a cigar from a silver case that was *also* probably worth more than her entire life. Clipping the end with his claws, he muttered, "I just couldn't watch that whelp grab at you any longer. If my anchor were here, he'd tell me to shoot him."

Dahlia had to work very hard to keep her expression neutral. Devon was busy with his drink, but she could never be too careful. Only the gods knew what he'd do if he thought she was gossiping about him. Or worse: laughing at his expense.

Mustering a perfectly inoffensive compliment, she replied, "Your anchor sounds very interesting, sir."

Mr. Bowan shot her a look from under his heavy brows as one of his men leaned over to light his cigar. She was pretty sure it was an insult that he didn't offer one to Devon, his host, but the man was too drunk to pick up on it.

Blowing out a cloud of fragrant smoke, he said, "Interesting is a word for it. Pain in my ass is what I'd call it." He leaned back in his chair. "What's your name?"

"Dahlia, sir."

"Like the flower?"

"Yes," she replied, surprised.

"Don't look so shocked." He didn't smile, exactly, but something in his hard eyes softened. "My anchor keeps fresh flowers in our house. He says it makes it feel less like a tomb. Dahlias—" Mr. Bowan tipped his head in her direction. "—are his favorites."

She had no idea why he was talking to her. Most of the VIPs ignored the servers or treated them like meat. Mr. Bowan wasn't exactly warm and fuzzy, but he spoke to her like she was a person, which was more than she could say for Devon.

Casting a cautious glance at her boss, who seemed to only just realize that his guest wasn't paying any attention to him, she asked, "Have you been to the flower market here, sir?"

Mr. Bowan took a long draw from his cigar before he shook his head. "No. Should I?"

"If your anchor likes flowers so much, I'd recommend it. There's a morning and night market. It's where all the florists in the city get their flowers every day and it's just stunning to walk through. Your anchor might have fun—"

Devon's grating voice rose above the music piped in through the speakers hidden in the awning. "Dahlia, unless you're offering Mr. Bowan a drink, shut the fuck up."

Her jaw clenched. Anger was a tiny burning coal in her belly, hot and useless.

Averting her gaze, she couldn't quite get her shoulders to slump in the way they probably should've. *Head down, tray up.* That was the rule. It helped to look meek and cowed. Normally she could fake it better, but something about tonight made it more difficult.

"Miss..." Mr. Bowan cast her an expectant look.

She tried not to move her lips too much. "McKnight, sir."

Turning his flinty gaze on his host, the old vampire sneered, "Miss McKnight was giving me some useful advice — unlike yourself. You haven't stopped spewing bullshit since I walked in here."

Devon slammed his mostly empty bottle onto the table. "What? It's not bullshit! San Francisco is the new—"

In a blatantly dismissive gesture, Mr. Bowan angled his body toward her. "What do you think, Miss McKnight? You seem smart. Do you think there's room for new commerce in the Elvish Protectorate?"

Cold sweat covered the back of her neck. *Fuck.*

She knew better than to get comfortable. Even the nice vampires could get her into trouble.

Feeling Devon's furious gaze on her, she carefully answered, "I... have no knowledge on the subject, sir. I'm just a server."

Mr. Bowan knocked the ash from his cigar onto the table, deliberately ignoring the ashtray only a few inches away. "How long have you been a server here?"

"Five years, sir."

"And how long have you lived in this city?"

"Ten years, sir."

"Ten years in the capital and five years working for vampires," he mused. "I'm impressed you lasted so long here. Shows grit. I bet you've got more than enough knowledge to at least have an opinion. So tell me honestly, Miss McKnight: do you think it's wise to move syndicate business into the EVP?"

Her stomach curdled. It was lucky she didn't have time to eat any breakfast before she started her shift. If she had, she probably would've thrown it up on Mr. Bowan's extremely expensive shoes.

"I..." Dahlia gripped her tray hard, fighting the urge to run. She was always so careful not to offend, not to over-step. How had she ended up stuck between two predators, being used as a tool to humiliate her boss?

Devon's going to kill me, she thought, shifting in her heels. A weak man was never more dangerous than when he'd been embarrassed.

As if reading her mind, Mr. Bowan held her stare and calmly assured her, "Don't worry about the whelp. I'm the wolf in the room, not him. So answer me, Miss McKnight."

Resignation crept over her in a slow, dreadful wave. Letting out a breath, she answered, "I... I think that the elves pay more attention than it seems. They know they can't stamp out crime altogether, so they allow what's useful to them. But they would never allow any organization to take actual power. They're so few of them. They can't risk it. If there was even a hint that the— the syndicate was actually building something here, they'd crush it."

Mr. Bowan's dark eyes gleamed through a cloud of cigar smoke. "So what would you suggest?"

"Suggest, sir?"

"Let's say I was foolish enough to want to expand my business here. How would you suggest I do so?"

He was toying with her. Or rather, with Devon, who looked like he was a few seconds from popping a blood vessel somewhere in his soft little brain.

Not answering wasn't an option. Mr. Bowan was right. He was the bigger predator in the room. And either way, she was screwed.

Tensing, she said, "If you *really* wanted to, you'd have to work within their rules. Elves care about appearances. If you stayed in the bounds of legitimacy — publicly, at least — it would be a lot harder for them to fight you. It'd have to be splashy and loud and come with a lot of charity work, but it could be done. The Solbournes are all about cooperation and tolerance these days. If you're bringing legitimate business to the territory, what can they do? Sometimes being a bigger target makes you harder to hit."

For the first time since the old vampire arrived, a smile curved the corners of his hard mouth. "And he's got you serving drinks."

"Dahlia, come here," Devon growled.

"She's going to stay where she is."

The hair on the back of her neck prickled when Devon lurched out of his seat. His face was flushed, his eyes glazed. She'd seen that look before.

"You can't tell me what to do with *my* employee in *my* bar," he snarled. All the tendons stood out on his neck. "She belongs to me."

Dahlia edged back a step, her pulse hammering, but stopped when Mr. Bowan gestured for her to stay still. "Don't worry about him, Miss McKnight. You're safe."

She cast a quick look around the room. None of the other servers would meet her eye as they pressed themselves into corners, making themselves smaller. All around them, Mr. Bowan's security was on alert, their stony gazes fixed on Devon, whose own men didn't seem terribly interested in what was happening.

I'm definitely not safe.

But before things could escalate further, one of Mr. Bowan's men announced, "Sir, Yvanna just arrived."

"You're very lucky, boy," the old vampire sighed. "If she'd been any later, I would've shot you." He raised his eyebrows at Dahlia. "Or let you do it, Miss McKnight. Now *that* would be fun to see. Smart girls always have a vicious streak."

Devon sputtered. "You can't *threaten*—"

Mr. Bowan's fangs gleamed in the low light when his lip curled. "I can do whatever the fuck I want. You're nothing. Your bar is nothing. Your family is nothing. The only reason I deigned to step foot in your shitty establishment is because it's neutral territory. So do yourself a favor and shut the *fuck* up so the grownups can do what they came here for."

"Oh, sounds like you've been having fun without me."

Dahlia turned her head toward the entrance to the rooftop, where a statuesque woman dressed in a forest green pantsuit stood.

Ice water poured down her spine.

She'd never met her. She'd never even seen her before. But one look at that face and the single lock of white hair by the vampire's temple and she *knew*.

The resemblance to her boogeyman was uncanny. While the woman was older, with fine lines around her eyes and mouth, she was the spitting image of *him*.

When Yvanna's pale gray eyes drifted her way, Dahlia dropped her gaze to the floor. Her mouth went painfully dry. A high-pitched buzzing blocked any sound from reaching her ears. She didn't hear the greetings that were exchanged or whatever it was that calmed Devon enough to put his ass back in his seat.

She tried to step back, to at least pretend like she could still do her job, but Mr. Bowan stopped her again with a single raised finger.

Oh gods, he's taunting Devon. She didn't dare look up to see, but she knew that her boss was grinding his teeth, seeing her stand there beside a vampire who'd disrespected him.

It wasn't like she wanted to be close to him, but the longer this went on, the worse it would be for her when Mr. Bowan left. The threat of being fired was the absolute least of her worries. A vampire whose pride had been wounded was far more dangerous than one who wanted to fuck her.

But even as she tried to think of a way to politely extract herself from the situation, she couldn't stop glancing at Yvanna, who'd settled into her seat like a supermodel ready for her photoshoot. There'd been no recognition in her eyes, no interest at all when they briefly looked at each other. If the woman knew about Dahlia's connection to her boogeyman, she didn't show it. But that didn't mean anything.

Her mind cartwheeled toward catastrophe. It didn't matter how many times she reminded herself that she'd never done anything wrong. All she'd ever done was exist.

You're fine. You're fine. Just keep still and don't say another word.

Movement caught her eye. Devon had gotten up from his seat again, but didn't appear ready to launch himself at Mr. Bowan anymore. Instead, he stalked to the far corner of the roof, where he pulled out his phone and began typing furiously. She suspected he was whining about how things were going to Duke, who'd probably set this whole thing up.

Duke had never been interested in the bar mostly because he was more focused on where the real money was made — mainly crime. Devon was too hapless to have gotten two obviously powerful players here himself, so she guessed it'd been his brother who orchestrated the meeting. *Why* he trusted his little brother with people they wanted to impress was beyond her.

Dahlia tuned back into the conversation just in time to hear Yvanna say, "...advantageous for the both of us, Alastair. You hate my nephew. I hate my nephew. I have a working womb. You have a young groom in need of a good match. I see no downsides."

Mr. Bowan smoothed his index finger over his white mustache. "Except for the extremely notable downside of tying your inferior family to mine, you mean."

Yvanna's fanged smile was as sharp as a knife. "You'd get our army. And I'm willing to pay for the privilege."

"Do I look like I'm wanting for firepower, Yvanna?" He tapped his cigar on the edge of the table again. "I'm not inclined to sell my niece's only son for something I don't need. Or at all. I'm fond of him."

"Every man has his price," Yvanna challenged, unperturbed by Mr. Bowan's flat tone. "You wouldn't have taken this meeting if you didn't think you could get something out of it."

"Maybe I just wanted to see the trainwreck up close." Leaning his elbows on the chair's armrests, he leaned forward like he was about to impart a secret. "We've known each other for a long time, so let me be honest with you. You're losing the war, Yvanna. Badly. I do hate your little shit of a nephew, but even I can admit he's going to win this one. You're a rat in a trap. And I don't work with rats. You'd be better off throwing in the towel and hoping he's merciful."

Dahlia had to give her credit. It was like the harsh warning completely bounced off Yvanna's shiny armor. "With the support of the Bowans, I could take the family back. All I need is a groom. The elders would back me if they saw I was blessed by Grim."

Dahlia was only following about half of that. Her mind was too full of alarms to try to make sense of what in the world Yvanna was referring to. All she could think of was her boogeyman and whether any of this had to do with him.

Involuntarily, her gaze drifted upward, toward Yvanna's striking, mature face. The breeze barely moved her black hair with its single streak of white that had been twisted in a perfect chignon. Their eyes met.

There was nothing but ice in Yvanna's gaze. It was a pure, flat contempt that sent Dahlia's attention skittering over the vampire's shoulder just in time to see the small black canister land on the floor behind her chair.

She didn't know what compelled her to shove Mr. Bowan's shoulder, and she had no idea what she said. Whatever it was, he listened. In less than a second, he'd slung an arm around her waist and dragged them both to the ground between the metal table and his chair. His body twisted around hers as she held up her tray like a shield, protecting his head.

It wasn't nearly enough to protect them from the blast.

This night is cursed, she thought, floating somewhere between consciousness and the sweet bliss of oblivion.

Her back hurt. So did her front. And her head.

Dahlia couldn't remember why. She was used to her feet screaming at her at the end of the night, but she hadn't been this uncomfortable since Cecilia convinced her to take that free pilates class. And the *smoke —*

She tensed and immediately regretted it. A searing pain radiated from her left shoulder. Acrid air wheezed out of her lungs as her eyes were forced open. Around her, the world was chaos.

Her vision was partially obscured by dark fabric, but she could see across the floor. Through smoke and dust, she could just make out the shape of Yvanna, laying on her side.

Or what was left of her, which wasn't much. Terror squeezed her throat.

Instinct clawed at her insides, compelling her to move, to crawl away from the carnage as fast as possible, but she couldn't. Something was laying on top of her, pinning her there, and the pain of even the slightest movements made stars burst in her stinging eyes.

Cold fingers tapped her cheek. It wasn't quite a slap, but it wasn't exactly gentle, either. "Stop moving," a hoarse voice growled above her. "You'll kill us both if you keep that up."

Her bleary eyes swung upward. Mr. Bowan stared down at her, his golden skin streaked with blood and dust. His eyes were a little wide around the edges, but otherwise he seemed perfectly composed as he informed her, "Miss McKnight, do me a favor and try not to panic, but I believe we've been impaled with a piece of that ugly table."

A dying bird sort of sound escaped her throat. *"We?"*

He looked meaningfully down. Dahlia tried to turn her head to see what he was talking about, but her vision was obscured by a jagged piece of brushed stainless steel. It took her a long moment to understand why it was covered in blood.

Like a giant serrated knife, the metal had run right through

Mr. Bowan and into her shoulder. His blood ran down the twisted surface in thick red rivulets to pool on her chest and around her wound.

Her vision went spotty again. "What— what do we do?"

"Fucking Amauris. I knew taking this meeting was a terrible idea." The vampire's lips pressed thin. "I'd like to get out of here before the authorities arrive, so we're going to have to separate. My men are going to assist. Since you saved my life, I'm going to try very hard to not kill you in the process."

He glanced up at someone she couldn't see and nodded. Not a moment later there were people everywhere, each one of them moving like they knew exactly what to do.

Panic made her legs spasm uselessly as she clawed at Mr. Bowan's expensive coat. "Wait, wait—"

No one listened to her. They had more important things to do — like quickly and efficiently yanking the metal out of Mr. Bowan with one hard pull. She didn't have time to wonder if it was the right thing to do because they'd ripped it out of her, too.

White-hot pain scoured every one of her nerve endings as a hot splash of blood covered her chest. A heavy hand pressed some fabric — a shirt, maybe — into her shoulder. She could barely feel her own fingers, but the faceless person dragged her hand up to hold pressure on the compress before they disappeared as quickly as they'd come.

Mr. Bowan grunted as he was pulled to his feet. She watched, her vision doubling, as two haggard-looking security guards pressed their coats into his front and back to stem the bleeding.

Looking pale but disconcertingly poised, he wheezed, "It was a pleasure meeting you, Miss McKnight. I sincerely hope you make it."

A hysterical bubble of laughter escaped her. "L-likewise, Mr. Bowan."

What will it take to make you leave me alone

UNKNOWN NUMBER

I see we're at the negotiation stage

You keep changing your number so I can't block you. When I ignore you, you send shit to my apartment (extremely creepy that you know where I live?????) and you obviously know where I work

Are we just listing facts now or what

I guess I'm just wondering why on Earth you think I'll ever actually want to talk to you, a stalker

Does it count as stalking if I'm not physically following you around

if you have to ask???

This is just how things are done. I've been pretty restrained, actually

in what universe is anything you've done normal, let alone restrained??

You're in the vampire world, pet. The rules are different

pretty sure laws still exist in Vampire World, boogeyman

That's honestly really cute

It'll take more than the law to get rid of me, pretty girl. Maybe try a gun

noted

THREE

THE HEALERS AT SAN FRANCISCO GENERAL CALLED HER LUCKY. Dahlia begged to differ. It would've been a lot kinder if the gods had let her die on that rooftop instead of subjecting her to Cecilia's idea of nursing.

All in all, the wound had been remarkably superficial. The metal had missed her heart, lung, and all major arteries. She was left with a big old hole in her muscle that was easy for the healers to fix. They'd initially been deeply alarmed by the amount of blood on her, but it was quickly discovered that most of it wasn't hers.

She only spent one uncomfortable night in the hospital because the healers were very good at their jobs. By the time Cecilia wheeled her out the doors and into the cab, she was exhausted but undamaged. There wasn't even a scar.

A slight concussion and the exhaustion that came with healing were the worst of her injuries, but you wouldn't know it by how Cecilia carried on.

If she wasn't randomly bursting into tears, she was clinging to Dahlia like a barnacle. It was nice to hold her hand when Patrol stopped by the apartment to grill her about the murder —

Assassination? Bombing? — but after a few hours, she'd been forced to send her friend on an errand to get a little peace.

"I left my purse in my locker," she explained. "Can you go get it for me? I want my phone."

"Ah, of course! Don't worry about it. Just rest." Cecilia tucked her into bed as tightly as a mummy, sniffling all the while, before she practically ran out the door.

As soon as she left, Dahlia climbed out of bed to take a shower. Luckily there was hot water this time. She needed it to get all the crusted blood in her ears and under her fingernails. The nurses at the hospital had done a wonderful job getting her clean, but there were some nooks and crannies even they missed.

She wasn't sure when the shock would hit. Probably soon. It had to, right? One didn't just see the mangled corpse of a woman a few feet away while impaled on shrapnel and be totally *fine.*

Dahlia pulled on her softest pajamas and climbed back into bed. Her hair was wet, but she didn't care what it'd look like when she woke up. It wasn't like she'd be going to work. The bar would be shuttered for a few days at the very least. Patrol had to do their investigation, though she doubted there would be much to find if the Vances weren't *complete* idiots, and the city would probably have to check that the building was still structurally sound.

She stared sightlessly across the studio at her little kitchenette, trying to summon some great existential crisis from her near death experience. Nothing came.

That wasn't to say she didn't think about what happened. She did. Obsessively.

She'd run through every second of the night a thousand times since she woke up in the ambulance to find an extremely handsome were packing her wound with gauze.

Patrol hadn't told her much, but they'd disclosed that the device used had been essentially a miniature hand grenade mostly likely intended for a single target. They hadn't needed to explain that she wasn't important enough to be that target. It'd been aimed precisely at Yvanna and did its job perfectly.

Of course, she wasn't the only injury. Just the worst, if one didn't count Mr. Bowan. Several members of security and one other server had been hit with shrapnel, and Devon had his right arm broken. It was a wound that took five minutes to heal, but you wouldn't know it by how he gassed on and on.

Dahlia counted the old, yellowed tiles of her sink's minuscule backsplash, thinking, *If Mr. Bowan and Devon hadn't started arguing, I probably would've died.*

Devon's chair had been right beside Yvanna's. She'd stood behind it, a scant foot away from where the explosive landed. If she'd done as Devon told her to, she would've ended up just like Yvanna — smeared across the rooftop.

Still nothing. Well, not nothing. I'm relieved. And pissed off. Who throws a fucking grenade to kill someone? Snipers exist!

Whatever had happened, she was unlikely to find out the truth about it. All she knew was that Mr. Bowan was right. Yvanna had lost the war. Badly.

She looked away from her kitchenette when her front door swung open. Cecilia had a key and she never bothered to knock. Her best friend burst into the apartment with Dahlia's purse slung over her arm, as well as several bags from the corner bodega.

"I know you're probably tired— Oh good, you showered! But next time wait for me. What if you'd fallen?" She blew out a breath. "Okay, anyway... I brought comfort food and your purse. Which do you want first?"

Her stomach rolled at the thought of food, so she sat up and held out her hand. "Purse, please."

"You can have the snacks later." Cecilia dumped the bags on the floor by the bed and passed the little black purse over.

Dahlia's pulse jumped as she dug through the minimal makeup and money she brought with her to work to find her old phone. She didn't dare check it with Cecilia so close, but it felt somehow heavier in her hand. She couldn't decide if it would be better or worse if there was nothing from her boogeyman when she turned it on.

Does he know? Were him and Yvanna really related, or did I just imagine the resemblance? If there's nothing, does that mean he's okay or does that mean something bad happened to him, too?

She'd never, in the years he'd invaded her phone and her life, showed him how much she cared. But the fear that lodged itself behind her breast bone was a huge, spiky thing and she worried that she might be forced to break her own rule to make it go away.

Trying to breathe normally, she gave Cecilia a wan smile. "Thank you. How was the bar?"

"Not too bad, considering." Her friend leaned down to fish around in one of the bags. Pulling out a strawberry soda, she cracked the can open and took a long sip. "Lotta Patrol milling around. One of them stopped me to ask what I was doing. When I told them I was there to get your things, they let me through." She shuddered. "Elves are so scary. Even when they're being nice. I almost peed my pants when they asked for my name."

Dahlia waved her hand at the soda. "Gimme some of that. I need to take my pain meds."

Cecilia handed it over with a frown. "How's your head?"

"Fine," she muttered around the pill under her tongue. "Just sore."

Dahlia normally liked Pink Pop, but when she took a large swig of the soda, she had to clamp her lips shut to avoid spitting it all over her friend and the nice bedspread she'd gotten at the discount store.

Coughing, she gasped, "What's *wrong* with that?"

Cecilia snatched the can away from her. "What are you talking about? It's the original flavor!"

"No, it absolutely isn't. That tastes like sugary gasoline!"

Her friend gave her a bizarre look as she took an experimental sip. Swallowing, she said, "It tastes normal to me. How hard did you hit your head again?"

"Not hard enough to change my tastebuds," Dahlia muttered. "Must be the shock, I guess. Or whatever they put in my IV."

"All right, if you're besmirching the world's best soda, you definitely should get some rest." Cecilia leaned over to press a kiss to Dahlia's cheek. "I love you and I'm, like, so fucking happy you didn't die."

Dahlia slung her arm around her friend's shoulders in a loose hug. "Someone's gotta take care of Oyster when one of your dates stuffs you in his trunk."

After a lingering embrace, Cecilia walked to the door, her can of soda in hand. "Yeah, well, they'd have to show up to kill me. Tony didn't."

"Your date stood you up?" Dahlia asked, outraged.

Opening the door, Cecilia turned her head to give her a heart-breakingly tender look. "I couldn't give less of a shit, dude. My best friend's alive. That's all I care about."

That really took the righteous wind out of her sails. Not all of it, but most.

Dahlia gripped her phone tightly as she leaned back into her pillows. "You go get some rest yourself, you sap. I'm not going anywhere."

She waited five seconds after Cecilia locked the door before she dared to turn her phone on. It took a second for it to boot up, but when it did...

"Shit."

She stared at the notifications streaming across the screen with horror. There were half a dozen calls, two video chat requests, and a cascade of texts. Obviously, he'd heard about what happened. Even if he wasn't related to Yvanna, *of course* he knew. He had eyes everywhere.

It was terrifying. *He* was terrifying. But her ridiculous, self-destructive heart still swelled with warmth at the sight.

He's alive.

Not that she really thought he was dead. She'd done everything in her power to *not* learn about him, but even she knew that Felix would be damn hard to kill.

They weren't friends and they weren't lovers. She'd only ever seen him in person the one time, when he showed up to retrieve that body bag during what now ranked as her second worst ever shift.

But they talked. A lot.

Not because she *wanted* to, but because he'd decided they should. She had no idea what drew his attention her way. All she'd done was serve him a drink. She didn't want to know how he'd gotten her number, only that he had.

She knew what he wanted from her. Felix wasn't a subtle man. He was a dangerous, unhinged one. He'd told her under no uncertain terms that she wasn't getting rid of him, but she still tried.

Blocking him hadn't worked. Telling him to go away hadn't, either. Turning off her phone for a week had only resulted in a shiny new one showing up at her apartment. She shoved it in a drawer and never touched it again.

Dahlia didn't want to say he'd worn her down because he hadn't. She hadn't cracked. She didn't respond to his relentless flirting or his many, many requests to fly her out to see him.

But... she did learn to like him. Just a little bit.

It was almost impossible not to when the man called her just to request her help with puzzling out a word game or texted her pictures of his perfectly organized closet to impress her.

If that'd been all he was — a strange, intense sort of guy who needed to be taught boundaries at the business end of a spray bottle — she probably would've given in a long time ago. His cyberstalking wasn't great, certainly, but it wasn't the worst thing she'd heard a vampire do when they liked someone. She'd had to help clean the grout in the women's bathroom, after all.

The real problem was that Felix was also a monster.

He didn't wear a mask. He didn't pretend. If she asked him, she was almost certain he'd tell her the number of people he'd killed and how he'd done it. He'd probably laugh, too.

And that's why she didn't ask. She didn't ask about anything. Not about what he did for work, where he lived, or what his last name was. Knowing details like that would only entangle her further — which was exactly what he wanted.

Dahlia knew she played a dangerous game with someone like Felix. Just like with Devon, she could read the signs all around her. Time was running out.

He'd never showed up on her doorstep. He didn't bother her loved ones, as few as those were. He didn't threaten her or endanger her job. But he could.

Objectively, Felix leaving her alone was the best option. No good could come out of his interest in her. She had no desire to be his blood bag, and she was fairly certain that becoming anything more would end with her dead in a ditch somewhere.

Men like Felix didn't have healthy, lasting relationships. They were fast cars headed for cliffs.

The problem was that she didn't really want him to go away. When she imagined what it would be like to open her door and find him standing on the other side, she wasn't afraid. She *wanted* to see him.

All of those conflicting feelings crashed through her as her shaking fingers typed out a message.

Just got my phone back. I'm fine.

The message had barely finished sending before a call came through. Knowing it was best to get it over with — and definitely *not* because she wanted to hear his voice — Dahlia answered.

"Tell me what happened."

There was a lot of noise. It sounded like a party was going on in the background, but you wouldn't know it by Felix's tone. There was none of the usual boyish playfulness that made his bloodthirsty nature so terrifying. It was cold and hard, each word a sharp little blade of ice.

Bewildered, she asked, "Are you mad at me?"

"Dahlia, I'm not fucking around. I don't have time. Tell me why you disappeared for twenty-four hours."

He sounded like a pissed off boss. She was under no delusions that the man was in love with her — or even capable of more than basic lizard-like emotions — but that stung. Did that mean he didn't really know what had happened at The Lush?

Or did he simply not care that she'd been one wrong move from death?

Suddenly not as keen to talk as she'd been a second ago, Dahlia hedged, "Not that I *have* to tell you anything, but some shit went down at work and my phone was locked inside. I only just got it back like five minutes ago."

There was a slight pause. Someone in the background hollered but she couldn't hear what they said.

Felix's voice, an always slightly rough, sexy rasp, was tight with annoyance when he said, "You weren't supposed to work this weekend."

Goosebumps rose on her arms. Her pulse quickened as she registered what he wasn't saying. "Alexa had a family emergency. We swapped shifts." She sucked in a shaky breath. Her voice was barely a whisper when she asked, "You knew, didn't you?"

A cheer came through the line. "Dahlia— Hold on."

She got the impression that he'd put his hand over the speaker, but she could still hear another man's voice nearby. Felix replied quickly before growling into the phone, "I have to go. We'll finish this later."

It was damn stupid for her eyes to sting so much. What did she expect? That he'd *care?* That he'd ask her if she'd been scared or upset?

She didn't want to know how he'd known about the attack. She didn't want to know if he'd planned or only heard about it beforehand. It didn't matter. She'd been worried about him for nothing, all while he hadn't even thought to warn her that there might be danger.

All of it was so fucked, but the worst part was that she wasn't even that upset that he'd let her walk into that. She was hurt that he didn't ask if she was okay.

Some mad part of her had actually picked up the phone expecting *comfort.*

Feeling raw, Dahlia wrapped an arm around her middle and pressed her forehead into her knees. *Oh, now I feel something,* she thought. *That's so great.*

"Enjoy your party." She was glad her voice came out as a flat monotone. Him hearing her cry would've been a fatal blow to what was left of her self-respect. "Goodbye, Felix."

She wasn't sure what he heard in her voice, but she supposed even lizards could pick up threats. Instead of hanging up right away, he paused.

In a more cautious voice, he said, "Dahlia, if you're—"

Hanging up on him wasn't nearly as satisfying as it used to be. There was no joy in it. No thrill of knowing he'd come back, demanding her attention again. She'd come to enjoy the way he chased her.

Not anymore.

She'd always known that he was just like every other vampire who looked at her a little too long. They didn't see her as a person. At best, they saw her as a buffet they could fuck. At worst, she was prey to be batted around until they got bored and killed her.

Dahlia refused to be either of those things to anyone, but most especially to Felix.

FOUR

She didn't turn her phone back on for over a week.

At first it was because that was the only way to avoid facing what she knew she had to do, which was find a way to cut off Felix for good. She hadn't been able to work out how to do it before, but she also hadn't tried that hard. Now she had real incentive: heartbreak.

The only problem was that she didn't have the energy to make good on any of her ideas. So she simply avoided it altogether. It wasn't like she needed her phone, anyway. Work wasn't happening, and she'd already decided that she had to quit.

Finding another job that would work with her school schedule would be a pain in her ass, but it was beyond time to get out of the vampire world. She should've done it when Felix started stalking her. She should've done it the first time she'd been asked to mop up blood.

She sure as shit would do it after being impaled.

Unfortunately, she barely had the energy to job hunt on her tablet. Dahlia chalked it up to the strain healing put on the body, as well as a mix of shock and the ridiculous heartbreak she didn't want to acknowledge. She slept a lot and ate very little.

At first, she just lacked an appetite. That wasn't unusual, given the stress of everything. Cecilia plied her with homemade pasta and cheese puffs and burritos from their favorite place, but none of it sounded good. All she could manage was white rice, cheese, and the protein shakes she stashed in the back of her tiny fridge for busy days.

Things devolved slowly.

Her minimal appetite devolved into outright disgust at the foods she normally loved. Even her lifeline of white rice and soy sauce betrayed her. She began throwing everything up almost as soon as it hit her stomach.

A dull but persistent headache dogged her. It got a lot worse whenever she dared turn the lights on too bright. It wasn't so bad, since she was used to a more or less nocturnal lifestyle, but the pain seemed to increase every day.

Then shakes came. And the fever. And the full-body cramping.

"I can't believe I caught the fucking flu on top of everything else," she moaned to Cecilia after puking up the only thing she'd managed to eat that day.

Holding her hair back for her, Cecilia fretted, "I really think you should go back to the hospital. This isn't normal. You're barely keeping water down now."

She'd shuddered at the idea. Not because she hated hospitals or anything, but because the idea of stepping outside her apartment was… uncomfortable.

It wasn't just that she was absolutely certain Felix would have someone watching it, but an instinct that had grown louder and more vicious every day. She couldn't stand the idea of being *exposed*. All she wanted to do was cover all her windows and hide under her bed.

So she shook off her friend's concern, praying that whatever bug she'd caught would pass.

But it didn't. One week bled into two.

Cecilia told her that the bar was open again — sans rooftop

lounge — and management had been asking if she was coming back. Devon had sent her a ridiculous bouquet, which sat rotting on her tiny kitchen counter. Whether he hoped to get her to return to work or it was just another ploy to get her to pay attention to him, she didn't know or care. She hadn't even bothered to read the card.

It didn't matter. Work didn't matter. Nothing mattered.

She couldn't think past the pain in her head and jaw. Food was a distant memory, mostly accompanied by the burn of stomach acid.

Sometimes she thought of Felix, whether he'd given up yet, but mostly she didn't. She slept for a long time. Too long.

When she woke after a nearly eighteen hour stretch of black, dreamless sleep to find two of her teeth coming loose, panic finally set it.

Swaddled in her favorite blanket, head down, and sunglasses on despite the fact that it was an overcast day, Dahlia allowed Cecilia to escort her back to the emergency room.

Solbourne General was a busy hospital that served every type of being living in the city. They handled all sorts of crises every day, most of which were far more serious than whatever illness had sunk its teeth in her.

So it came as something of a surprise when the nurse in charge took one look at her and immediately whisked her away. The lights in her room had to be dimmed before she could bear to take off her glasses, but it didn't do much good when a nurse shined a pen light into her eyes. Dahlia puked her guts up onto the shiny floor.

She didn't remember all that much after that. There was a pinch of an IV in her hand, then a flurry of activity as an increasing number of healers, doctors, and nurses moved in and out. They all appeared too busy to talk to her, which was fine. She was too miserable for speech.

She did start to feel a bit like a spectacle, though, when the third cluster of nurses stopped by her door. They whispered to each other and offered her strange, excited smiles before they hustled off.

She wasn't sure what they put in her IV, but she started feeling a little better. The real improvement came, however, after her blood tests finished.

Her doctor came in with a tablet tucked under one arm and a plain silver bottle in the other. He smiled benignly at her from beneath the shadow of his glasses.

"Well, we just got the results in," he announced, sounding unsettlingly excited. She wished she'd been assigned a healer instead. They at least had warmth to them, but there were a lot more non-magical doctors around, so she couldn't be choosy.

"I'll need to run a couple more tests, but you are absolutely healthy."

Dahlia looked up at him balefully from the hospital bed. Her stomach had caved in. Her skin was plastered with a film of cold sweat and the reek of illness. Every time she ran her tongue along her upper teeth, they wiggled. And when she dared to touch the roof of her mouth, it felt like a hot lump of lava was about to explode from her soft palate.

Healthy was the last thing she felt.

"There's no fucking way that's right," she croaked, wishing she had the strength to throw the IV bag at the doctor's smug little face.

The doctor crossed the room. Using some button on the floor, he propped up the head of her bed, forcing her into a sitting position. "I know you *feel* awful right now, but that's perfectly normal. Here, drink this. It should help immensely."

Dahlia shied away from the warm bottle he tried to put in her hand. A little white straw poked out from the top and spun in a jaunty circle as he forced her fingers around it.

"I can't keep anything down," she explained for the tenth time. "Not even water anymore. I can't drink this."

"I promise you, you can." The doctor watched her closely, his expression intent. "Just try one sip. If you really can't keep it down, we can try something else. But I need you to taste it."

Grimacing, Dahlia forced herself to put the straw between her lips. She was fully prepared to throw up again — hopefully on the doctor's clogs — but that didn't happen.

Glorious, incredible, life-saving flavor burst across her tongue. Rich like toffee, salty like her favorite chips, as perfectly balanced as the luxury coffee she couldn't afford — she'd never tasted anything like it.

She'd never been so hungry in her life. In an instant, Dahlia became a feral animal. She hunched over the bottle and sucked hard, draining every last drop in a matter of seconds. Bliss was a haze in her mind, blocking out all the pain and discomfort of the last two weeks.

Fullness, perfect and without the churn of bile she'd become used to, settled her stomach at last.

Slumping against the bed, she pressed the empty bottle against her sweaty cheek and breathed, "Oh gods, what *was* that?"

The doctor let out a strange sort of chuffing sound. His wide smile was lit by the cold glow of his tablet's screen as he rapidly typed something on the glass. "Incredible. Absolutely incredible. They talk about this in med school, but you never really think you'll see one — especially in this territory. The odds are astronomical."

"What are you talking about?"

The doctor glanced up from his screen. "That, Miss McKnight, was *synthblood*."

She was pretty sure her brain short-circuited. It had to, because he couldn't have said that. She was just so used to the word that she heard it everywhere.

"Huh?"

He nodded glibly. "The transition is always difficult, but it's made a lot worse if you don't get proper nutrition in time. No wonder you got so bad. You were starving, and every time you tried to eat regular food, it was like putting regular gasoline in a diesel engine."

Gasoline in a... What the fuck is he talking about? No one uses gas anymore.

The doctor tapped his screen with a little too much enthusiasm. "But we caught it, so you'll make a full recovery! We just need to get you on a regular synth diet and perform a minor outpatient procedure. You should start seeing an improvement immediately."

It was like she sat at the bottom of a pool. Every word he said reached her, but they were all distorted. None of them made any sense.

She looked down at the bottle in her limp hand, too confused to be disgusted. "Why would I need to be on a synth diet? Only vampires drink synth."

"Well... yes," the doctor replied, finally lowering his tablet to really look at her. He cleared his throat. Rolling his shoulders back a bit, he said, "Miss McKnight, I saw on your chart that you were recently admitted to the ER for a puncture to your shoulder, concussion, and other mild injuries. Were you at any time during the incident that caused those wounds exposed to a vampire's blood?"

The image of the jagged piece of metal pinning her and Mr. Bowan together flashed in her mind. And afterward, when his men pulled it loose, blood had rained down on her in an awful splash. She'd been covered from her from chin to belly button.

Dahlia nodded slowly. "A bit, yes."

Appearing to need a second to collect himself, the doctor turned his back to find one of those odd little rolling stools medical professionals liked so much. He dragged it across the floor and perched on the cushion before continuing.

"It's rare — *really* rare — but the vampirism virus can be transferred accidentally if enough blood is exchanged."

She gave the doctor a blank stare. "That's not possible."

"I'm afraid it is," he replied, not sounding particularly

regretful or sympathetic. "Our tests confirmed you've been infected and are in the last stage of transition. All that's left is for your incisors to fall out."

His words were starting to come through clearer. That was bad. She didn't want that. Clarity meant reality, and she was starting to suspect that reality wasn't something she could face.

Dahlia's sweaty fingers clutched the bottle hard enough to dent the cheap aluminum. Her vision swam. "My— my teeth are going to fall out?"

"It's totally normal! Your fangs should come in within a couple hours or so. They're already in there, pushing against the old nerves. That's what's causing you so much pain." He patted his knees in the way people did when they were about to leave. "Of course, there's no need to wait for nature to take its course there. The process can be quite painful. We'll do it for you here with a local anesthetic. You should be good to go."

Standing up, he ignored the way she'd begun to hyperventilate and walked to the door. "There are a few more tests I need to run, and you should come in for a check-up next week, but otherwise you should be back to normal very soon."

"Normal?" Her voice came out choked, like the word was a bunch of broken glass in her throat. "How can I be normal when I'm— when—"

"You're a vampire?" The doctor cracked the door open, but he didn't leave right away. Keeping his hand on the knob, he turned to give her a close-lipped smile. "This isn't the end of your life, Miss McKnight. It's the start of a new one. Try not to worry too much. I'm sure you'll be fine."

Did you not like my gift

I know it's the one you wanted. Send me a picture with the necklace on. Clothing optional but strongly discouraged

Keep ignoring me and I'll just send more diamonds. You know I love getting your attention

—CALL BEGAN SATURDAY 1:05 AM
—CALL ENDED SATURDAY 1:43 AM

Is it weird that I kind of like it when you yell at me

absolutely yes

So maybe I shouldn't say it made me hard when you told me to fuck off

I WILL throw my phone in the ocean

I'll just buy you a new one again. I love getting you gifts

You could find a woman who actually likes getting gifts, you know

Ah, but she wouldn't be you

Call me when you're done with work

no

Why not

I don't like talking to you???

Liar

Why are you so obsessed with my work

Nice swerve.

I'm flexible like that

I can't wait to test that out for myself

But for the record, I'm obsessed with your work because you spend your nights in a dangerous bar full of horny vampires who don't take rejection well. Thinking of you walking home by yourself gives me fucking hives

You'd know all about horny vampires who can't handle rejection, wouldn't you

I'm an expert on the subject

If I hired a private car for you, would you use it to go to work

it's literally six blocks away from my house

so no

We wouldn't have this problem if you quit and let me take care of you

you know how many vampires have used that line on me? Dozens. Hasn't worked yet

Names.

Names, Dahlia. Now.

enjoy your night, boogeyman 🖤

—MISSED CALL SATURDAY 1:50 AM
—MISSED CALL SATURDAY 1:52 AM
—MISSED CALL SATURDAY 1:55 AM
MESSAGE TRANSCRIBED FROM A VOICE NOTE:

Gods, I really can't wait to bite you, brat.

FIVE

THE NEWS FROM SAN FRANCISCO WAS GOOD — FOR ALL OF FIVE fucking seconds.

Felix liked finishing things. He enjoyed puzzles, word games, fitting things in exactly the right size organizer, and, of course, the satisfaction of a good kill. It didn't matter if he was the one who pulled the trigger or not. If it was done on his order, it was his.

And there was no one he'd looked forward to killing more than his aunt Yvanna.

Knowing that it was done in the very same bar where his piece of shit uncle Julius had been poisoned three years prior? Even better.

It's done, he'd thought, viciously pleased by the photos of Yvanna's nearly unrecognizable corpse. *The war's over. We can finally fucking breathe.*

His men were already whooping and hollering, their greedy fingers going for the stash of potent alcoholic synth he kept in his office, but Felix didn't join in their celebration. In that moment, the only thing he wanted to do was talk to his girl.

Finally. Finally. Finally.

His pulse throbbed in his neck. The gland in the roof of his mouth burned, as it always did when he thought of the tart little waitress he was obsessed with.

Felix wasn't used to delayed gratification. He didn't *do* self-restraint. When he saw something — or someone — he wanted, he took it.

And he'd never wanted someone like he wanted Dahlia McKnight.

The only thing that stopped him from having his men put a bag over her head and gently escorting her onto a private plane was that he couldn't guarantee her safety while Yvanna lived. That normally didn't bother him, especially when the women he took to bed knew the score, but with Dahlia…

The thought of her becoming a casualty of the war that raged between him and Yvanna over control of the Amauri empire had made him pause. He couldn't enjoy her if she was dead, and Felix hadn't put as much effort into her as he had just to have her snatched from him.

So he'd bookmarked her for later.

She'd be his spoils of war and his reward for putting up with Yvanna's bullshit for so long. As soon as things stabilized and word filtered out that he was the uncontested leader of the Amauri family, he'd take a little trip to San Francisco to pick up his prize.

He couldn't keep her. Not forever. Not even for a few months. But he'd take what he could before he was forced to send her away.

He'd be taking a blood bride soon enough, and there wouldn't be room in his life for the two of them, no matter how many times he tried to convince himself he could make it work.

To form an alliance with another powerful family — a necessity in the cut-throat, bloodline-obsessed syndicate world — he'd have to take one of the few blood brides available and pray they wouldn't make him miserable. There was a shortlist waiting for him on his phone at that very second, with photos and bride prices and points of negotiation for each family.

From what he'd learned, that was why Yvanna had been in The Lush. She'd been hoping to make a match that could turn the tide of the war — with the *Bowan* family, of all people. He doubted she would've succeeded, since those uptight twats thought they were so much better than Amauris, but it was a ballsy play nonetheless.

It was just too bad for her that he had a reason to keep a very close eye on that city, and on *that* bar in particular.

It'd been shockingly easy to set up the hit. The only real complication was making sure it happened on a night when his girl was off.

Getting that full-body itch that came whenever he went without hearing her voice for too long, Felix stepped away from his plush leather armchair and the men who caroused around it. He stood by the large window overlooking the Amauri mansion's grounds and held his phone to his ear.

It wasn't unusual for her to ignore his calls. Dahlia liked to keep him on his toes, and he enjoyed letting her. Usually.

Felix scowled at his wavering reflection in the glass as his call went directly to voicemail. He checked the time. She would definitely be up already. Even on her nights off, she was up and moving around by then.

It wasn't normal for her phone to be off. She typically only did that when she was working, and he'd triple checked that she wasn't. He'd even made sure her friend Cecilia was off, just in case.

Dahlia never talked about her, probably because she was afraid he'd use her as leverage, but there was vanishingly little he didn't know about his girl. Those two were practically inseparable, so he was pretty sure she'd rip him a new asshole if he accidentally killed her.

Ignoring a rowdy call for him to join the party, which was just the prelude to what would no doubt be at least a week of celebration, Felix rang one of the two men he'd assigned to guard Dahlia.

As much as it bothered him, he'd had to hire out to get her protection. He hadn't wanted to lead any trail back to himself, just in case his enemies realized how highly he valued her. It would be just like one of the crusty elders to put a hit out on her to try and teach him a lesson.

In their world, no one was off limits except mates, what they called anchors. And a tasty little treat like Dahlia? She was easy pickings.

The men he hired were supposed to be good. Not as good as the sworn Amauri soldiers, but good enough. One was an arrant — a non-magical human like Dahlia — who watched her apartment during the day, and another was a vampire. It was the vampire's job to watch her at night.

With how much he was paid, there was absolutely no reason he shouldn't have been available to take Felix's call.

And yet somehow it went to voicemail, too.

Sensing something was off, he called the arrant in charge of the day shift. He was very, very lucky he answered on the second ring.

"Hello?" Maxwell sounded groggy but alert enough. There was a slight pause as he checked his phone and realized who he was speaking to. "Oh, uh, sorry, sir. How can I help you?"

Felix flexed his fingers on his phone. "Where's Stevenson?"

"Sir?"

"Stevenson," he snapped. "He's not picking up his phone. Where is he?"

"Um…" The arrant seemed to wake up a little more. "I think he took the night off, sir. I don't know where he is."

Felix went very still. "He took the night off."

It wasn't a question, but the arrant babbled like it was. "Well, yeah. The charge wasn't working tonight, right? He takes those nights off. She sticks to her schedule, so he didn't think it'd be a problem."

"He didn't think it'd be a problem." A red veil slipped over his mind, muting everything around him.

I don't know where she is.

On this night of all nights, when Yvanna and her lackeys were in his girl's city, she'd been left without a guard. And now he couldn't reach her.

Something expanded in him. It was huge and hot and explosive. A lesser man would've called it rage, but for Felix, it was the wild joy of a wildfire — a certainty that he'd be scorching the earth and leaving nothing behind.

"Listen to me very carefully," he said, deceptively calm. "You are going to get out of bed. You are going to find your charge in the next hour. If you can't, you'll report back to me. Once you've done that, I have another job for you."

At last sounding like he'd grasped the gravity of his situation, the man rasped, "Sir?"

Felix stared blankly out at the sprawling courtyard of his estate. The beat of his own heart was all he heard when he ordered, "You're going to hunt Stevenson down and shoot him in the fucking face."

SIX

"You have to at least pretend that you're having a good time," Milo muttered.

Felix took a sip of his synth and flipped his second in command the bird. "Fuck off. I'm the boss. If I want to look miserable at this boring party, I will."

Milo sighed. Squeezing his hulking frame into the chair beside Felix's, he scolded, "You haven't even tried talking to the elders tonight, man. You know you have to. That was the whole point of this."

Reconciliation, they'd called it. The old fucks were all too happy to smile and pinch his cheeks and drink his booze in *his* house now that there were no other contenders for the throne.

He might've taken the opportunity to enjoy rubbing his victory in their faces if he didn't feel like he was coming out of his skin. And if he wasn't certain *they* would take the chance to push their candidates for his blood bride under his nose.

It was one thing to know he'd have to take one and quite another to feel like he was being forced into it. Especially now.

His synth tasted like ash on his tongue as he took another long swallow. It hadn't tasted right since he met Dahlia all those years ago, but he could usually force it down. He barely managed it tonight.

Milo gave him a long look. He was good at making people do things with just a look like that, probably because everyone except Felix found his massive scar and pale eye unsettling. "She still not talking to you?"

"Does it look like she's talking to me?"

Felix tracked the movement of a gaggle of his distant cousins as they drifted toward the bar in the corner of his ballroom. Some of them were too young to drink alcoholic synth, but he had little doubt they'd try. He certainly had, and his grandmother had somehow always known. And whooped his ass for it.

He missed the old bat. It did a man good to have a strong woman around.

"You still plan on picking her up next week?"

"Obviously."

Milo braced his elbows on the small round table Felix had posted up at. Clasping his hands together, he cautiously began, "I really don't think it's a good idea to—"

"It's incredible that you believe repeating the same point six times means I'm going to start listening. Maybe you should try for a seventh, for science." Felix pulled his phone out of his pocket. His molars ground together.

He liked Milo. Milo was one of his only real friends. Milo was his cousin. Milo was a good second in command. Milo was smart and loyal to the bone.

He also wanted to kill him more often than not. Especially when he tried to get Felix to leave Dahlia alone, which happened roughly once a week.

In the itty-bitty part of him that was reasonable, Felix understood that his cousin was doing what he'd always done: trying to protect him from himself. Milo was the only one of the inner circle who knew how deep his obsession with the little blonde server went, and if Felix was forced at gunpoint, he'd even say that he trusted the man with her safety.

But that didn't mean he planned to listen to his advice.

In a quiet voice, Milo warned, "You can't keep her, Felix."

"You don't think I know that?" He unlocked his phone. Killing his cousin wasn't an option, so he had to calm down. Checking up on his girl was like a little calm down pill, so he quickly navigated to the chat he'd opened with her new security team.

The efficacy of his calm down pill wasn't quite as potent when she continued to ice him out for some reason, but it soothed him all the same.

Or it would've, if there hadn't been a notification waiting for him.

He'd been informed by the day crew that she and Cecilia had gone to the hospital in the afternoon. The update had driven him crazy, but he'd done his best to remind himself that normal people went to the doctor all the time.

Maybe she'd cut her finger chopping... whatever it was she ate. Maybe she had a gyno appointment and needed moral support while a doctor shined a light up there. Most people didn't only go to the doctor for bolt gun wounds, stabbings, strangulations, concussions, poisoning, or missing eyes. That was just the people he hung out with.

Milo said she probably just had a cold or needed a shot. Felix couldn't explain that even something minor like that made him antsy. He didn't need his second being more concerned about where his head was at than he already was.

Gods help him if people started to think he'd gone soft.

The news that she'd returned to her apartment several hours later should've soothed some of his worry, but he couldn't shake it. Dahlia had never been exactly forthcoming when she'd been sick in the past, but she'd been opening up more lately. She'd even let him send her soup once.

It was pathetic to feel so triumphant about something like

that, but he had. And when she'd said thank you in that sad, sick voice, only to fall asleep on the phone with him...

He'd sucked up every little bit of her vulnerability like it was the sweetest blood. The more he got, the more he craved.

Felix had never had to work so hard to get a girl before. If they didn't want him, he walked away, unbothered. But something about Dahlia kept him coming back for more.

She'd never told him to go away. Sure, she'd blocked him. She'd ignored him. She'd asked him what he thought he was doing, pestering her like he did. But she never told him to fuck off.

He was certain she loved him, and he'd been looking forward to proving it to them both.

Except now she wouldn't speak to him. Her phone was off. He'd sent her another new one, hoping for some sort of reaction, but she hadn't even answered the door to accept it.

He knew she was alive because he'd been given detailed reports of what could be seen the rare times her blinds were opened, but that was it. She'd become a ghost.

It pissed him off.

You aren't allowed to hide from me, he silently warned her as he scrolled through her team's updates. *You aren't allowed to be sick and not tell me. You aren't allowed to —*

"Huh."

He glanced at his second, who was frowning at his own phone. "What?"

Milo's brow was furrowed. He didn't look overly concerned, but he was stoic on the best of days, so it was hard to tell what was going on in his brain. "Our man in the Bowan house just got back to me."

All business now, Felix placed his phone face down on the table. "Tell me what he said."

"Alastair had the Patrol report on the hit pulled," he explained, eyes flickering as he scrolled through the message.

"Looks like it was just finished. Gods, elves move fucking slow. But that's not every—"

Milo cut himself off. His face, already pale, drained of what little color it had. Muttering to himself, he said, "You've got to be fucking kidding me."

Instincts prickling, Felix sat up straight in his chair.

The Bowans were an old, aristocratic syndicate family. They'd been top dogs once and still had a considerable amount of power, but they hadn't adapted well to the modern age. They were still a force to be reckoned with, though, and Felix had groaned when he found out Alastair, the head of the family, was the one to be injured during the hit.

They'd had to pay out the nose in tribute to make up for the damage and smooth ruffled feathers, but it could've been worse. Accidentally killing Alastair would've resulted in outright war. They were all lucky the old bastard managed to limp home.

Felix supposed it wasn't necessarily unusual that the Bowans were looking into the incident, perhaps hoping to find out what Patrol had learned. He would've done the same thing. But something in Milo's sudden stillness set his fangs on edge.

There wouldn't be anything to find. His assassins were good, if a little showy. But not everyone could be Harlan Bounds or Atticus Caldwell. They were the best assassins the syndicate ever produced, and they'd been sworn to the Amauri family under control of Julius.

It was a damn shame his uncle was such a fucked up prick that he'd pushed two of their best killers to break from the family. He'd definitely deserved every bit of retribution Harlan gave to him in that bar, but that didn't make their loss smart any less.

Luckily, he still had good men on his side. Even if they were a pain in his ass.

"What?" he demanded, rapidly losing what little patience he possessed.

"They pulled the file to corroborate a tip," Milo answered,

each word slow and measured in a way that filled Felix with dread. His cousin always chose his words carefully, but when he talked like that, it was *always* bad news.

And the way Milo avoided his gaze? It had to be very bad indeed.

"Apparently, a server was injured. Substantially."

"So?" Felix didn't love the idea of innocent bystanders getting hurt, but it wasn't earth-shattering, either.

Milo took a breath before he met Felix's stare. "The Bowans have gotten word that there… that there might have been blood exchanged with the server. And that server just tested neutral." He swallowed. "Our spy said they're planning to mobilize."

It took him a second to follow what his second was trying to tell him. Working it out just as slowly as his second, Felix said, "The Bowans wouldn't care if one of their men accidentally turned someone. They'd only care if…"

"If it was Alastair's blood."

Felix narrowed his eyes. Relaxing a bit now that he knew the sky wasn't falling down, he leaned back in his seat. "Well, shit. He should send us a crate of guns or something. Sounds like we handed him a shiny new heir, no effort required."

The old man didn't have a direct heir, so they'd really done him a favor. Turning was a damn nasty business and unreliable, since the odds of it working were slim. Most vampires relied on good old fashioned procreation to make the next generation, but Alastair Bowan had been handed a gift: an heir of his given blood.

If it turned out the new vampire really was venom neutral, making them a coveted blood bride, too… They'd be worth more than their weight in gold.

Only blood brides could procreate with another vampire, making them highly prized by families who cared too much about their bloodlines. They tended to be female, but there were grooms, too.

If Alastair suddenly had an heir *and* they were venom neutral, it'd make that new vampire the single most prized bride on the market.

And the most hunted.

Godspeed and good luck, you poor wretch, he thought. *You'll need it.*

Reaching for his synth, it took him a moment to realize Milo hadn't relaxed. If anything, he looked even grimmer, which was saying something.

Speaking against the rim of his drink, Felix said, "There's more."

"Your girl went to the doctor today, right?"

His muscles locked. Speaking took some effort when he could barely unclench his jaw. "Yes."

Looking a bit like he'd resigned himself to taking out one of his kidneys with his own claws, Milo told him, "The tip came from a doctor at San Francisco General. An hour ago."

The noise of the room whited out. There was nothing but static in his ears as the facts tumbled together.

She wasn't supposed to work that night.

The twenty-four hours after the hit had been some of the longest of his life. He hadn't even known that she was in the building until she texted him the following night. All she'd said was that she didn't have her phone, and since she'd refused to speak to him since, he hadn't gotten any further details about that night or where she'd been.

Her silence drove him to distraction, but he'd been reassured that she was well. Physically, at least. He didn't have time to follow up in the two weeks after the hit as he stabilized his control on the family. Whatever was going on in that enigmatic blonde head, they'd hash it out when he snatched up his prize.

Felix's grandmother would've called him careless. She was always saying he missed the bigger picture.

The droning in his ears got louder and louder. Setting his

bottle back on the table with a gentle tap, he asked, "Do they know the name of the server?"

Milo let out a breath. "Dahlia McKnight."

ASSHOLE
—MISSED CALL WEDNESDAY 3:05 AM
—MISSED CALL THURSDAY 12:47 AM
—MISSED CALL FRIDAY 2:20 AM

I know it's been a few weeks, but are we really back to the ignoring your man thing

you're not my man

lmao

see, because if you WERE, you wouldn't idk go radio silent for SIX WEEKS and then act like everything's fine and normal

you'd tell me when you were busy and let me know when you could that you're okay and not dead in a fucking ditch somewhere because you're a stupid evil little man with an ego the size of Solbourne Tower and too many guns

a man I was in a healthy, fulfilling, consensual relationship with would make sure I knew that he was fine, even if he had a lot going on. He'd answer his phone at least ONCE in the SIX FUCKING WEEKS that had elapsed

MY MAN would stop for a second to think how I might worry about him and not want to cause me any distress, or at the very fucking least consider that I might assume he'd ghosted me and might move on with my life in the meantime

maybe I got a new fucking man while you were off doing gods know what. You ever consider that?

So what I'm hearing is that you really, really missed me

Fuck off, Felix

I missed you too. Now answer your man's call

—CALL BEGAN FRIDAY 2:45 AM
—CALL ENDED FRIDAY 8:58 AM
CONTACT NAME CHANGED TO BOOGEYMAN

Sleep well, pet

I still hate you

SEVEN

DAHLIA THOUGHT SHE WAS PRETTY GOOD AT HANDLING CRISES. She'd grown up in a home that had one at least once a week, if not more.

House burned down? Happened twice. Not a big deal. It wasn't like she had much to miss in the first place.

Mom's in jail again? Good thing Dahlia could usually pack her own school lunches.

Cousin Ricky blew up his car? That was just another Wednesday.

She'd been forged in the fires of a chaotic, often dangerous household, and while it came with copious negative consequences, it also made her damn good in a crisis. She never questioned that she'd be able to make things work. Rent would be paid, one way or another. There would always be food in her fridge. She'd get her degree.

Maybe she'd be sleepless. Maybe she'd eat nothing but rice and peanut butter. Maybe it'd take her twice as long as everyone else to get her education.

But she'd do it, damn it.

In her short life, she'd never met an obstacle she couldn't

overcome — until the day the doctor told her she'd been turned into a vampire.

Dahlia thought she could be forgiven for having a minor mental and emotional collapse.

And that was before the doctors and nurses finally convinced her to do the tooth extraction. It'd taken hours and hours of denial-fueled negotiation for her to consent. She hadn't wanted to believe it.

She *refused.*

Being arrant in a world of dragons and vampires and elves and witches wasn't exactly a walk in the park, but it was who she was. Who her family had always been. They didn't have much, if anything, to be proud of except for the fact that they were scrappy survivors living in a harsh world.

Even if Dahlia hadn't spent five years working in a vampire bar and witnessing some of the worst of them, she wouldn't have wanted to be a vampire. She *liked* who she was.

Or she had, until one bad night ruined her life.

The doctors sent her home with numbing gel, an ice pack, two fewer teeth, and entirely new identity to grapple with.

Well, maybe that's not fair, she thought, eyeing the small stack of glossy paper sitting on her kitchen counter. *They also gave me pamphlets.*

After they'd pumped her for as much information as possible, they'd sat her down for a disturbingly nonchalant rundown of what her life would be like. The biggest and most obvious change was that she'd be on a strict synth diet for the rest, but there were others.

No more sunlight. No more junk food. No more casual dating.

She had to worry about things like *drinking from people* and venom and how complicated it would be to have kids. That last part stung the most. She'd hadn't even begun to process it yet.

That was on the list, she thought, touching her finger to a brand new fang. It was damn sensitive, but the doctor assured her any discomfort would go away within twenty-four hours.

Dahlia had it all planned out. She and Cecilia would move to San Francisco together. She'd get her degree. She'd start a business. Then she'd have a couple cute kids around the same time as Cecilia.

Her kids would have a soft life and never have to worry about whether someone would be around to help with homework.

But how would she have kids now? Everyone knew vampires were infertile until they found an anchor. It wasn't like finding a regular partner to hopefully stick around after knocking you up. It took months of injections of a vampire's venom to make their bodies compatible, and that was only *after* convincing a person to be your personal buffet for life.

Maybe another person would've been initially more upset about the horrific diet change, but Dahlia had been around synth and blood for so long that it only made small ripples in her mind. What she really cared about was her future, which now appeared almost unrecognizable.

Cecilia was the only person in the hospital who seemed to understand. While the doctors and nurses went on and on about the dangers of too much sunlight or the risks of being reckless with her new venom, Cecilia held Dahlia's hand and looked at her with so much sympathy it made her want to sob all over again.

They'd spent the rest of the day and most of the night curled up together in Dahlia's bed. They didn't talk. They just put Dahlia's tablet between them and watched several episodes of a soap opera about a coven of witches embroiled in several torrid love affairs.

Cecilia had asked if she wanted her to stay over, but Dahlia knew she needed time alone to process, so she'd sent her friend to her own apartment around two in the morning. They were used to the nocturnal life, but Cecilia had been up to take her to the hospital since noon. By the time she shuffled off to her own bed, she looked almost as tired as Dahlia.

Left alone, her mind spun in circles of denial, anger, and acceptance.

A shower helped. So did another bottle of synth. Finally clean and full after weeks of illness, she forced herself to crack open her windows to air out her tiny apartment.

"You can grieve," she muttered to herself as she sat on her floor. The guts of her tiny closet were spilled out around her in piles of vintage silk, fur, chiffon, and wool. "Some bad shit happened to you. You're allowed to be upset. But you can't let yourself drown in it. Dahlia McKnight doesn't throw pity parties."

Cool, wet air blew into her apartment as she sorted everything into piles. She should've been resting, but after weeks of sickness, she rode the wave of renewed energy the synth had given her.

Reorganizing her closet gave her something to do with her hands while she muddled through her feelings.

She hadn't wanted to give the doctors more information about what happened to her, but she'd been given little choice. Dahlia wasn't reckless enough to give Patrol the names of those who'd been in the rooftop lounge that night and they hadn't asked, assuming an insignificant server probably wouldn't know, but she'd been convinced by the doctor to spill the details.

"It's important for your health that we know who donated the blood," he'd cajoled her. *"If there's some sort of problem or rejection, we can consult their records. You never know — it might just save your life one day."*

Even then, it'd taken his assurance that nothing would get leaked back to Patrol before she coughed up the name.

Dahlia gently rolled up a silk scarf, a treasure she'd found at an estate sale, her thoughts on what it meant to have someone else's blood in her. She knew more about vampires than the average person, certainly, but there was plenty she'd never bothered to learn.

I have no choice now. How fun.

She wondered if it would mean anything to Mr. Bowan if he knew he'd accidentally turned her. It seemed unlikely. She was just a server he'd had the misfortune of meeting once. What would he care?

Dahlia stood up from her cross-legged position and began hanging her clothes back up, this time by color rather than occasion as she'd done the last time she reorganized. Growing up with next to nothing, there was little she treasured more than her wardrobe, which was painstakingly assembled via thrift stores, bargain shops, estate sales, and swaps.

The rich colors, the sumptuous fabrics, the vintage craftsmanship... All of it made her feel special in a way nothing else in life had. When she wore her beautiful clothes, she was more than just a girl from a broken home. She was a beautiful woman making her way in a glamorous city.

I can still be that, she thought, trying to summon some sort of positivity. *Things will just look a little different.*

She'd have to get a new job, but she'd already decided on that, so it wasn't too much of a shock. There were many shops open at night. She'd worked retail in the past. Surely she could get a job at one of them. Until then, she had a healthy savings account for emergencies. She could take a couple weeks to get her bearings before she threw herself into real life again.

Her rent would still be paid. She'd still have food — synth, now. School would start up again in a few weeks. She could easily switch to being fully online, though she'd miss being in a classroom.

The rest... well, the rest she'd just have to figure out in time.

Feeling marginally more calm, she'd just finished carefully aligning her shoes and bags on the floor of her closet when the knock on her door came.

Dahlia heavily considered not answering it. She hadn't

ordered anything, and there was no reason for her landlord to come around. The gods knew he avoided the rundown apartment building like the plague, lest one of his many disgruntled renters corner him and demand improvements.

It was most likely one of Felix's deliveries. When she ignored him for long enough, he tended to get more and more extreme in his bids for attention. A phone was just the start. He'd once sent her a necklace with a diamond bigger than an egg. She'd been so terrified of having it in her apartment that she'd forced him to take it back.

In the past, the ploy had always worked. Whether she accepted his gifts or not wasn't the goal. It was getting her attention.

Which was exactly why she'd been refusing everything. She wasn't about to bend this time. She wouldn't give in.

She was done with the game Felix played.

Not that it matters now. He won't want a vampire.

A staggering pang of loss struck her as another knock came, more insistent this time. It'd been one thing to decide to cut him out once and for all. It was quite another to know *he* wouldn't want anything to do with her now.

Vampires don't date other vampires.

They couldn't. Or at least, she'd never heard of any of them doing so.

Vampire venom was poisonous to them, and they couldn't feed without releasing it.

And vampiric relationships were all about feeding. Especially the shallow ones.

Felix wouldn't want anything to do with her if he couldn't fuck and feed. He'd toyed with her for years, and though she'd grown feelings for him, she'd never been delusional enough to think he wanted more than those two things from her.

Her throat went painfully tight. Gods, they'd never even gotten close to dating. And she'd broken things off with *him!* So why did it hurt so much to think that there was no possibility of anything between them now?

Dahlia stood there in the middle of her apartment, her silk pajama shorts and flowy top fluttering in the cool breeze, frozen by the prospect. A part of her didn't want to see whatever outrageous thing Felix sent her, but another, bigger part was compelled by the fact that it would probably be the last gift she ever received from him.

She padded across the floor. If it was too much, she promised herself that she'd return it anyway. But if it was tolerable, she'd make it a keepsake for the strange, dangerous era in her life when she entertained a vampire suitor.

It was a deeply unpleasant shock to find no delivery man on the other side of her door.

Dahlia's grip tightened reflexively on the door handle as she fought the urge to step back. "Devon?"

EIGHT

HE STOOD ON HER LITTLE WELCOME MAT, HIS BLOND HAIR disheveled and his eyes just a little too wide. He was dressed more casually than she'd ever seen him. Instead of his tight shirts and slacks, he wore joggers and an oversized coat, like he'd thrown on whatever he could grab before running out of his house.

Devon sucked in a sharp breath. His pale eyes skimmed over what he could see of her from between the partially open door and the wall.

"Hey, Dahlia." He laughed, running a hand through his hair. "Sorry for dropping by unannounced."

Dahlia wasn't really surprised he showed up. If anything, she'd expected him when it became clear she wouldn't be returning to work. But something about his body language made her instincts scream an alarm.

When he braced his hands on the door jamb and leaned closer, his scent became overpowering in a way it never had before. It was cloying and burnt, like brown sugar and cigarettes and clothes a day overdue for the wash.

Stomach rolling in a too-familiar way, Dahlia curled her

suddenly cold toes against the cheap flooring. "Um, what are you doing here?"

"I heard you're not coming back to The Lush," he answered. His gaze flicked over her shoulder. "Can I come in? I was hoping we could talk."

Her nails bit into the wood of her door. Every instinct warned her not to let him inside, and not just because he was a threat. Her skin crawled at the idea of letting this man into her private space.

Not caring if she came off as rude, she told him, "I really don't think there's anything to talk about. I'm not coming back."

It unnerved her when Devon didn't pout or throw a fit. Instead, he smiled at her. "Oh, I know. You're too good for that place. I've been telling you for months."

Wrong-footed, she was too busy trying to figure out a way to end the bizarre visit to stop him from shouldering past her. "Hey! I didn't say you could come in," she snapped, watching him stroll into her tiny studio like he owned the place.

He took a long look at her cheap stick-on wallpaper, thrifted drapes, and carefully DIY'd light fixtures. Her apartment was cozy and beautiful, full of rich reds and maroons and touches of burnished gold. She'd designed every inch to fit a loose *femme fatale's boudoir* aesthetic and she didn't appreciate the way Devon looked at it like he'd just stepped in something foul.

The look of disgust only lasted a second, however. As soon as it appeared, it was replaced by something else. Something *hungry*.

Devon took a deep breath. Then another. And another.

Color rose high on his lean cheeks. Flushed and visibly excited, he turned on his heel to give her another one of those big, unsettling smiles. "I always knew you were special. You know, Duke told me I had to leave employees alone. Pissed me off, but thank fuck I listened to him! He'll change his tune about how bad things went with the Bowans when I tell him what I've got."

Dahlia didn't dare move away from the door. "What are you talking about?"

He tilted his head toward her kitchenette. The pack of synth the hospital had sent her home with sat on the counter, missing one bottle, beside the vase of withered flowers he'd sent her.

"You enjoying your new diet along with those fangs?"

All the blood drained from her head in a rush. For just a moment she'd forgotten. She hadn't even thought to try and cover her mouth.

Not that it *mattered*. What did Devon care if she was a vampire or not? She'd effectively been taken out of the dating pool, and she wouldn't be welcome back at her position in The Lush.

She hadn't done anything wrong, either. There was no shame in having some seriously bad luck.

And yet she felt it crawling up the back of her neck like cold, clammy fingers. The way he looked at her was far worse than how he'd done it before. He'd always objectified her, but now he looked at her like she was meat.

But that doesn't make any sense. If anything, he should be pissed he can't have me.

Suddenly aware of everything from her thin pajamas to her brand new pair of fangs, Dahlia pressed her back against the door and eyed Devon like the intruder he was.

"What do you want?" she demanded, annoyed that her voice came out a little high.

"I bet you're starving. I know I am. You smell like the stuff dreams are made of, baby." Devon shucked his oversized coat and tossed it on her bed, completely carefree. He wore a thin, v-neck t-shirt underneath it — and a gun.

She sucked in a sharp breath. The situation had been serious before, but the shoulder holster and its gaudy, too-big bolt gun made it *very* serious.

Keeping her eyes on the gun, she muttered, "Devon, I don't know what's going on, but I need you to leave."

Patting the gun like a prized dog, he assured her, "Ah, don't worry about this. I only brought it in case anyone else shows up. Can't have anyone horning in on my claim."

It was on the tip of her tongue to ask if he even knew how to use a gun like that — a big dick handgun with a mean kick, as her cousins would say — but she'd seen how quickly Devon could explode in anger, so she held it in.

Instead, she calmly asked, "Your claim on what?"

Devon put his hands on his hips and flashed his fangs in an expression that was part smile and part sneer. "You."

Dahlia's mind was working overtime to catch up to what in the world was going on. Everything was a bunch of broken pieces in her head. She'd only just caught up to the fact that he knew she'd been turned when another realization hit her: he hadn't been surprised.

Cold sweat dewed on her freshly cleaned skin. *How?*

The only person who knew was Cecilia, and her best friend would quit The Lush before she gave their bosses Dahlia's personal information. The only possibility that made any sense to her was that the brothers had somehow put together what had happened that night on the roof, but the timing was deeply suspicious.

The doctor knew, she realised. *But why would he tell my boss? And even if he did, why does it matter to them?*

None of it made any sense, but most especially the way Devon looked at her as he prowled toward where she stood.

"I'm a vampire now," she warned, though he obviously already knew.

It didn't stop him. If anything, it made him more excited as he boxed her in against the door. The muscles of her thighs flexed, preparing to run, but when the butt of that monstrous gun touched her side, she froze.

No matter what he said, the threat was there.

Devon placed his palms flat on the door on either side of her head. Leaning down to whisper in her ear, he said, "I know, baby. That's why I'm here." The sound of him drawing in another deep breath made her shudder. "You smell *divine*. I always heard you taste better than regular blood. I can't wait to get my first taste."

Her pulse thundered in her ears. "You— you can't do that. My blood's—"

"Even more delicious now than it was a couple weeks ago," he purred. "Or at least, that's what people say. I've never gotten the chance to try a bride before."

Bride? The word pinged off of some distant, nebulous memory, but she didn't have time to work through what it might be.

Feeling like an animal in a snare, she glanced from side to side, trying to figure out her best escape route that wouldn't get her shot. Devon was clearly into some stuff she'd never heard of. She'd always been told that vampires couldn't feed each other without dying, but maybe there was some kink for it she'd never been privy to.

Or maybe Devon had just lost his mind. It seemed equally likely.

Dahlia had never been bitten before. She was one of the very few servers at The Lush who hadn't tried it at least once. Many were more than happy to trade a single feeding at the end of their shifts for an extremely hefty tip. She'd heard it was more pleasurable than it sounded and provided a lovely little buzz.

But she'd never been curious enough to risk it even before Felix warned her that he'd be extremely unhappy if he found out she'd fed someone else. She was even less inclined now that she knew doing so would kill her.

"Devon, you can't bite me," she told him, trying to sound reasonable and not as scared as she felt. "That'll kill me. I thought you liked me. You don't kill people you like."

He laughed a loud, braying laugh. "It won't kill you. It'll feel really good, I promise. But maybe you're right. You should bite me first. You're probably starving. And I'm a gentleman."

Dahlia balked when he pressed down on the top of her head, trying to guide her mouth to his neck. "Have you lost your mind? It'll kill you, too!"

She'd always figured Devon was a consummate coward and would probably run at the first sign of any real danger, but he didn't bat an eye at the thought of her injecting him with her brand new venom.

Even if she hadn't been warned explicitly against it, her stomach turned at the thought of feeding on *him*. Nothing about him appealed to her on any level.

"You won't," he crooned.

Bracing her forearm against his chest, she tried to wedge a bit of space between them. "How? What's going on?"

Devon winked. "It'll just take a couple bites and no one will be able to take you away. The Bowans will *have* to make a deal with us."

A little spark of temper went a long way to burning up her fear. Pushing hard on his chest, she watched him stumble back a step and took the opportunity to slip to the side. The fire escape couldn't be trusted and there was no way out besides the door, but she had to put what little distance between them she could.

"What does Mr. Bowan have to do with this?" she demanded, skirting around the kitchenette and toward the bathroom. Worst came to worst, she could lock herself in and yell for Cecilia to call for help.

Devon tracked her progress around the room with a slow spin on his heel. "How about I explain it all to you at my place?" He offered her an indulgent smile. "You come home with me, baby, and we'll work everything out."

"No, thanks," she snapped. "I'm happy here. My boyfriend wouldn't like it if I went anywhere with you."

Devon's eyes narrowed. "You don't have a boyfriend."

"You don't know that." She held his stare as she inched toward the bathroom. The lock was flimsy and the door wouldn't do anything to stop a plasma bolt shot, but it was better than nothing.

"You never smell like anyone," he challenged, shoulders hiking in a defensive, angry posture she'd seen dozens of times. They were headed into dangerous territory, but she couldn't think of what else might deter him. "There's no scent here. And even if there was, it wouldn't matter. You're mine."

Some reckless idiot inside of her actually compelled her to scoff aloud. "You don't know my boyfriend. He's gonna flip his shit if you touch me, Devon."

Only one part of that was a lie. Felix had never been her boyfriend, but he *would* lose his mind if he discovered another vampire had been encroaching on his territory.

It'd happened before. She'd once made the mistake of complaining about a serial grabber at work. The next night his face appeared on the news. He'd been dumped in front of a hospital missing his hands.

A vein began to throb in Devon's neck. His excited flush had deepened into a darker puce. "Tell me his name, then."

She'd never said it aloud. She'd never even told Cecilia. Dahlia had kept whatever existed between herself and Felix close to her chest. At first it was because he was dangerous. And then it was because she didn't want anyone telling her to stop.

Her heel just edged over the tile of the bathroom floor when she said, "Fel—"

A fist pounding on her door cut her off. Dahlia froze, caught for a split second by the thought that it might be Cecilia.

She wouldn't knock, she reminded herself as Devon whirled around.

She watched with dawning horror as he clumsily unholstered his heavy gun and reached for the doorknob. Tearing it open, he'd barely raised his gun when a deep voice drawled, "Hello, fucker."

The flash of a bolt going off reached her before the whine of the discharge did, and a full second before Devon's body dropped to the ground in a heap, most of his head missing.

Dahlia slapped her hands over her mouth to muffle her scream. Her body locked as a man in a long black coat stepped over the body and casually tucked his gun away. He was tall and lean, with wide shoulders and a head of wavy black hair that curled around his ears and neck. A distinctive white lock of hair was a jaunty little swirl that just brushed his eyebrow.

His nose was straight. His eyes were a cool gray. And when he put his hands on his hips and looked at her, he smiled like he didn't have a care in the world.

Recognition was a lightning bolt through her entire body.

Even if she hadn't spent three years as his reluctant penpal, she would've recognized him from that awful night in the bar, when they dragged the bloated, poisoned body of his uncle Julius out onto the dance floor and he'd taken a drink with it sitting at his feet.

She'd know her boogeyman anywhere.

"Hi, pet," he greeted, rocking back on his heels like a little boy too excited to stand still. "D'you miss me?"

BOOGEYMAN

What'd you do yesterday

> are we really going to pretend like you
> don't know
>
> like you don't see everything I do with your
> beady little boogeyman eyes

First, my grandma said I have big beautiful eyes
and she only lied about 75% of the time so it
must be true

Second, of course I know, but a good partner
still asks

> please excuse me

What are you doing

> laughing myself to death

I hope you appreciate that you're the only
person in the world allowed to laugh at me

> I'd appreciate it more if you didn't need it so
> badly

Who needs to be laughed at

> everyone. It keeps a person humble

There's your problem. I'm amazing. I have no
reason to be humble

And neither do you

You're fucking perfect, Dahlia

NINE

FELIX TOOK IN THE LITTLE APARTMENT WITH A SWEEPING GLANCE. "This is nice. I like your wallpaper."

Dahlia didn't reply. She stood stiffly in the doorway of the bathroom. There was no relief at the sight of him, but he hadn't really expected any. His girl wasn't the type to appreciate a man riding to her rescue.

He had little doubt that she could've taken care of the blond twerp, but as soon as he got word that Devon had been seen entering her building, he knew it was finally time to give him what he deserved.

It was too bad for him. Dahlia would've been more merciful. Felix didn't do that sort of thing.

It didn't matter that Devon didn't know about Felix's claim. What mattered was that he'd been bothering Dahlia and other women on his staff for a long time, and finally making a move on her had given Felix the perfect excuse to rid the world of his unique brand of garbage.

No one could fault him for it. A claim was a claim, and one placed on a blood bride was a beast all its own. Even if she'd just been his anchor, Felix wouldn't have been judged for his quick execution, but the fact that she was his blood bride made it more than justified.

It was expected.

Ignoring the body on the floor, he did a small circuit around the apartment, taking in all the little details she'd never shown him through the lens of her phone's camera. Of course, he knew her shopping habits. He checked her payment records weekly, just to see what she'd been up to and make sure she didn't need some help.

He didn't do it to keep control over her but because he was a pathologically curious sort of person. Knowing things was his favorite hobby, and knowing *Dahlia* had surpassed anything he'd ever enjoyed before.

Felix loved knowing that she bought the same coffee every week. He loved that she never splurged on anything new, but was willing to shell out her hard earned money at estate sales or thrift stores. He loved seeing what textbook she'd been forced to buy that semester and where she ate lunch with Cecilia that day.

Every single one of those purchases told him a story. It told him what she valued, what made her happy, and what she deemed necessary. More importantly, it told him what her weaknesses were. It was vital information for a man like him.

And he could admit that he just liked it. Because he liked her. A lot.

The roof of his mouth pulsed angrily as he circled around her bed. She still hadn't made a sound, but the feeling of her awareness of him, her nearness, made the craving for her almost unbearable.

Dahlia had always smelled good. He noticed it the night they met, when Harlan Bounds so kindly handled his uncle for him.

She smelled of vanilla and brown sugar and suede and whatever fancy shit she used in her hair. One whiff of her and a flash of that scowl...

He'd been caught, hook, line, and sinker.

It was a beautiful kind of torture to be in her space, especially now. If she smelled delicious before, it was nothing compared to what Alastair's blood had done to her.

All venom neutral vampires smelled sweeter than the rest of their kind. There was no instinctive disgust when he sucked in her scent. No instinct telling him to avoid drinking at all costs. No competitive urge to show dominance or strength. There was only hunger.

Blood brides were hard-wired to be delicious.

While vampires as a whole were designed to be predators, *they* were designed to prey on *vampires*, and that meant everything about them was meant to appeal. To entice.

His mouth watered as he slowly turned to face his girl. The ache in his fangs was persistent and growing, along with other parts of his body, but it couldn't quite distract him from the dark circles under her eyes or the hollows of her cheeks.

He was so happy to see her that he'd been briefly distracted from his fury. The sight of her standing there, trembling in her skimpy silk pajamas, brought it roaring back.

"You're in some serious fucking trouble," he bit out. "When were you going to tell me you were sick?"

The thought of what she must have been through in the last two weeks sent a wave of awful, prickly feeling over his skin. A vampire lived or died based on how well they cared for their anchors, blood bride or not. It was a hard-wired survival imperative. A vampire couldn't feed on a sickly, neglected mate, after all.

It was his job to keep her safe. It was his job to provide for her. It was his job to see to her needs, whatever they were.

He'd been forced to keep his distance while his war with Yvanna dragged on, but that didn't mean the instincts were muted. Even knowing he couldn't keep her, he'd felt them like a knife between his ribs every day as he lay in bed, staring at his ceiling and gnashing his teeth.

To know she'd not only been on that roof the night of the

assassination but also silently suffering as Alastair's blood took hold really, *really* pissed him off.

And when she still refused to say anything? A fuse lit.

Felix stalked across the room. Her cornflower blue eyes went wide as she watched him approach. Bare feet slapping against the cheap bathroom tile, she scrambled backward until her spine hit the edge of the sink.

He didn't stop.

Felix crowded her against the sink. She leaned as far back as she could, but it didn't do much. Cupping her cheeks, he pressed his thumbs into the corners of her mouth.

"Show me," he growled.

The brat sucked her lips between her teeth instead.

Gods, that stubborn shit made him hard. He loved it when she looked at him like that — scared but scrappy. Determined to be a pain in his ass at every turn. He'd seen it in her that night in The Lush. Just a spark. Just one look.

That was all it took for him to know she was perfect.

But this was serious business. They only had a handful of minutes before Bowan men came down on their heads like a hurricane, and he wasn't eager to start another war just as he finished one.

Well, he *was*, but not with Dahlia around. She needed to be safely tucked away in the Amauri house before he started shooting.

"Dahlia, I'm already mad at you. You really want to make things worse? Open."

He half expected her to keep fighting him, but she didn't. She let out a shaky sigh and closed her eyes. Reluctantly pulling her lips out from between her teeth, she flashed just a hint of fang before attempting to hide them away again.

Felix's pulse jumped as he pressed his thumbs into her upper lip, forcing her to reveal the full length of her dainty little fangs. They were pearly white and smaller than he was used to, but fit her perfectly.

A rush of blood made him light-headed as he stared at them. He hadn't had time to secondguess the news that his girl had been turned. They'd taken an m-gate — a magical tear in space-time — to get to her before anyone else could. There hadn't been a moment to really think about any of it.

Of course he smelled the change in her scent and he saw the synth on her counter, but until that moment, it hadn't really sunk in that it was *real*.

Dahlia was a vampire.

Dahlia was *his*.

An elation unlike anything he'd ever felt popped in his chest like Charter Day fireworks. He'd been so focused on making sure she was okay and that he got to her first that he hadn't allowed himself to truly consider the fact that he'd been given everything he'd ever wanted.

The war was over. The family belonged to him. Dahlia McKnight would be his until the day they died.

And after, too, if he had anything to say about it.

Easing her full lip down over those beautiful new fangs, he breathed, "This is the best night of my fucking life."

Dahlia's eyes popped open. Rearing her head back, she looked at him like he'd pissed in her synth.

"What are you *talking* about?" Before he could explain, she started slapping at his chest and arms. "Why are you here? How did you even— What is going *on*? How does everyone know that I'm— I'm— And you killed Devon! In my apartment! Felix, what the fuck—"

His girl wasn't a crier. She was a stiff upper lip, lick her wounds in private sort of woman. So it really alarmed him when she stopped slapping him and started crying the big gulping and shaking kind of tears.

"Wh— what is going *on?*" she repeated, batting at him weakly. "Go away, go away, go away!"

Very aware of his men standing guard nearby, Felix reached back to close the bathroom door. No one needed to see Dahlia like this. She'd be mortified if she knew they were there, and selfishly, he wanted to keep every bit of her vulnerability to himself.

Hoisting her up onto the edge of the sink, Felix stepped between her legs and wrapped his arms around her shoulders. He rested his chin on top of her head and let out a pleased sigh when her breath puffed over his exposed throat. It wasn't the time to be turned on, but he couldn't exactly blame his cock for being excited. It'd waited three long years, after all.

She was nearly enveloped by his coat, which was a necessity in San Francisco's bullshit excuse for a summer. She didn't exactly relax, but she didn't push him away, either.

"Shh," he soothed, petting her silky blonde hair covetously. She was so damn pretty. Dolled up or bare-faced. Dressed in her favorite outfit or wearing her pajamas. Grinning or ugly crying. It didn't matter.

Dahlia McKnight was a *mcknockout.*

Her voice was adorably watery when she demanded, "What are you doing here, Felix?"

He glanced at their reflection in the mirror and smiled. They looked damn good together. "I'm rescuing you, of course."

"How did you even know—"

Just like that, his smile turned into a scowl. "That you'd been turned? Not because you told me, that's for sure."

Dahlia pushed his chest until he reluctantly dropped his arms. Clutching fistfuls of her hair, she stared at the floor in wide-eyed disbelief as she croaked, "How does everyone *know* that? I just found out today and— and Cece is the only person who knows. She wouldn't tell anyone. So how did Devon and you find out?"

There wasn't time to get into the ugly details, but he knew that he'd never get her anywhere willingly if he didn't at least partially explain the situation.

Rubbing his hands up and down her arms, he said, "The vampire underworld is big and made up of more than just us.

There are factions who make it their business to keep eyes on places like hospitals — and keep doctors in their pockets. The information was sold to whoever has their claws in Solbourne General, then leaked through informants and spies. Nothing stays secret for long when everyone's willing to be bought."

Dahlia's expression was heartbreakingly shocked. "The doctor?"

"The doctor," he confirmed.

"But why? Why does anyone care?"

"A lot of reasons," he hedged, feeling his phone buzz in his pocket. No doubt it was Milo telling him to move his ass. "But we don't have time to get into all of them here. We need to get you out of here. Now."

Dahlia leaned away from him again. Giving him a suspicious look, she asked, "Why?"

"Because if that dipshit—" He jerked his thumb toward the bathroom door. "—knew, that means *everyone* knows. We won't just have the Bowan cavalry riding in, but every piece of shit in a thousand mile radius."

She made a face. "Bowan? Why would Mr. Bowan care?"

They *really* didn't have time to get into the intricacies of vampire culture, so instead of answering, he clapped his hands together and announced, "Time to get a move-on! Pack a bag with essentials but don't worry about the rest. I'll have everything shipped home."

TEN

HE EXPECTED HER TO HOP OFF THE COUNTER AND GET TO WORK, BUT that was wishful thinking. Dahlia had never listened to him in the past. It didn't seem likely she'd start now.

"I'm not going anywhere with you," she said, like it should've been obvious.

Felix gave her the look a statement like that deserved. "You are."

"I just saw you kill a man, Felix. You've lost your mind if you think I'd go *anywhere* with you!"

"I'm confused about the part where you thought you had a choice. Maybe I wasn't clear enough." He leaned in close. Speaking slowly so she couldn't miss a word, he explained, "As of today, you've officially become the most wanted vampire in the entire syndicate. I'm gonna tell you why that is, but not here and not right now. Because if we don't leave soon, you're going to see me kill a lot more than that blond idiot."

She paled a little, but her chin hadn't lost its stubborn angle. "How do I know you aren't lying to get me to do what you want?"

That rubbed him the wrong way. Felix was a lot of things, but a liar wasn't one of them. He was an upfront sort of monster. That didn't mean he was trustworthy, but it did mean she ought to believe him when he told her what was what.

Taking a step back from her, he demanded, "When have I ever lied to you, Dahlia?"

She said nothing, but her gaze shifted to the side. It was strange to know someone as well as he knew her and yet not have a clear read on her physical tells. Her expression was tight, but he couldn't decide if it was one of resignation or preparation to fight some more.

He looked forward to unraveling all those subtle intricacies. Just not tonight.

"Time's up, pet."

She let out a squawk of alarm as he hoisted her off the sink. Giving her lovely ass a swift pat, he pushed her toward the door. "Bag. Clothes. Woman shit. Now."

Dahlia jolted toward the door, only to stop with her hand on the knob. Her shoulders tensed. Without turning to look at him, she whispered, "I... don't want to go out there."

He arched a brow. "Why?"

She let out a sigh. He'd heard that exact same one from Milo thousands of times. It was the *"Felix, please be normal for five minutes"* sound.

"The *body*," she stressed.

"Ah." He'd already forgotten about the smoking ruin he'd left on her floor. Devon had been an obstacle. Now that he was gone, Felix had moved on to more important things.

Guiding her back a step, he said, "Please hold."

With her standing behind him, he cracked the door open and poked his head out. A quick inspection revealed that his men had already done their job. There wasn't a trace of the body on her floor, and the scent of singed flesh and plasma had been cleared out by the breeze drifting through her open windows.

Stepping out, he held the door open for her. He shot her a

sharp smile. "Funny. I don't see a body. You must've been mistaken."

Dahlia peered around the door jamb like she expected Devon to pop up and grab her. Surprise warred with relief when there was nothing and no one to see. He could practically hear the questions dancing on the tip of her little pink tongue. A smile cramped his cheeks when she stubbornly held them in.

Smart girl. Only a fool asked questions about where bodies disappeared to, and his girl wasn't one of those.

Clapping his hands again, he cajoled, "Get to it, pet. We should've been out of here ten minutes ago."

She gave him another one of those withering looks. He wondered if she'd keep it up if he told her how much it turned him on.

Probably not, he decided as he watched her scurrying around.

Felix loved her spine. He loved that she knew the risks of pissing off a man like him and still stood up for herself.

In his world, the currency was prestige and protection. It paid to suck up to the biggest prick in the room. Alliances and matings were all built on the idea of giving and receiving protection in some sense — financial, physical, or political.

That meant that for most of his life, the people he met were either trying to get something from him or trying to kill him. Even his own family.

Especially his family.

But Dahlia was different. She'd never asked him for anything. She had nothing to gain from his downfall. She stood stubbornly outside of the bloody world he intended to rule, and because of that, she treated him with absolutely zero respect.

He *loved* it.

"Where are we going?" She didn't sound enthused, but she didn't stop shoving silky bits of fluff into her overnight bag, so he counted it as a win.

"Home." Felix peered into her closet. It took some effort to resist the urge to press his face into the clothes. He wanted to roll around in her scent like a blissed out cat.

Something hard thumped his back and clattered to the floor. Felix glanced down. A lone black leather heel lay on its side by his feet.

After scooping up the sexy projectile, he turned to find Dahlia glaring at him. "Where's home?"

"Somewhere safe." Her apartment was so small, it only took him a handful of steps to hand the heel back to her. Spying the other one in the bag, he pressed his tongue to the roof of his mouth in a vain attempt to ease the ache.

Why she thought four inch tall black leather stilettos were essential, he had no idea. He was simply grateful.

Dahlia snatched the heel from his hand. Pointing it at him like a weapon, she demanded, "Where, Felix?"

He rolled his eyes. "To the Amauri estate. There's a witch waiting in the back alley with an m-gate at the ready. It'll take us directly to my house in United Washington. Happy?"

She scoffed. "What does my happiness have to do with any of this?"

A little of his good humor bled away. He didn't like that, but he also knew better than to make promises to her about what their future would be like. Even if she believed him — unlikely — there was no guaranteeing anything in their world. Most especially happiness.

"Time's running out," he prompted her. "Do you have everything?"

Dahlia did another quick sweep of the apartment. After snatching her makeup case off the bathroom counter, she zipped up her bag and turned toward her closet. "I just need to change and we can—"

"Don't. I like the short-shorts." Felix snagged her bag and strode to the front door. Tossing it out to Nash, a rough-looking behemoth and one of the trusted cousins he'd left standing in the hall, he said, "We're leaving. Is Genevieve ready?"

Nash nodded. "Yes, sir. But we should hurry. There's movement two streets up."

Felix nodded. Turning back around, he found Dahlia in the middle of ignoring what he'd told her. She was rummaging around in a small chest of drawers, her fingers curled around what looked suspiciously like a pair of pants, when he swooped down on her.

She sputtered indignantly when he pressed his shoulder into her middle and lifted her feet off the ground. Her smooth legs flailed uselessly in front of him as he adjusted his grip.

Her movement stopped abruptly when his fingers settled in the crease between her ass and her thigh, putting his fingertips right where they belonged: in the hot cleft of her silk-covered cunt.

"Careful, pet," he warned, rubbing his index finger along the gusset of her sleep shorts. "Don't squirm too much. You don't want to ruin these pretty pajamas, do you?"

Speaking through her teeth, she informed him, "I can walk!"

He clicked his tongue against the back of his fangs. "Not without shoes. No girl of mine is walking barefoot on that nasty-ass hallway carpet."

A fist bounced harmlessly off his side. "I have shoes!"

"Yeah, but I like this better." Her thighs clenched around his hand as the scent of her arousal perfumed the air — unmistakable and raw. A deep purr erupted from his chest as he stroked her again, more firmly this time, and teased, "I think you do, too. I bet I could get you off just like this."

She made a choked sound of outrage, but she didn't try to deny it. They both knew what he felt between her thighs, and it wasn't just warm silk.

Felix's cock throbbed behind his fly. He couldn't wait to get home and show her just how right he was.

Carrying her to the door, he told her, "You know what? I've changed my mind about ruining these shorts. I'll just buy you a new pair."

There wasn't time for her to come up with a response. In a moment they were out her front door. Speaking to the guards flanking them, he ordered, "Have all her things packed and shipped back to the house."

"Wait, wait—" Whatever she was about to say was cut off by his shoulder jamming into her stomach as he jogged lightly down the stairs. He did his best to not jostle her, but there wasn't anything for it. Taking an elevator was a rookie move, since it was the easiest thing in the world to trap a person in, and they didn't have time to go slow.

Nearing the ground floor, he said, "We'll need to double security on the house. I want two men on every post twenty-four hours a day. Tell Milo that I don't care who you have to pull. Once Bowan finds out we've got her, he's going to throw one massive fucking hissy-fit and we need to be ready."

Several firm grunts of assent bounced off the emergency stairwell's walls. Nash asked, "How long do you think it'll take, boss?"

There was no impatience in his tone. It was a question of preparation from a man who'd only just finished fighting in one war and was now being asked to fight another.

They both knew that honor demanded Alastair fight until the last man to get his daughter back. The key to avoiding war was to act fast. There was only one way to end things without one side annihilating that other, and that was to make it impossible for Dahlia to be separated from Felix.

She needed to cleave to him — mind, body, and soul. When she became his bride in all ways, there would be nothing for Alastair to do but accept it.

So it wasn't unreasonable for Felix's men to wonder how quickly he could move the process along. They were all exhausted. No one wanted to fight another war so soon, and no one wanted to die when there was a pleasurable alternative to be had.

The problem was that he couldn't force Dahlia to do

anything. Not really. Not when it'd ruin the only truly good thing in his life.

Feeling the beginnings of a tension headache in his temples, Felix answered, "As long as it needs to."

No one said another word, but he could feel their collective frustration simmering in the air as he pushed open the metal emergency door. The alleyway behind Dahlia's apartment building was damp and ripe with the scents emanating from the dumpsters on either side of the door. Orange light from the streetlamps shimmered in murky puddles, contrasted by the depth of the navy blue shadows that stretched along the filthy asphalt.

Genevieve and her guards stood a little ways away, their backs against the opposite wall.

The witch was his single most expensive employee. Not only did he have to pay her exorbitantly for her services, but she had to be guarded at all times. Taking a shot at her was like slashing the tires of the getaway car, so protecting her was costly but absolutely necessary.

All of five feet tall, olive-skinned, tattooed, and with the sharp, fox-like features all witches somehow seemed to possess, Genevieve looked out of place standing between two hulking vampire guards. It wasn't helped by the fact that her dark hair was pulled up in a jaunty ponytail and she wore her customary uniform of over-sized sneakers, cardigan, and short pleated skirt. And when Nash, her dedicated bodyguard, resumed his normal place at her side, she managed to appear even more ridiculous.

She looked like a damn co-ed rather than the risky invest-ment that had paid off again and again in the year since he'd found her.

He nodded at her. "Fire it up, pipsqueak."

Completely unfazed by the now loudly protesting woman strung over his shoulder, Genevieve finished up whatever game she'd been playing on her phone and tucked it into her sweater pocket.

"Where are we landing?"

Normally he avoided tearing a hole in space inside his house, as it tended to wreak havoc on antiques and minor things like structural integrity, but instinct was instinct. He was practically coming out of his skin having Dahlia exposed. The urge to get her somewhere safe and private was impossible to fight.

"The foyer," he answered, giving Dahlia a reassuring pat on the ass.

One of the things he liked about Genevieve was that it was impossible to tell by looking at her that she was a force of nature. With her small stature, preppy clothes, and sunny attitude, it was all too easy to underestimate her.

But all it took to correct that was seeing her in action one time.

All of his men except Nash took several quick steps back as the witch pressed her hands together. In an instant, the air in the alley grew heavy and full of static. He could feel the magic racing over his skin in little invisible arcs of electricity as the scent of garbage was overpowered by the metallic, blood-like stench of power.

Dahlia clutched his coat in tight fists, her body stiff with apprehension over his shoulder. He skated his free hand down her leg in a comforting caress as Genevieve threw her hands apart.

An explosion of light and magic filled the alley, burning away the shadows. A gate had been opened as easily as one might part a curtain.

He stepped forward just as Dahlia's tremulous voice reached him. "Felix, I've never been through an m-gate before."

"Shh. I've got you. Just try not to throw up on my back, okay?" He did a little hop, hoping to startle a laugh out of her as she bounced. "I like this coat."

His girl didn't laugh, though. She did something better.

Dahlia gripped his coat tighter and pressed her face into his back. Her voice was small when she said, "Please don't let go of me."

Felix pressed a fierce kiss to her side. "Never," he promised, stepping into the gate.

is everything okay? You sounded stressed

Just tired of family bullshit.

anything I can do to help

You can finally let me see those perky tits I've
been dreaming of for two years

ah there he is

gods forbid the boogeyman get too close to an
actual feeling

I have lots of feelings. Big ones. Thick ones.

your cock doesn't count

I strongly beg to differ

ELEVEN

SHE WAS FAIRLY CERTAIN THAT FELIX WAS JOKING WHEN HE TOLD HER not to throw up on his coat, but as soon as he stepped through the m-gate, the threat became very real.

Dahlia wasn't used to magic. Her small town had been mostly arrants, and even after moving to the city, she'd never had much contact with the magically gifted. The Lush didn't pay her enough to afford things like magically enhanced clothing or jewelry or tech. Even the relatively common sort of magic was foreign to her.

An m-gate was nothing close to common.

Passing through one was a bit like having her whole body sucked through a straw and shot out the other side like a spitball. One second she was nothing but atoms molded to fit a new shape and the next she was Dahlia again, presumably with all her bits and bobs, thrown over Felix's shoulder in what looked like the foyer of an opulent, Gilded Age mansion.

She was so disoriented that it took her a minute to realize he'd set her back on her feet.

The world swayed in a sickening wave before it righted itself. The cool marble under her toes helped center her as she swallowed a mouthful of bile.

"Not so bad, huh?" Felix gave her one of those wicked smiles and flicked her nose. "Welcome home, pet."

Weaving a little, she peered around him as a series of vampires stepped through the gate, followed by what had to be the witch. The tattooed brunette gave her a cheerful wave before clapping her hands together. The tear in space disappeared with a soundless explosion of energy that rattled the crystal chandelier above their heads.

One of the vampires handed Felix her bag. She only had a second to notice his hand was tattooed with a strange swirling pattern before Felix ushered her toward a staircase so covered in gold and marble, it was a miracle it didn't collapse under its own weight.

A crimson runner cushioned her bare feet as Felix turned his head to dismiss the assembled crew. She didn't notice the distant hum of music and chatter until he said, "Good work, folks. Sorry about the detour. Go back to the party and have some fun while you still can."

More confused than before, Dahlia flicked an apprehensive glance toward the side of the foyer where the music was loudest. "There's a party?"

"Sort of a victory celebration," he answered, urging her up the stairs with a hand on her lower back. "Why? You wanna join?"

She blanched. "No. Gods, no."

After the day she'd had, all Dahlia wanted to do was lock herself in a closet and scream until she lost consciousness.

Felix nodded. "Good. I hate telling you no, but I really don't feel like killing anyone else tonight."

A chill swept through her at the casual reminder of what he'd done to Devon.

Dahlia wasn't a saint. She was probably not even a good person. There was no seed of compassion in her that made her regret his ignominious death in the way she should've. He'd been a mean, handsy prick who enjoyed tormenting his staff.

The gods only knew what else he got up to when no one was looking.

But she was an animal at heart, and all animals could recognize death when it stared them in the face. Felix had killed someone right in front of her. He didn't care what she saw, which meant she was in an incredible amount of danger.

Trying not to sound as nervous as she felt, she asked, "Why would you have to kill someone at your own party?"

Felix made a thoughtful sound in the back of his throat. "Because someone would take one look at you and try their luck. Can't have that, can I?"

She'd always known that Felix was a special sort of monster, but the casual way he talked about it made her gut churn.

Felix murdered people the same way she might take out the trash. It was nothing but a minor inconvenience.

And I followed him here.

Because he was the monster she knew. Because when he walked into the apartment, something in her brain just... clicked.

But she should've thought it through for a second more. Sweat gathered between her shoulder blades as he nudged her to turn right at the top of the stairs. She barely noticed the silk wallpaper or the paintings in their gilded frames.

Moonlight cast pale shapes on the ground through tall, antique windows partially shaded by heavy velvet drapes. She padded through those little puddles of light sightlessly.

What have I done?

She wasn't exactly paying attention to the route, but even if she had been, Dahlia doubted she could've remembered her path through the winding corridors of Felix's home. They seemed to go on forever, and he pushed her along at a speed that made it impossible to keep track of any landmarks.

"Is this your *house?*" she asked, bewildered, as he nudged her down yet another hallway.

"Yep. My grandmother built it and then left it to me when she died. What do you think?"

Dahlia shrugged stiffly. "It's big."

He snorted. "Not big enough. Do you have any idea how many cousins I have?"

"Your family lives here with you?"

She wasn't sure why that surprised her so much. Maybe it was because nearly all the vampires she'd ever met were loners. She'd always been under the impression that they liked their private space and weren't inclined toward living in groups.

"Not all of them all the time," he answered, at last gesturing to a grand set of double doors at the end of a blessedly short hallway. "But the house was built to hold everyone, their anchors, and their kids in the event of an emergency. Every Amauri has a room. Sometimes they use them, sometimes they don't. Tends to be that the single folks live in the main house and then move out when they find someone, but it varies."

Dahlia blinked. "Oh. That's kind of nice."

She'd certainly never had a home to fall back on when things got hard. Her family was in the wind. No one told her outright that she wouldn't have any help when she moved out at eighteen — it'd just been assumed by all involved. She couldn't remember the last time she'd spoken to any of the McKnights, and it certainly hadn't occurred to her to give them a call when the rat bastard of a doctor told her the news.

Having a house where every family member was welcome at all stages of their life was a lovely thought.

Or at least it *was* until she remembered that one of the Amauris had blown up Yvanna. Family meant having a place to crash, apparently, but not safety from being brutally murdered.

As if he could read her mind, Felix blithely continued, "You haven't met all the cousins — or the elders. This time last year, half of them wanted me dead. The other half only slightly less so. They were just happy to let someone else do it." Stepping around her to grasp the shiny gold door knobs, he pushed the doors open and nodded for her to go in ahead of him.

Dahlia swallowed. "And you still let them live in your house?"

It was his turn to shrug. "Family's family."

She had no idea what to say to that, so she walked into the room instead. A suite out of her vintage dreams sprawled before her, draped in silks and lit by milk glass lamps designed to look like lilies. A white marble fireplace stood between towering mahogany bookshelves. Arrayed around it were antique couches and well-loved leather wing-back chairs.

When she dared to look up, she found a ceiling bursting with hand-sculpted plaster molding. The designs were heavily floral, but only a few of the flowers were recognizable to her. They were interspersed with pomegranates spilling their seeds, bats in flight, and a massive gilded disk in the center — a moon, perhaps, or Grim's symbol. Maybe both.

This wasn't the home of someone who was rich. This was the home of someone who was *filthy fucking rich.*

"You know, I'm totally fine staying in a hotel," she croaked, skin crawling at how out of place she felt standing in what was essentially a palace. "I'm sure no one would—"

"You want us to go to a hotel?" Felix grimaced. "That's a nightmare for security, Dahlia. Milo would have my ass if I told him we were staying anywhere but the house."

He kept trying to push her toward what she could only assume was a bedroom, but Dahlia planted her bare feet and swung around to face him. "Not *us,*" she clarified. "Me."

He gave her a blank stare. "I'd stay here and you'd go to a hotel?"

"Yes."

"I don't understand."

"What don't you understand?"

Felix raised his eyebrows. In a voice that implied it was a perfectly normal thing to say, he answered, "Why you think I'd let you go anywhere by yourself."

Dahlia stared at him for a beat, at a loss. It wasn't entirely because she was completely overwhelmed by everything that had upended her life in so little time. The truth was that she simply didn't know how to act.

Standing so close to him, hearing him say some bullshit she should've expected after knowing him for so long, the strangest dissonance overtook her.

They'd spoken for hours upon hours on the phone. They'd shared thousands of text messages. He sent her gifts and she'd eased him to sleep at dawn with rambling stories from the bar.

In many ways, despite her best efforts and all good sense, Felix was one of her closest friends — second only to Cecilia, of course. And if she was honest with herself, he was a lot more than that.

But when she stood there in the palatial suite, Dahlia realized she didn't *actually* know him. The man standing before her was a stranger. He wore the face she knew, but that face had always been safely contained within the bounds of her phone. That raspy voice was piped through a speaker. Those words were just text on a screen.

Trying to assimilate the two Felixes that existed in her head and in the room was disorienting in the extreme, and it took a hammer to her confidence. If they'd had this conversation through the phone, she wouldn't have hesitated to roll her eyes and argue her point, but standing there...

Dahlia had no idea how to talk to him.

Her tongue pressed flat against the roof of her mouth, which hadn't stopped aching since Felix burst into her home. She wasn't sure if it was the stress of everything or the mouthwatering scent that hung in a cloud around him. Either way, it added to her discomfort. Averting her gaze, she curled her toes into the antique carpet and asked, "So what happens now? What are you going to do with me, Felix?"

Her bag hit the floor with a dull *thunk.* She looked up to find him shrugging off his long black coat. He certainly didn't need it in the muggy heat of an east coast summer or in the carefully climate controlled mansion. A crisp black button down stretched taut over his lean stomach and wide shoulders as he tossed it carelessly over the back of a couch. Keeping his eyes on her, he unfastened the buttons at his wrist and began to methodically roll up his sleeves. Corded forearms were revealed one delicious inch at a time.

Like he wanted a report on the weather, he demanded, "Tell me how you're feeling."

He looked perfectly calm, but something about his stare and the quick, efficient flicks of his claws as he fixed his sleeves by his elbows made her begin to back away. "Uh, fine?"

He didn't follow her, but his gaze tracked her progress as she slowly inched back toward the fireplace. "Are you in any pain? How are your fangs? I bet those pretty little things are sensitive right now."

Dahlia touched the tip of her tongue to the roof of her mouth again. The flesh there was hot and swollen. It appeared to be getting worse by the second. There was a peculiar pressure not unlike how she'd felt before her fangs came in, as if something was just dying to be released.

It wasn't quite painful, but it wasn't far off.

"The roof of my mouth hurts a little," she admitted, touching her lips with the tips of her fingers. "There's a weird pressure. I thought that'd go away after they took my teeth out."

For a split second, Felix's easy demeanor slipped. A vision of who he really was came through as his smile turned predatory. "How do I smell, pet?"

Good. Better than good.

The thought popped up instantly, a bubble of something hot and primal from a deep, dark place in the back of her mind. A pulsing ache throbbed in her gums.

She hadn't had a whole lot of time to process it or anything about him really, but it was impossible to ignore the way he smelled. When he carried her over his shoulder, his scent filled her lungs until she was dizzy with it.

Felix smelled like smoke. He smelled like caramel. He smelled like clean skin and good bourbon and even better sex.

It made her hungry in a way she'd never experienced before. It wasn't just a growly stomach and the compulsion to fill it. It was something older. Something raw. It made her itch with an urgency to curl her fingers into his flesh and hold on, maybe, or drag him into a shadowy place and climb him like a tree.

It was the need to eat, true, but it was also the relentless urge to fuck.

For someone who'd never had those impulses tied together, it was deeply unsettling. She'd loved a good lasagna, but she'd never wanted to *screw* one. Seeing as she had more than enough confusing shit to deal with in a day, Dahlia elected to ignore all of it.

"You smell fine," she answered, stumbling a little when she bumped into one of the couches.

"Fine, huh?"

Felix's eyes didn't twinkle. There would have to be some warmth in him for that sort of thing. Instead, they gleamed with a sinister sort of knowing that hadn't seemed quite so bad through a phone screen but when viewed from as few feet away was greatly alarming.

"You know why I dug up your number all those years ago?"

Dahlia licked her lips. "Because you were attracted to me?"

"Because you looked and smelled like *mine*." He took a handful of measured steps toward her. His boots didn't make a sound, but she wouldn't have been able to hear it if they did. Her heartbeat was too loud.

A wave of heat rolled through her as he stalked around the coffee table, his focus on her complete. "What are you doing?"

"I'm gonna do what I should've done the night we met."

TWELVE

DAHLIA HAD BEEN ATTRACTED TO MEN BEFORE. SHE'D FELT THAT gnawing touch-hunger of the lovesick and the bright spark of need for an attractive stranger. Nothing compared to the tension between herself and Felix.

It was the cruelest twist of fate that gave them the most combustible sort of chemistry she'd ever experienced.

"Felix," she rasped, putting a hand on his chest. He looked calm, but his heart raced under her palm. "Stop. Whatever we had— Nothing can happen. Not anymore."

Gods, she really hated the way her eyes welled up and her voice cracked. If she started crying, he'd think he'd won her over — a secret she'd been hoping to take with her to the afterlife, just to spite him.

But she was wrung out. There was nothing left to hide behind. Her entire life and identity had been swept away, and the part that upset her most was that she'd lost something she'd never wanted in the first place: *him.*

An irrational sort of anger crackled in her chest when he didn't appear to listen to her. He just kept on coming. Felix pressed close, until his hands found her hips. He gave them a squeeze and guided her backward.

"Why aren't you listening to me?" she demanded. "I'm a vampire, Felix!"

He slid his palms up and skated them beneath her loose, silky top. The heat of his skin burned a path over her fluttering belly and the curve of her ribs. "I am very aware," he murmured, cupping her breasts with a greedy, possessive squeeze.

It was getting hard to think past the throb in her mouth, which had synced with the one between her legs. Her anger was there, but it was almost indistinguishable from the burn of lust as he delicately rolled her nipples between his thumbs and forefingers.

He hunched his shoulders enough to put his lips by her ear. "I should wait until my doctor confirms it tomorrow, but I'm just not that patient. I've waited years for this, pet. I'm not going to bite you tonight, but I *am* going to get a taste of you."

"What are you—"

She yelped when he abruptly dragged her shirt over her head and threw it aside.

Stepping back to get a good look at her, he continued in that same cool, unruffled voice, "There's a lot you don't know about being a vampire. It's a good thing you have me to guide you, pet. Now… plant your ass on that couch."

She didn't mean to sit. It just sort of happened.

The light in the sitting room was dim. Only a gold glow was cast from the milk glass lamps on the walls. They threw long shadows across his face, and when he smiled down at her from his great height, all she saw was the dark hollows of his eyes and gleaming white fangs.

There was no reason for his slow crouch to be as hot as it was. Felix took his time placing his hands on her knees and prying them apart. Dahlia's face went scarlet. She didn't need to look down to know that the dove gray silk of her pajama bottoms was shamefully soaked. It clung to every fold and crease.

Situating himself between her legs, he lazily spun a finger in the air, gesturing toward her lower half. "Whatever these are called, I want you to order ten of them tomorrow. Never been a big panties guy, but I find something about the things it's doing to your pussy *extremely* compelling."

It wouldn't have surprised her if he was rough with her. Felix was a man who took what he wanted, and he'd never been coy about the fact that he intended to sleep with her. Apparently not even the threat of her now inedible blood and risk from her bite changed that.

But he wasn't rough. Instead, he smoothed his hands up her inner thighs, pushing them farther apart, and framed her cunt. Thumbs delicately tracing the damp outline of her folds, he purred, "You've had a rough night, pet. Let your man make it better."

An electric jolt coursed through her from head to toe when he pressed the pad of his thumb down and rolled it in a slow circle over her clitoris. Dahlia's toes curled in the expensive carpet as the wet silk slid over her sensitive skin.

"Felix," she gasped, "that's— We shouldn't—"

The fingers of his other hand feathered down to her silk-covered opening and gently pressed in. "Oh, we definitely should. We should've been doing this years ago."

It would've been torture at any time, but now the steady rise of pleasure was accompanied by the pounding ache in the roof of her mouth and gums. Urgency made her squirm and clench her teeth hard. She couldn't speak anymore. Only breathy noises escaped her locked jaw as he dipped his fingers inside her again and again through the barrier of her pajama bottoms.

"My poor pet," he crooned. "Look at how desperate you are. I'm not even touching you and you're wiggling like you need to come."

She'd hardly say he wasn't touching her. He'd thrust his fingers as far in her as the silk would allow, and he'd never stopped playing with his other hand, his fingertips skillfully strumming over the taut bundle of nerves. He used the resistance and slip of the wet material like a master. It seemed to amplify every sensation rather than dull it.

A particularly painful stab of pressure made her slap her hand across her mouth. It seemed like the closer she got to an orgasm, the worse the pressure grew. She would've thought it'd make chasing the edge more difficult, but it did the opposite. With each flash of pain, she lurched closer to giving Felix what he so clearly wanted.

His smile was knife-sharp as he dropped a hand to the waistband of his slacks. The sound of his belt unbuckling made her core clench hard. "Something wrong?"

Her breasts heaved as she forced words out from between her clenched teeth. "I don't know what's happening. My mouth— It *hurts.* And I feel like something's gonna happen if I don't do... I don't know. I don't know what I need to do."

She was mortified to hear it come out like such a pitiful whine.

Something flickered in Felix's gray eyes. "It's okay, pet. It's all normal. This will help, I promise."

She caught a glimpse of the ruddy, swollen head of his cock peeking out from the top of his briefs a moment before he rose onto his knees. When he freed it from its confines, he let it fall against the apex of her thighs with a wet slapping sound.

Something in her went still for all of a heartbeat before an animal sort of need exploded to life in her belly. Dahlia's fingers curled into claws and dug into his bare forearms, forcing him to bend over her as he began to torture her with his cock instead of his fingers.

Firmly rubbing himself up and down her slit, he chuckled, "This really is the best night of my fucking life."

Some small part of her rational mind still existed. It wailed in the background, telling her to slow down, to ask questions, but the roar of blood in her ears drowned out everything except her absolute focus on him.

Felix pressed his lips to her cheek. It was close to her mouth but just shy of a kiss. When she tried to turn her head, desperate to taste him, he moved back. "Sorry, pet," he muttered, "I can't risk my fangs getting too close to you until we get the all-clear. I can't imagine I'm wrong, but I'm not going to play around with your safety."

When she could only manage a confused, frustrated whine, he grasped her jaw and turned her face away, allowing him to drop a series of open-mouth kisses to her cheek and sweat-slicked neck. Speaking against her pulse, his voice finally lost its cool composure. "I know you want to bite, and I'll let you as soon I can, but tonight this is just going to have to be enough."

Her muscles strained, trying to fight his grip on her jaw. Dahlia tried to thrash, to buck him off so she could move freely, but he was far stronger than her. She wasn't even sure what she wanted to do or why she needed to move so badly until he mentioned biting.

Blind need eclipsed everything else. The need to sink her teeth into any part of him she could reach. The need to lock her legs around his waist. The need to feel him buried inside her.

And most of all, the need to *feed*.

Dahlia scored his arms with her nails, desperate to mark him as he nudged her shorts aside. "You'll feel better if I fuck you," he promised. Leaning back a bit, he firmly turned her face toward him again, but he didn't release her. A flush made his pale cheeks glow as he pinned her with his stare.

He told her in a strained voice, "Your instincts are telling you that you need me. They're telling you that you need to claim me. They're telling you I'm yours, even if the rest of you doesn't understand what that means yet. A bite would make everything better, but we can't do that right now, so this is the next best thing."

His jaw clenched. It didn't look like he wanted to continue, but he did. "If you really don't want to do this, then we can stop here. I'll put you in our room and lock you inside with some synth. I don't want to, but I will."

It didn't feel like there was much of her left that was capable of understanding him, but some small measure of reason made it through the haze of lust and hunger that had overtaken her.

Do I want this?

Her body pulsed with an unequivocal yes. The rest of her had to dig deep to answer.

She would never admit it aloud, but she'd thought about sleeping with Felix hundreds of times. Even knowing what he was and what he expected, she hadn't been able to stop herself. She doubted anyone subjected to his level of obsessive attention could hold out longer than she had.

The fact that she'd never given in to his dirty talk or taken their video calls further than a tease was a miracle considering how many dawns she'd gone to sleep with her hands between her legs, imagining it was his.

The truth was that she'd never been brave or reckless enough to take that step over the line with him, and she'd been reluctantly impressed by his respect for that hesitance. Yes, he pushed and he prodded, but never seriously, and never with any annoyance. Stringing him along, seeing how far she could push him before he snapped had been a dangerous game too tempting to ignore.

But even now, with the head of his cock gently pushing against the slippery entrance of her cunt, he didn't push. He waited for her to say yes.

She didn't know what madness compelled Felix to ignore the fact that she'd been turned, but Dahlia decided she didn't care. What was the worst that could happen? It wasn't like he could get her pregnant, and he certainly wasn't going to ask for commitment in the morning.

For this one night at least, she was going to fulfill the fantasies she'd never shared with him.

A rush of satisfaction made her head spin as she trapped his hips between her thighs. He still held her head firmly, but her arms were free, so she wrapped them around the back of his head, drawing him in. When he stooped over her, his body blocked out the light. They made a cozy little cave together, which pleased the part of her that desperately wanted them somewhere small and dark and saturated in the scent of sex.

"Please, Felix," she whispered, rocking her hips. "I want it."

A deep rumble rattled from his chest and into hers. "That's my girl."

Felix was gentle with their foreplay, but not with this. Holding her wet pajama bottoms to one side, he thrust in to the hilt in one vicious stroke.

The breath exploded out of her as the stretch and burn registered. The discomfort was a low drone in the back of her mind — nothing but static as the rest of her screamed with victory.

Elation unlike anything she'd ever felt made her blood fizz in her veins. Her fingers curled in Felix's wavy black hair as he set a pace of slow, deep strokes. He never let up on her jaw, no matter how hard she unconsciously strained against his grip, but he gave her everything else she could've asked for.

His free hand found its way back to her shorts. Bunching the gusset in his hand, he sawed it back and forth in time with his thrusts. Pleasure burst with each pass.

Lips moving restlessly against her neck, he hissed, "You're mine, Dahlia. Everything about you has been mine since that night in the bar. Everything you are belongs to me. Your body. Your blood. Your perfect cunt."

She didn't realize she was nodding frantically until he growled, "Use your words, pet. I want to hear you say it."

How he expected her to talk when he had a hand on her jaw and he'd decided to hammer her cervix like he wanted to break the damn thing down, she had no idea.

A high whistling note was all she managed as lewd sounds filled the sitting room — wet ones, the slap of their bodies coming together, and the ominous, rhythmic creaking of the antique couch they were at serious risk of ruining.

Felix pulled out of the circle of her arms. Dodging her frantic clawing to get him back, he straightened up enough to peer down at where they were joined. His lips parted on a ragged breath. "Now that's a sight. I'm the luckiest fucker on this planet."

Her mind went fuzzy. An animal urge to mark him swelled in her chest, dislodging all the oxygen she'd managed to drag in. Unable to bite, Dahlia made a furious sound and attacked his black shirt.

Buttons flew in all directions as she tore the sides apart, revealing a shocking expanse of pale skin and a swirl of crimson. It took her a second to realize it was a tattoo — a splash of blood, maybe — before her instinct took over again.

Felix hollered a curse when she raked her nails down his chest to the base of his cock, leaving livid tracks of red in her wake.

"My sweet girl. You want to give me gifts?" He leaned back a bit, angling his hips, and drove himself deep. Stilling, he gave her a sinister half-smile. "Every time you mark me, you get a reward."

He didn't give her a second to try and guess what that might be.

Felix set a new pace. This one was all force — short, shallow thrusts at an upward angle. Stars exploded in front of her eyes.

Dahlia didn't realize she'd tilted her head back until it hit the fine polished wood frame of the couch. She scratched at the hand on her jaw, her nails leaving scores in the across his knuckles and the powerful muscle of his forearm as he pounded at her g-spot mercilessly.

Her orgasm was just as violent. It struck her like the crack of a whip over and over, seemingly endless. A rough, breathless laugh filled her ears as he forced her abused cunt to give him more, to keep the ripples going until her thighs began to shake.

Tears leaked out of the corners of her eyes. She snapped her teeth again and again, but there was nothing to bite, and the frustration was enough to make her scream as Felix emptied himself inside her with a drawn out groan.

When he finally stilled, he hunched over her shaking body again. Dahlia's limbs snapped inward automatically, seeking shelter in the shadow of him. He made soft shushing sounds as he turned her face away from his neck.

"How is this better?" she cried, overwhelmed by the pain in her mouth now that the pleasure was fading.

Felix pressed a kiss to her thundering pulse. "Vampires are possessive. It's how we keep our food to ourselves. Knowing everyone will see that I'm off limits won't fill your belly, but it'll satisfy other parts of you."

Dahlia squinted at him. It was hard to see his face from the angle he held her at, and her tears made everything blurry, but she still managed to get a peek of the raised welts she left on his neck and collar bones.

The pain didn't go away, but she was baffled to feel it dull, just a little, as her gaze traced the red marks her nails left on his skin.

"My mouth still hurts," she complained, not wanting to admit he was right.

Felix stroked her sweaty hair away from her face. She almost hated how soothing it was, and when he nuzzled her temple... Dahlia tried not to think of anything at all.

"I know." He almost sounded genuinely upset by that. Felix slid his arms under her knees and around her back. Lifting her up and standing in one impressively athletic motion, he soothed, "We're going to get you some synth. It should ease the pressure for a little while. You can drink it in the bath."

Sniffling, she wrapped her arms around his neck and asked, "Is there lots of hot water?"

He gave her an odd look, but he still answered, "As much as you'd like, pet."

BOOGEYMAN

Your apartment building is shit

> you know I love reminders that you're watching me. Makes me feel all warm and fuzzy inside

> also screw you??? You try finding a nicer apartment on my salary in this city

I meant the security. It's basically wide open

Tell me you have your own locks on your door

> why? You worried about me, boogeyman?

I take care of my things, pretty girl

I've found you a better place. You'll love it and I'll be happy because it's got actual security. You get to keep every penny of that shitty salary because I'll be paying rent. I'll have movers swing by tomorrow

> lol

I'm not joking

> I didn't think you were

> no thanks on the upgrade

Why in fuck

> I'm not interested in being your kept pet, Felix

Too late for that

THIRTEEN

FELIX STARED AT THE CURLED UP FIGURE OF HIS BRIDE IN HIS BED with deep satisfaction.

He could've put her in the bedroom connected to his. It'd been designed for her, technically, with all the womanly shit his future bride would need ready and waiting.

He'd never intended on keeping his bride close. It was always supposed to be an arrangement of mutual benefit, not one of affection. She'd have her life and he'd have his. They'd meet in the middle for feeding and breeding, but that'd be all. Even that would wither after an heir was born.

It was all he could stomach.

Maybe in another life there might've been a chance for him to warm up to his faceless blood bride, but that chance was shot in the face when he met Dahlia McKnight.

He fully intended on doing what he had to. Felix couldn't afford the luxury of indulging in his feelings, and he'd worked too fucking hard to sacrifice his place as head of the family for anything. Even her.

So he'd planned everything out with meticulous attention to detail, as was his way, to keep the faceless woman as far from him as possible.

Separate bedrooms. Separate responsibilities. Separate lives.

His bedroom would always belong to Dahlia, even after she left his life. No other woman would sleep between his sheets or curl up amongst his pillows.

It never occurred to him to think he might get lucky enough to keep her there.

His fingers itched to trace every inch of her. The fall of her golden hair over the cream pillowcase and the gentle slope of her bare shoulder peeking out from beneath the blankets made his mouth water.

Fucking her wasn't enough. It'd never be enough. He needed everything she had to give.

He'd always had a greedy heart. Felix was rarely satisfied, his restless ambition always jumping to the next goal, the next challenge. It was the thrill of winning that spurred him on. Every prize only made him hungrier for a bigger, better score.

Nothing was bigger or better than having Dahlia McKnight as his blood bride.

It was so good that it was literally unimaginable. He wasn't one for believing in miracles, but it was hard to see it as anything but.

The object of his obsession had been neatly packaged into his perfect bride. Now she'd never escape him.

Felix forced himself away from the bed and into his closet, where he found a new shirt to replace the one his girl had ruined. A fond smile curved his mouth at the memory, but it came with a small pang of worry that sped his steps toward the door.

As much as it pained him to leave her, he forced himself out into the hall. He doubted he'd be back any time soon. Sleep would have to wait. There were too many arrangements to make.

The Bowans would know about his little heist soon, if they didn't already, and they all had to be ready for what would come when the inevitable demand for her handover was refused.

They'd handle it. The new generation of Amauris — his cousins — had seen him through the war against the old guard and that viper, Yvanna. They'd come out of it stronger than they'd gone in, their bonds and loyalty solidified by spilled blood. They could take a few Bowans.

What concerned him most at that moment wasn't the fact that he'd stolen Alastair's daughter, but her care. Tough as she was, Dahlia had clearly been through too much. He'd barely been able to get her out of the bath before she passed out, her too-thin body exhausted even after she forced down a bottle of synth.

Felix didn't do well with worry. He did much better with lists. Tasks. Logical steps leading to a clear end point.

So he made his list as he stalked to his office, where Milo and his half-brother Luis were waiting for him.

Their gazes immediately landed on the vicious little marks Dahlia left on his neck and collar. He'd deliberately left more buttons of his shirt undone than usual just to show them off.

Luis, the older of the pair, let out a low whistle. He sat in one of the low leather chairs arrayed around a glass coffee table, his long legs spread and his tattooed arms draped over the armrests. Like usual, he looked like he couldn't care less what was going on, but Felix knew him too well to buy it.

"That was fast," he chuckled. His smile was bright white against his golden skin. "She must be something. I can't wait to meet her."

Felix held up a finger as he strode to his desk at the far end of the room. "Watch it, shithead. That's *my* bride."

Luis had always liked danger a little too much. It was allegedly part of his charm, and also why he teased, "I don't see a bite yet. I might still have a chance."

Milo stood against one tall bookshelf, his big body stiff and his frown thunderous. "You *want* Felix to kill you?"

"I could probably take him," Luis glibly replied, waving one scarred hand in his half-brother's direction.

"Trust me when I say that even if you managed to kill me —
and you'd have to — you wouldn't be able to handle Dahlia."
Felix sat heavily in his desk chair. His skin crawled with the
urgency to get back to her, and even though he knew for a fact
Luis was only joking, a wave of possessiveness made him grind
his teeth.

I like Luis, he reminded himself. *He makes me a lot of money. It'd
be annoying if he died in a mysterious, gruesome accident.*

Like he could see the murder in his eyes, Milo let out a put-
upon sigh and meandered over to the chairs in front of his desk.
Though he was the younger sibling, Milo seemed to always
place himself between Luis and danger — in this case, Felix.

Luis propped his feet up on the coffee table like the animal he
was. "Is she the little secret you've been keeping?"

"She's mine," he answered shortly. It was all he or anybody
needed to know.

Milo leaned his elbows on his knees. "Are you sure she's
neutral?"

The gland in the roof of his mouth pulsed with renewed fury.
Felix snorted. "Yeah, I'm pretty fucking sure. Just standing next
to her makes it feel like my fangs are going to explode."

If she wasn't venom neutral, her scent would've put him off
immediately, regardless of their prior relationship. It was pure
survival instinct for vampires to be disgusted at the idea of
wanting to fuck or feed on each other. Even allowing that
perhaps her body hadn't completely finished its transition, he
would've felt it.

Still, he'd restrained himself from biting her. He didn't want
to. In fact, he couldn't remember ever wanting anything more
than that when he had his cock buried in the vice of her wet cunt
and she practically begged him for it.

He was absolutely certain she was venom neutral, and yet...

"I need Alvin to take a look at her. I trust my nose, but I'm
not risking poisoning her because I can't wait one night to get a
sip. She needs to be tested. Actually, she needs a full work-up.

Everything. I want to be sure she's completely healthy before I touch her. Once that's done, I want Marietta to get her settled. My girl's going to need a friend to answer questions and get her things to make her feel at home. Whatever Dahlia needs, she gets."

He paused before adding, "And I want the bed taken out of the bridal suite. She can do what she wants with the space but she's not sleeping there."

Felix drummed his claws on the desk, the list unspooling in his mind in order of most urgent to least. "Milo, I need a full report on what the *fuck* went down at The Lush. This worked out in our favor, but the fact that a fuck-up of this scale happened to *my girl* is unacceptable."

She was there. She was there. She was there.

The knowledge that Dahlia had been on that roof with Yvanna and he hadn't even known was like fine grains of glass under his skin. He knew his girl was stubborn and didn't trust him, but to not say anything at all about the fact that she'd clearly been injured was—

He forced himself to take a deep breath.

Felix didn't do self-loathing or regret. That meant looking back on shit that was done and couldn't be changed. What he *did* do was cause and effect. Actions and consequences.

Action: He'd been careless.

Consequence: His girl was put in harm's way.

Action: Dahlia hid what had happened to her.

Consequence: He'd make sure she never did that again.

"I want her hospital records sent to Alvin and then I want them wiped," he continued. "Luis, you'll pay a visit to the doctor who sold her out first thing tomorrow night. No one should have the information on her that he does."

The brothers nodded, all business now.

Milo said, "I got all her records while you were gone. You want them?"

"Are they just from today?"

"No. There's normal check-up stuff, but there's also a visit to the ER the same night as the hit."

Any remnant of the pleasant after-sex buzz that had stubbornly clung to him vanished. Hand stilling on the desk, he murmured, "Tell me how bad it was."

Milo blew out a breath. "Boss, maybe you—"

"Now."

Grimacing, he said, "She got lucky. When I compared the Patrol report to her hospital record, I was able to piece together where she must've been when the explosive went off. She was standing across from Yvanna, presumably close to Alastair. I don't know what happened between those two, since he's not in the report, but she arrived at the hospital with…"

He trailed off. Milo wasn't one to mince words or hesitate, so the fact that he really didn't want to tell Felix what had happened to Dahlia made his stomach churn.

Keeping his voice flat, he prompted, "Finish."

"The intake notes say she was impaled by a piece of a metal table. There was a major puncture wound in her left shoulder and several shrapnel wounds on her face and limbs. She also had a minor concussion." He rubbed his jaw again, his gaze averted. "Where Alastair fits into that… I don't know. She told the doctor that she was absolutely certain it was his blood that got in her wound, though."

Impaled.

Dahlia had been impaled. And she hadn't told him.

It wasn't just fury that made his mind go blank. It was betrayal. Another more well-adjusted person might've called it hurt, but he wasn't one of those, so the fact that she hadn't trusted him enough to tell him she'd been catastrophically injured registered as an insult.

He'd spoken to her the next night and she'd sounded off, but he'd chalked it up to the fact that she'd been rattled. After years of back and forth between them, he just *assumed* that she'd be smart enough to tell him if she so much as got a paper cut. It seemed obvious to him that being impaled by a fucking table warranted at least a phone call.

Dahlia had actively and knowingly shut him out when she needed him. She hadn't trusted him to care for her when she was at her most vulnerable. She'd tacitly informed him that he was unfit, unworthy, and unwelcome.

She'd tried to reject him.

The air in the office was heavy with the weight of his anger. No one spoke. No one even moved as he stared out into the middle distance, processing this new information and assimilating it into his plans.

Luis and Milo shared a look. All the good humor had left the older of the pair. He liked to tease and pick fights, but even Luis knew how serious it was to have an anchor, a *bride*, hide something of that magnitude.

Still not looking at them, Felix said, "Tell me what you would do in this situation."

Neither man answered him for a beat. Surprisingly, it was Milo who spoke up first.

"I'd lock her in the house until she understood how stupid that was. You can't hide shit like that from your man. How are you supposed to keep her safe if she won't tell you when she's been hurt?"

Luis snorted. "Lock her in the house? Grow up, man. You want to make her understand? That's what a little bit of pussy torture is for. She won't make the same mistake twice if you tie her to your bed and leave a vibrator on her for a few hours."

Both options had their appeal, certainly, but he doubted either would work on Dahlia. Locking her in a cage wouldn't break her, and neither would a bit of pleasure-pain. She was too fucking stubborn.

Felix sighed. He'd just have to find his own way to settle things between them.

FOURTEEN

For the first time in weeks, Dahlia woke without a headache.

Her limbs were heavy with the remnants of sleep rather than bone-deep exhaustion. There was no pain in her stomach or gnawing emptiness. She was perfectly content, swathed in soft sheets and surrounded by the delicious scents of smoke and caramel.

It took her a while to register the fingers combing through her hair or the almost undetectable vibration of a purr rattling against her back.

"There she is." Felix's voice was a deep, husky whisper.

No, she thought, desperately clawing at the last vestiges of blissful sleep. *No, I don't want to be awake yet.*

It meant facing every terrible way in which her life had blown up in her face. It meant getting answers for all the questions she didn't want to ask.

It meant facing *him.*

A sharp twinge between her thighs felt a lot like her body saying, *"Good luck avoiding that."* And when she swallowed, her tongue pressed against the backs of her new fangs, forcing the reality of her situation on her until the weight of it threatened to push the air from her lungs.

"You can't ignore me forever," he informed her. Claws drifted through her hair, their tips gently scraping her scalp. "It's time to face the reckoning, pet."

Something in his voice made a shiver of unease run down her spine. Dahlia's eyes opened. The shapes of the giant four-poster bed's canopy were unfamiliar. So was the room beyond the crack in the bed's drapery, with its polished mahogany furniture and shimmering silk wallpaper.

She knew she wasn't in her bed, but when she opened her eyes, Dahlia resigned herself to the fact that she was in a completely different *world.*

Curling her fingers into the pillow under her cheek, she croaked, "I want to go home."

"We both know that's not an option." Felix's soothing strokes never broke their rhythm, but the rest of him shifted a bit closer, until she could feel the texture of his clothing against her bare back.

"Why?" she pressed, still not brave enough to turn and face him. "Why can't I just go home and pretend none of this ever happened? You know I'd never tell anyone about Devon. I don't care that he's dead. I'm not going to run to Patrol. I just want to be left alone."

"That's not how it works."

"Why not?"

Instead of answering her, Felix sighed. "We've got an appointment to keep, pet. It's time to get up."

The sheets were pulled off her body in one swift, ruthless motion. Dahlia yelped and curled in on herself, hiding her naked body from the cool air. Felix *tsked* and gave her a light swat on the ass. "None of that. The doctor will be here in a few minutes."

Finally swiveling her head around to face him, she demanded, "Doctor? Why am I seeing a doctor?"

Felix was already climbing out of bed. His back was to her, so she couldn't read his expression when he answered, "You were just turned into a vampire, Dahlia. You need to be checked by someone I trust to make sure everything's all right."

He said it so casually, like she'd twisted her ankle instead of the world-shattering change she'd undergone. It was the same way he'd acted the previous night. Like it didn't matter. Like it was nothing.

At the time she'd been too confused and overwhelmed to really register it. Now she was well-fed and rested. She had more than enough energy to be pissed off.

Sitting up, Dahlia snatched a sheet and wrapped it around her torso. "That's it?" she snapped. "That's all you have to say about it?"

Felix parted the drapes on his side of the bed and slipped away. She watched him go, a gradually enlarging ball of red-hot feeling burning in her chest.

He doesn't care.

Of course he didn't. Felix wasn't capable of caring. She'd known that for years. What for a normal person would've been displays of affection and concern were merely the expression of instinct for him.

If he wanted to keep her safe, it was because he needed her to be healthy to feed on. If he asked her how she was, it was the strictly necessary maintenance to keep her connected to him.

It likely didn't even occur to him that she might be upset or traumatized by what had happened to her. All he cared about was what it meant for him — which was almost certainly why the doctor had been called. He wanted to confirm that she was officially a waste of his time.

Why he showed up to her apartment when he did and why he'd bothered to take her home, she had no idea. In that moment, she wasn't even sure it mattered.

Dahlia blinked back the sting of tears. She hated that she'd allowed herself to fall into his little game. There'd never been any hope of her winning. Even if he never got what he really wanted, she was always going to be the loser.

And I had sex with him last night. Gods, I'm an idiot.

The sudden drawing back of the drapes on her side of the bed made her jump. Felix stood there, his wide shoulders silhouetted by the golden light from the lamps, one arm outstretched toward her.

"Here," he said, tossing her a bundle of red silk like it was a football.

Without looking at him, Dahlia snatched it from her lap. It was a decadent crimson robe. Refusing to ask where it came from or who it belonged to, she clenched her jaw and shrugged it on over the sheet. When all her bits were hidden from him, she swung her legs over the edge of the bed.

Remembering the path to the bathroom, she brushed past him without a word, intent on scrubbing the staleness from her mouth. The fact that her toiletries and make-up kit were waiting for her on the marble counter was a small relief.

She still looked like she'd been sick, but a little blush and some concealer went a long way. As did a quick styling of her hair. It wasn't about looking good for him or anyone else. It was about having some control over the disaster that was her life.

By the time she emerged from the bathroom, Felix had disappeared and she was a little bit more composed.

Unfortunately, the rest of her things were missing. Her clothing, wallet, and phone were nowhere to be found in the luxurious bedroom. That left her in just the robe.

The sound of Felix's voice drew her back into the sitting room. Keeping her gaze very firmly averted from the couch they'd soiled, she spied him standing by the door with another man.

Trying not to feel awkward in just her robe and nothing else, Dahlia crossed her arms and waited for them to notice her.

She'd barely completed the motion before Felix's attention swung her way. Those gray eyes snapped toward her instantly, like he knew exactly where she'd be on instinct alone. Something in her throbbed at the sight of him — a deep, fundamental yearning that went beyond lust or hunger.

Dahlia was disturbed by the impulse that fluttered behind her ribs. It was a giddy urgency to be near him as quickly as possible, to run her hands all over him and check that he was well.

It made his lack of regard for her even more galling.

Digging her nails into her arms, she met his smile with a scowl. There was no damn way she would act like that. Not when he didn't care enough to ask if she was all right.

Clapping a hand on the stranger's shoulder, Felix gestured toward her. "Alvin, this is Dahlia. Dahlia, this is R. Alvin Turner III. We just call him Alvin. He's the family's doctor."

Alvin gave her a small, close-lipped smile.

He was a tall man with sandy blond hair, sun-kissed skin, and a smattering of freckles across his nose and cheeks. She could tell at a glance that he wasn't a vampire, but something in his eyes made the hair stand up on the back of her neck none the less.

Nothing about him screamed of a threat. The man wore slacks, loafers, and a neat white button down. His hair was perfectly parted and his body language was easy. He looked like every rich man whose daddy bought him a sailboat for his birthday and never had to work a day of retail in his life.

But the very things that would've made her dismiss him on sight made him stand out starkly in Felix's sitting room. Standing there in his preppy outfit, she got the distinct impression that it was a costume meant to disguise the glitter of sharp intelligence in his eyes.

"It's nice to meet you, Miss McKnight. I hear you've had a tough couple of weeks." The doctor's voice was smooth and warm, non-threatening in a practiced way that only made her more wary.

Anyone who looked like *that* and was still somehow trusted by Felix was someone to watch.

"Uh-huh." She didn't bother pretending to be polite. "Sorry you came all this way, but I don't need to see a doctor. I'm all set on my check-ups this year."

The corner of Alvin's mouth lifted. "I'm sure you've had your fill of doctors recently."

Recalling that she'd been sold out by the piece of shit doctor from the ER, Dahlia found her upper lip curling over her fangs. "You have no idea."

The men made brief eye contact. Some wordless exchange passed between them before Felix tilted his head toward one of the couches around the fireplace. The doctor made his way over to it.

Setting a well-oiled leather bag on the coffee table, he sat down. "I promise this won't take more than a few minutes. We just need to check that your system is adapting as it should."

Dahlia was unmoved. She remained in the doorway to the bedroom, the muscles of her shoulders tightening. "We, huh?"

If he noticed the edge in her voice, he didn't acknowledge it. Alvin popped the latches of his bag and began to pull out some equipment she had no name for.

"Me and Mr. Amauri," he explained, tossing her an absent smile. "I read your records and it looks like you went through the transition mostly unassisted, which raises some red flags. Obviously it wasn't your fault, but in cases like this, the prefer-ence is to have medical supervision as soon as possible. You're young and healthy, so I'm sure you're fine, but I'll need to check your heart, blood pressure, reflexes, venom gland, and the like."

She took a deep breath. "That's interesting. I wonder how you got my private medical records, Dr. Turner, since I don't remember giving them to you." She narrowed her eyes. "Or *Mr. Amauri*, for that matter."

The doctor looked up from his task of meticulously orga-nizing his instruments to give her a glib smile. "It was handled for you, of course."

Before she could give the doctor the response that shit

deserved, Felix stepped up behind the couch. "Dahlia, just do this for me."

"What do I get in return?"

Felix rolled his eyes. "What do you want?"

Knowing it wouldn't work but trying anyway, she demanded, "Take me home."

"Try again."

"Drop me off at a hotel."

"Still not happening. Try again."

Holding his amused stare, she bit out, "A car."

Felix's smile turned predatory. His low chuckle made her toes curl. "You want me to buy you a new car, pet?"

Hoping her cheeks weren't as flushed as they felt, she shot back, "So I can drive as far from you as possible? Yes."

He spread his hands on the back of the couch and dipped his chin in an exaggerated nod. "A new car it is. Now come sit so we can get this over with, hm?"

Once again, it somehow didn't feel like she'd won anything when she walked stiffly over to the couch and perched on the edge of the cushion. She stoically endured Alvin's impersonal inspection of her, trying not to wrinkle her nose at his smell as he leaned over to check her pupil dilation or press her tongue down with a popsicle stick.

He didn't smell... bad. But he didn't smell mouthwatering, either. Alvin smelled like citrus and fresh water and a little bit of mint. Nice, clean. Not for her.

Dahlia's eyes swung involuntarily back to Felix, who hovered over the couch with his arms crossed, his attention fixed on the doctor's every action. The roof of her mouth gave an angry pulse.

Alvin, who was peering into her mouth with a pen light, made a thoughtful sound. "Gland looks good, but it's pretty inflamed. Are you experiencing discomfort?"

He withdrew the tongue depressor, allowing her to speak. "A little," she begrudgingly admitted.

The doctor nodded. He didn't appear surprised as he reached for his bag again, withdrawing a small plastic cup and a strange little instrument with a rubber tip encased in sterile wrapping. After donning a pair of gloves, he instructed her to open her mouth again.

"I need to take a sample of your venom so we can test what type it is. I'm going to massage your gland a little and it should empty a sample into my vial. Hopefully it'll help with a little of the pressure you're feeling, too."

Dahlia frowned. "The doctor at the hospital did that already. With a blood test, I think."

Alvin nodded, his fingers working deftly to unwrap the strange little instrument with the rubber tip. "That's the usual way of doing it, yes, but my test is both less invasive and a lot faster. And it's always good to have a second opinion on these things, don't you think?"

"*Your* test?"

"Alvin comes from a long line of doctors who specialize in vampires," Felix cut in, laying a steadying hand on her shoulder. "Blood's some sort of weird fetish for them. Good for us, though. Alvin has spent his career studying better ways to treat us. And stitching us up when someone gets stabbed."

"Blood's only a fetish for me, not my father. He's more interested in the aphrodisiac effects of venom." Alvin said it with perfect sincerity, his handsome, rich-boy-next-door face completely at odds with the admission. "Now open, please."

Still trying to work out precisely what kind of freak Doctor Turner was, Dahlia opened her mouth again and tried not to grimace as he inserted the tool. The rubber tip pressed against her soft palate. She had no idea what magic trick he pulled, but with only a slight amount of pressure, there was a release.

It wasn't quite pain and it wasn't quite pleasure that blinded her as a spurt of her brand new venom splashed into the plastic cup. It fell somewhere in between.

Dahlia gasped, shocked by the burn in her gums. Felix

cupped the side of her head, stroking her hair, and made a soft, soothing noise. With him, it was impossible to say whether his comfort was one hundred percent sincere, since he always sounded a bit like he was laughing at her, but the way his grip tightened made her think it was real.

Alvin withdrew both the instrument and the cup. She stared at the clear, viscous fluid at the bottom with a grimace. It couldn't have been more than a teaspoon, but it was more than a little disgusting to suddenly produce *any* amount of new bodily fluid.

Kissing the crown of her head, Felix whispered, "You did great, pet. Not so bad, right?"

She looked away as Alvin dipped a cotton swab and began to dab her venom onto what looked like some sort of disposable test. "That's so gross." Pointing a finger at Felix, she hissed, "I want a silver car. And it better be fast."

He nodded. "I was thinking red, but my girl gets what she wants. Always." It did funny things to her when she realized there was no ever-present undercurrent of laughter when he said *that*. The madman actually meant it.

Dahlia blinked. *Huh.*

Alvin cleared his throat. "I also wanted to ask you about something I saw in your records. It says that you are absolutely certain Alastair Bowan was the blood donor. Can I ask how you know that? It sounded like there was a lot of blood on the roof during the... incident."

"Incident, huh? That's a nice way of putting it." Dahlia didn't look at Felix again as she flatly explained, "There's no doubt in my mind that Mr. Bowan's the one who turned me. I was standing next to him when I saw the explosive land behind... uh, the woman. Yvanna. I managed to warn him and we took cover together."

The air in the room thickened with tension, but she couldn't tell if it was from her own lingering anger or whatever Felix felt hearing what happened that night.

She rubbed the spot on her upper chest where the metal pierced her. There was nothing there, but sometimes she swore she could feel it. "A piece of a metal table went through him and into me. I woke up with us pinned together. When his men pulled it out…" She spread her hands. "A lot of blood fell on me — and the big fucking hole in my shoulder."

Alvin listened attentively, his face impassive. A slow blink was the only sign that her story made any sort of impact before he inhaled sharply. "Yep, that'll do it."

Her gaze skated involuntarily toward Felix, trying to gauge his reaction. His expression was blank, his shoulders relaxed. It was like he had no feeling at all about what had happened to her.

Hurt punched through her all over again. Dahlia gritted her teeth to stop her chin from wobbling as she looked away.

Alvin checked his watch before he leaned over the coffee table, his attention on the odd-looking test. He made a thoughtful sound and scooped it up to examine more closely.

"What's that do?" she asked, desperate for distraction. "You said something about a venom type, but no one's explained what that is."

"Venom comes in a set number of sub-types — a lot like blood types, which you're probably familiar with. It's synthesized from blood, actually," he explained, "so your blood type and a variety of other factors can change what category your venom falls into and what you can be given in terms of medication and blood transfusions in an emergency. The most common are C, L, and R. There are sub-types within the sub-types, of course, but for our purposes we only need to know if you fall into one of those categories or outside of them."

Dahlia leaned over a little, suddenly interested in what the test had to say. "What happens if I don't fit into any of those types?"

Alvin tilted the test her way. On several small depressions

arrayed in a line, she could make out a shiny dot of her venom. "Then you'd be the rarest: N."

"What's N stand for?"

"Neutral," he answered. "It's equivalent to being a universal blood donor. It means that your venom would be essentially non-functional. The pleasurable effects still work, but it's non-toxic to other vampires. Not great for self-defense, but there are definitely benefits. Someone with the N type can feed on another vampire and vice versa without any negative repercussions. Vampires call them blood brides, since they typically tend to be women — though the connection there is unknown. I suspect it's more confirmation bias than anything, since men tend to be under-tested."

He offered her a sunny smile, like they were discussing his favorite thing in the world and not the various properties of a little gland nestled in the roof of her mouth. "Anyway, female blood brides can carry another vampire's offspring to term, which is pretty extraordinary. Many vampires believe a venom neutral person is blessed by Grim. But I'm sure Mr. Amauri will tell you all about the cultural stuff. That's not my area of expertise."

As he spoke, an alarm started ringing in her mind. Quietly at first, then louder, until she struggled to follow along, too distracted by the hideous racket.

Alvin checked his watch again. Making a satisfied sound, he held the test up for his inspection. The divot at the very end of the line had turned a livid, sour apple green.

Her gaze darted back and forth between the test and Alvin's face. "What's that mean? That color looks bad."

He gave her a winning smile — all white teeth and sun-kissed skin and impersonal satisfaction. "Congrats, Miss McKnight. You won the lottery of venom types." He showed her the test again, like she was supposed to know what that green dot meant. "You're type N."

you were born a vampire, right?

BOOGEYMAN

I was. My mom says I came out biting

why does that not surprise me

do you ever stop and think it's weird to get your
food from other people

Do you ever think it's weird to eat a steak?

ok that's fair

Why the sudden interest? You thinking about
what it'll be like when I finally sink my fangs
into you?

absolutely not.

No need to be scared, pet. I'll take good care
of you.

FIFTEEN

"Explain what's going on, Felix. Now."

She was pissed. Felix could feel her ire radiating in the air like heat waves off hot concrete.

He shut the door and flicked the lock in place. No one would bother him in his private space unless invited, but it never hurt to be extra sure. Especially now.

Felix turned slowly back to where Dahlia sat on the couch. Her cheeks were flushed, her eyes narrowed. She looked rumpled and so fucking beautiful in that silk robe he'd gotten her. When she looked at him like she was ready to rip his throat out, it only made him harder.

"Being venom neutral — it means something, doesn't it?" she demanded, watching him stride toward her with slow, purposeful steps. "That's what you were talking about last night, and that's why Devon kept trying to— Gods, how did any of you even *know*? Weren't you too busy bombing your own family members to pay attention to what happened to me?"

Felix weathered her tirade calmly. Sinking into the seat opposite hers, he leaned back. "You want me to explain or do you want to keep yelling at me?"

He swore he could see a vein throb in her neck when she hissed, "Oh, buddy, you haven't seen me yell yet."

Gods, he loved her.

Felix shifted his legs a little, trying to ease the discomfort of his pants' seam cutting into his cock. He didn't want to suffer an accidental amputation just when he got the chance to use the damn thing again.

Gods knew he'd waited long enough. He hadn't touched another woman since he met Dahlia. Even if he wanted to, he couldn't. Vampires were single-minded when they locked onto a potential anchor, and he was no different. No one tempted him the way she did. No one ever would.

Anticipation burned sweetly in his veins. His claws tapped a steady, patient rhythm on the armrest of his chair — a countdown beat to taking everything he wanted at last.

"Let's start at the beginning," he said, his tone conversational. Relaxed. The complete opposite of everything burning inside him. "You know me, but you don't know what I do or who my family is."

"I've put together what you do, Felix. I'm not missing any brain matter."

"You know I'm in the vampire syndicate and I'm a criminal," he corrected her. "You don't know that I'm the head of the Amauri family, which controls much of the underground gambling and arms trade on the east coast. I deliberately withheld that from you because for the last three years I've been in a war with my Aunt Yvanna, who wanted control of the family and our operations after my grandmother passed." He paused, sniffing. "Not that you ever asked."

Dahlia shot him a withering glare. "Because I didn't want to know. Still don't."

He waved her comment away, unbothered. "The risk that you could be targeted for revenge was high enough that I decided I wouldn't further our relationship until the fighting stopped. I put you on ice until I could be sure you'd be safe."

"Put me on ice." Dahlia leaned over to grab a silver dish off the coffee table. She whipped it at him with impressive speed and force, but he was just a bit faster. Felix leaned away, letting the dish sail harmlessly over his shoulder to dent the wall beside the fireplace.

"I'm not a fucking steak, Felix!" she seethed.

He arched a brow. "So you would've preferred I put you in danger, then?"

"Here's a thought: You could've left me the fuck alone."

Felix gave her a long look. "That was never an option."

When Dahlia simply sat back again, arms crossed, he continued, "The hit at your bar ended the war. You weren't supposed to be there. I made *sure* you and Cecilia were off that night."

She jolted, the angry flush in her cheeks draining away. "How do you know about Cece?"

Felix held her gaze steadily. The mask he normally wore slipped, revealing the dark, watchful predator underneath. "Pet," he murmured, "I know everything about you. You're mine."

"She doesn't know anything." A desperate note entered Dahlia's hushed voice. "I've never told her— She has no idea I've been talking to you. Please just leave her alone."

Instinct kicked in his chest. Her distress was a sour note in the air, making his muscles tense like he needed to be ready for a fight. It'd make his life a lot easier if he could use her best friend to keep her compliant, but Felix had never been interested in Dahlia's surrender.

"Cecilia is safe," he promised her. "From me, at least. Whatever she gets up to on her own is her business."

She still looked a bit queasy, but Dahlia seemed to accept that he was sincere. Still, she whispered, "She's the only family I have, Felix. I can't lose her."

"Well, that's not quite true."

"The McKnights don't count."

He grimaced. "I wasn't talking about them."

"Then who?"

Felix rubbed his thumb over the corner of his jaw, watching her carefully. "The Bowans."

"Mr. Bowan? What does he have to do with this? Besides the obvious, I guess."

"When Alastair's blood infected you, two things happened." He held up a finger. "First, in the eyes of the vampire world, you became his biological daughter. That means that as far as vampires are concerned, your name is now Dahlia Bowan, your father is Alastair Bowan, and you are the heir to the Bowan family. Which happens to be an extremely old and powerful one, I might add. Congrats on your upward social mobility."

He held up another finger and continued before Dahlia could let fly the barrage of questions and denials he suspected were bubbling up her pretty throat. "Second, you *also* became venom neutral, which is... Well, we should probably both buy some lottery tickets, because the odds of those two things happening in one shot are astronomical."

Her lips barely moved when she asked, "And what does that mean for me?"

"You heard Alvin. You can mate with another vampire, Dahlia. That means you can theoretically link anyone who claims you to the Bowan family. To some nuts, it means that you can make pure vampiric offspring, too. It's fucked, but it's what they think." When Dahlia gave him a disgusted look, he spread his hands in a *don't blame me* sort of gesture. "When that doctor sold your information, he effectively announced to the entire syndicate that a new princess was just put on the market — one valuable enough to kill for."

"So..." She paused, seemingly to try and catch her breath. It didn't work very well. "So Devon..."

"I didn't stop to ask, but he would've been stupid to pass up the chance to tie himself to the Bowans through you. And that's why Alastair wanted to snap you up, too. He can't have you running off with just *any* vampire."

The implication that *he* was one such unsuitable match hung heavy in the air.

It didn't matter that the Amauris had amassed an incredible amount of influence and money under his grandmother's leadership. They would always be the newcomers on the block, the ones who didn't abide by tradition or respect the rules designed to keep them in line with the old guard.

Alastair didn't like change. He didn't like new ideas or fresh blood running the game.

Tough shit, old man.

It filled Felix with a deep and malicious satisfaction to know that the old prick was gnashing his fangs, furious that he'd gotten to Dahlia first. Alastair had never liked him. He doubted that would change anytime soon.

"Now!" Felix clapped his hands together, startling Dahlia badly enough that she jumped. "We have one more topic to discuss."

Dazed and pale, she looked around the room with wide eyes, like some monster was about to pop out of the wallpaper and bite her. "There's *more*? What could possibly—"

Her mouth snapped shut when he reached under his jacket and extracted a sleek black bolt gun. Calmly setting it on the table between them, grip angled toward her, he leaned back into his seat and crossed one ankle over his knee.

Felix spread his arms over the back of the couch and dropped the mask — for good this time.

"You shouldn't have been at the bar that night," he said, voice flat and hard. "But fine. You didn't know what I had planned. That's not your fault. That was a miscalculation on my part and one I won't be making again. But you know what I *can't* accept, Dahlia?"

He was impressed by the way she kept her gaze away from

the gun. A weaker person wouldn't have been able to keep from looking at it, sitting there like a bomb about to go off on the antique coffee table. Not his girl. She held his gaze, her expression tense and her lips thinned. Afraid, maybe, but too damn proud to back down.

It was inconceivable that he'd ever let some worthless fuck have her. Another vampire would try and break that spirit. All Felix wanted to do was make it stronger. He always had, from the moment they locked eyes in that bar.

When she said nothing, he smiled with too much fang. "You didn't tell me you'd been hurt. I should've been your first fucking call. Not Cecilia. Not your mother. Me."

Speaking through her teeth, she said, "You're not my boyfriend, Felix."

"You're right. I'm not. I'm your mate. And you didn't trust me with your care when you needed it most." At last, the anger bled through the cracks in the ice. It rolled through his voice — all the rage and fear and hurt he barely understood. "You were fucking *impaled*, Dahlia! And then when you started feeling sick, you hid that, too. You know what that tells me?"

There was a vicious undercurrent in her cool reply. "That we're not dating and never have been, presumably."

"It tells me that I didn't properly explain to you how this is gonna be." He sucked in a sharp breath, trying to calm his temper. It didn't do shit.

"See, when a vampire finds his anchor, his bride, his *mate*, what-the-fuck-ever, we don't do anything halfway. They are the center of our world, Dahlia. We would starve without them, so their care is *everything*. Their complete trust that their man will protect and provide for them is essential. It's written in our DNA. That means that when, say, an anchor hides shit from her vampire, it's an insult of the highest degree. A declaration that he's unfit. That he's unworthy."

Dahlia sputtered. "You just spent ten minutes telling me all the things *you* have been hiding from me! How am I the one in trouble here when *you* set off a bomb in *my* bar and didn't bother to tell me?"

"You weren't supposed to be there!" he snarled, the threads of his control finally snapping. "I never — *never!* — would've put you in danger. Not for any opportunity. Not even to end the war! I would've found some other way. I would've called it off or told you not to go in. The fact that you even thought I'd—"

A bitter taste like sour, clotted blood filled his mouth. Felix stood up and paced away, his hands on his hips. He kept his back to her when he finished, "Here's how this is going to go down. You have two choices, Dahlia. You can accept that it's you and me, now and for the rest of our fucking lives, or you can take that gun and shoot me in the head."

"Felix, *what* — "

He faced her. Striding back to the couches, he stopped by the corner of the coffee table and stood there, hands still on his hips, his eyes locked with hers. "You heard me. Shoot me. You think I'm unfit to be your mate? You think I can't care for you or give you what you need? Then there's only one way you're getting rid of me, because I'm not walking away."

When she didn't move, her expression and body frozen, he lowered himself to his knees in front of her. She made a choked sound of protest when he shoved the gun in her limp hands. He kept his palms down on the couch cushions, his head up and neck bared. Felix's lip curled.

"Those are the stakes, pet. That's how serious this shit is. You either grab that gun and put me down, or you start trusting me. Your call."

It was harsh. He knew it was. But he also knew his girl. Sexual torture wouldn't work, and locking her up like an unruly toddler would just piss her off.

No, the only thing Dahlia had ever responded to was power. True, raw power. And there was nothing more true or more raw than putting a gun in her hand and letting her decide what happened next.

What he loved most about his girl was the fact that he genuinely didn't know what she'd choose. He wagered there was a fifty-fifty chance she took him up on the offer.

"What's it gonna be, pet?"

Her fingers curled loosely around the grip, but they didn't stray toward the trigger. "I... I don't want to *kill* you!"

"It's not about wanting. If you really think you'll never trust me, if you *really* don't want to be here, then that's the only option. I'm not going away. I've proved that again and again. You want to be single? You want to be with another person? Someone is going to have to shoot me, because I'm not letting that shit happen while I'm still breathing."

"Felix, this is dramatic even for you." A hysterical edge had entered her voice.

Good, he thought. *She's starting to get it.*

"It's the truth." He placed his hands on her knees and slowly pried them apart. Her robe slipped away, revealing soft thighs and a stomach that trembled with every frantic breath.

Felix held her stare as he lowered himself down to her soft pink center. The scent of her arousal perfumed every breath even as she made those little sounds of outrage.

"Are you kidding me? You give me a gun, tell me to shoot you, and now you want to go down on me?"

He pressed his lips to the soft curve just below her belly button, his eyes closing. The gun hovered over his head, locked in her frozen hand. "Can't a man enjoy his last meal?"

"You've lost your— Ah!"

Dahlia's back arched when his tongue slid between those perfect pink folds, arrowing straight for her clitoris. Vampires had special tongues designed for sucking blood from small wounds. It was an anatomical quirk that worked beautifully for other things, too, like eating out stubborn women who couldn't decide if he should live or die.

He didn't bother looking up to see if she dropped the gun or not when she fisted a hand in his hair, holding him in place as she ground her hips into his mouth. Felix kept her legs spread wide on the couch cushions, consumed by the taste and slick heat of her.

Feathering his tongue, he applied rhythmic, sucking pulses directly to her little pearl of nerves, trying to wring out as much pleasure from her as possible. Dahlia gasped, the muscles of her thighs tensing under his hands.

"Felix— *Felix.* That's not— I have a gun in my hand! You can't do that!"

He paused, tongue swiping slowly from top to bottom to collect as much of her taste as he could. Pulling back a scant inch, he told her, "Then put the gun down, pet. Unless you'd rather not finish. If you don't want me to make you come or have my venom in your veins in… let's say a minute and thirty seconds, then shoot me."

"You can't… you can't bite me." The words came out disjointed, chopped up between panting breaths. "And you *cannot* make me come that fast."

The competitive bastard in him roared to life. "You're wrong on both counts. You're venom neutral, pet. We can bite each other as much as we please. And as for making you come… Want me to prove it to you?"

He could see the logical, cautious part of her warring with the inherent need to compete with him and prove him wrong, but Dahlia was just as bullheaded and competitive as he was. The smart part of her didn't stand a chance.

Her eyes gleamed with challenge when she slipped one thigh over his shoulder. Pearly white fangs — perfect, dainty, and sharp — caught the light when she replied, "You know what? I do."

He flashed a smile. "That's my girl."

At this rate, he was going to have to reupholster the couch.

Felix doubled his efforts, alternating between fast, sucking pulls and gentle swipes of his tongue. When she began to tense up, her thighs twitching by his ears, he pulsed his tongue as fast as he could. Dahlia bit out a curse. Her fingers dug into his hair, nearly ripping it out by the root.

Blind need burned through him. Felix tore his mouth away from her delicious cunt and plunged his fangs into the plush skin of her inner thigh.

Three years. Three years he'd dreamed of what it'd be like the day he finally got to taste her.

It was better than he imagined.

Dahlia jerked, a babbling plea escaping her as his venom released with a hot pulse in his gums. Stars popped in front of his eyes. His hips rolled in jagged thrusts, moving in time with the ejection of venom as he came in his slacks.

Felix groaned, long and loud and appreciative. He hadn't felt that kind of relief in years. There was no other vein for him than hers. To finally be able to bite her was… *exquisite.*

When he had nothing left to give her, Felix smoothly extracted his fangs and began to draw from her in reverent little sips. A vampire's stomach couldn't hold too much blood at one time, so there wasn't a danger of killing her, but worry for her health was an ever-present throb in the back of his mind. Careful not to take too much, he savored every drop.

Her blood was rich and sweet, with a slight bite that made his mouth water for more. He'd never tasted a blood bride before, so he couldn't say whether her flavor was different from how it'd been when she was human, but it didn't matter. She was the most incredible thing he'd ever tasted.

Reluctantly finishing his meal, Felix sealed her wounds with several languid licks. Pressing a kiss to the sweet little puncture marks now adorning her creamy thigh, he looked up to find her sprawled out over the back of the couch, the gun dangling from one limp hand.

Her chest heaved beneath her robe and the fingers in his hair went slack. Felix licked his lips as he rose up to grip the back of the couch by her shoulders, caging her in. He dipped his head to press a kiss to her lips — soft, satisfied, and plainly smug.

"Under a minute," he purred.

Dahlia's tongue darted out to lap at his mouth. The sweet tastes of her blood and cunt drifted between them, passed from him to her. When she spoke, her voice was ever-so-slightly slurred. "Do I get to keep the gun?"

SIXTEEN

FELIX LEFT HER TO REST — AFTER CHANGING HIS PANTS. KNOWING he'd come without even being touched went a long way to soothing her bruised ego.

She just wished it helped with the rest.

Her mind was too full as she stepped into the shower. Not even the incredible water pressure, multiple shower heads, or sex bench could distract her from the clamor in her head.

Venom neutral. Blood bride. Bowan.

Only a few weeks prior, finally allowing herself to be bitten would've been earth-shattering. Now it seemed like the most normal, obvious part of the mess that her life had turned into.

And pleasurable. Can't forget that.

Dahlia's face heated as she dried off in the glittering bath room. Even the towels were luxurious. They were the fluffy, perfectly soft and extra large kind one normally experienced in high end hotels. Not that she'd ever been to those, but she could imagine.

Out of all the catastrophes that had been thrown at her in the last two days, finally giving in to Felix — temporarily, at least — was the least of her worries. That didn't make her pride smart any less. And it certainly didn't mean she intended to *stay*.

Leaving would be hard, though, and not just because he didn't let her keep the gun.

Exiting the bathroom, she padded into the bedroom, fully intending on pilfering some of Felix's clothes. She couldn't negotiate or sneak her way out if she was nude, which was probably why her bag had gone mysteriously missing.

Dahlia didn't see the woman standing by the bed until she rounded the corner. Dressed in a killer crimson pantsuit and sky-high heels, the woman was bent over the bed organizing what appeared to be a dozen black shopping bags. Nearly jumping out of her skin, Dahlia had to grip the towel wrapped around her head to stop it from falling off.

"I'm sorry— What are you doing in here?"

The woman straightened and turned on one pencil-thin heel. She was voluptuous, with sensual curves and a mass of wavy black hair piled on top of her head. A streak of white curled down over her brow to touch one rounded cheek, giving her a disheveled, almost impish look that made her already stunning features a thousand times more dangerous.

Her full mouth quirked in a wide, fanged smile. "There you are! Took you long enough."

Before Dahlia could even think to step back, the woman moved with surprising speed in her heels to barrel down on her. Soft hands cupped her cheeks, squeezing until her lips puckered. The woman sing-songed, "Oh, you're *gorgeous.* Just gorgeous! Felix doesn't deserve you at all. That nasty little goblin. He has the best luck."

Even if she could've spoken, Dahlia had no idea what she would've said to that. Other than perhaps agree. Felix *was* a nasty little goblin.

That thought was promptly catapulted from her mind when, with absolutely no preamble, the woman yanked the tie of her robe from around her waist. The robe parted instantly, revealing Dahlia's freshly washed body beneath.

The woman let out a low, appreciative whistle. "Damn.

That's a great pair of tits. Not as good as mine, but great none the less. You've definitely got me beat on legs, though. And you smell *delicious.* Congrats on that."

Dahlia was so used to being naked with Cecilia that she only felt confusion as the woman inspected her with a critical eye, her fingers holding the lapels of the robe apart.

"Uh, who are you?"

"Oh, I'm Marietta," she replied, dropping the sides of the robe to put her manicured hands on her round hips. "I'm Felix's cousin. One of many you'll meet, but definitely the best one. He told me to help you settle in, so here I am."

Dahlia closed her robe. This woman couldn't have been more different from the statuesque Yvanna, but the resemblance was there. Wiggling her finger in front of her face, she asked, "Does everyone in the Amauri family have the…"

Marietta crossed her eyes to look at the white curl hanging stylishly in front of her face. Giving it a blow, she chirped, "Almost! It's rare that one of us is born without it, but it happens. Mostly it shows up by the forehead, though it varies. My cousin Nash has it in his eyebrow and the side of his head, and Luis got a little in his beard."

"Makes you easy to pick out in a crowd, I guess," Dahlia muttered.

"My mom calls it our red flag." Marietta wrinkled her nose with amusement. "But enough about us. I can't believe a *Bowan* is joining the family. You're going to have to tell me everything about how in Grim's name my cousin pulled that kind of coup off."

"There are a lot of things wrong with what you just said." Dahlia ticked the reasons off on her fingers, her bare foot tapping against the expensive rug. "I'm not a Bowan. I'm not joining the family. And Felix didn't pull off anything other than a successful kidnapping."

If she expected Marietta to argue or show any shock, Dahlia was sorely disappointed. The woman tilted her head back and laughed. "Of course he did! As if a woman like you would ever give him the time of day."

Despite her best efforts, a snort escaped her. "That's what I keep telling him."

"I bet he *loves* that. Amauris enjoy being told no," Marietta said, head shaking. "We tend to take it more as a challenge than anything."

"I've picked up on that, yeah."

"Well, Bowan or not, I hope you don't make anything easy on him. Can't have his ego getting too big now that he's finally head of the family."

Since Marietta seemed like the chatty type, Dahlia dared to ask, "Why has it been so hard for him to become head of the family? He told me he's been fighting a war for years."

Marietta turned back to the bed. Pushing aside one of the heavy curtains, she began rifling through the sea of bags that hadn't been there when Dahlia went into the bathroom to take a shower.

"He was Dora's favorite, but he's young. She knew that when she made him her heir, but I really don't think she understood how against him some of the family was. Or how ambitious. The elders didn't think he had the experience to lead the family, and with Julius and Yvanna around, they figured there were better options." She shrugged as she began to extract clothing from the bags. Silk, velvet, fur — they spilled out across the bed in a rainbow of luxury.

Marietta didn't sound bothered when she continued, "Luckily Julius was picked off early. He was a crazy old fuck and would've driven the family into the ground, so it was great to hear he'd been poisoned by Bounds. Yvanna was a lot harder to handle. She was ice cold and smart to get some powerful people on her side early. The problem with her was that none of the cousins — mine and Felix's generation — could stand her. She treated everyone like they were disposable. She would've sold any one of us for pocket change."

Turning to Dahlia, she held up a slinky slip dress made of burgundy silk. "Here, put this on. I think it should fit, but you can't wear a bra with it."

She took the dress, but she barely registered the soft material in her hands as her mind churned with the new information. "I met Yvanna. Sort of."

"My condolences, then." Marietta pulled out a sleek black thong and tossed it to her. "She was a cunt and I'm glad she's dead."

No love lost there, Dahlia thought, eyeing Marietta with newfound caution. Her demeanor was care-free and cheerful, which made the casual way she spoke of Yvanna's death that much more unsettling.

Clearing her throat, she jerked her chin toward the bed. "Tell me this isn't all for me. I recall bringing my own clothes, so that would make this extremely unnecessary."

Marietta cast her a sly look. "I thought you said you were kidnapped. Seems strange that you'd be given time to pack a bag."

She could feel the flush settling into her cheeks. "He coerced me and threw me over his shoulder. It counts."

"Sure it does." She winked, making Dahlia's face flame hotter. "And don't worry about the clothes. Felix told me to go crazy, so I did. You know how big your closet is? Even with the stuff you already own, this won't even make a dent."

The panties were halfway up her legs when she muttered, "Closet? What closet?"

Marietta jerked a thumb toward a small door Dahlia had overlooked by the bed. "The one in your room."

Tossing the damp towel and robe down on the bed, Dahlia wiggled into the dress. It fit like a glove. Because of course it did. Felix had shown her again and again that he knew everything about her — from her favorite foods to what dress size she wore.

Gods, he's creepy.

But her hands still smoothed over the silk, greedy for the

texture, and that stubborn warmth in her chest couldn't be dislodged, no matter how hard she tried.

Shaking herself, she padded to the door. It blended nearly seamlessly into the wall. The only sign that it was there at all was the gorgeously wrought brass doorknob shaped to look like a lily.

Pulling it open revealed a room that mirrored Felix's, except instead of red silk wallpaper and upholstery, everything was done in creams and golds. There was also a notable absence of a bed.

"That's your suite," Marietta explained as she came up behind her. The scent of raspberries and dark chocolate hovered in the air as she leaned over Dahlia's shoulder. "It's got its own sitting room, office, entertainment area… Nice right? Felix should have your things moved in by tomorrow, probably, so you can start planning what you want to do with it."

Dahlia stood in the doorway, frozen, her hand limp on the lily door knob. It appeared that she'd at last hit her limit.

Staring blankly out at the suite, she said, "I think there's been some confusion."

"Hm?"

"I'm not staying here."

"Oh." Marietta made a thoughtful noise. "Would you prefer I have everything put in Felix's suite? I'm sure he wouldn't mind. We can just chuck his shit in his office."

Dahlia sucked in a deep breath. Her fingers spasmed on the cool brass flower. "No, Marietta. I mean I'm not staying *here*. I don't want my things moved in. I want to go back to my life in San Francisco."

"Ah. Well. That's trickier."

Rounding on her, Dahlia demanded, "Why? Why can't I go home and forget any of this happened? Can't I just leave?"

Marietta's red lips pursed. "Not exactly."

The truth settled in like a frost, chilling her in a slow, awful wave of prickling ice. "So I'm a prisoner."

"You're not… *not* a prisoner." Marietta spread her hands and opined, "But in the grand scheme of things, aren't we all?"

"For fuck's— No, we're not!" Dahlia pushed past her, heading for the bags. "Where are the shoes? I need shoes."

"Why? You gonna run?" Marietta didn't sound particularly worried about it, merely curious. Maybe even a little amused. "That won't be easy. Felix has the guards on high alert in case Alastair tries to snatch you back."

"Oh, that's fantastic," she seethed, ripping through bags until she found a pair of devastatingly beautiful black leather pumps. Shoving her foot in one, she snarled, "One man is holding me prisoner and another is trying to kidnap me so he can do the same. I must be the luckiest woman in the world."

Marietta crossed her arms in front of her heavy chest and cocked an eyebrow. "If what Milo told me is true, then you're not far off. But listen, it's not as bad as all that. Felix and Alastair will work things out. They both want what's best for you. Probably. Felix I'm, like, seventy-five percent sure about."

Shoes on, Dahlia straightened to her full height and leveled the other woman with a severe glare. "Marietta, let me be so, so clear: the day I let men decide what's best for me is the day they put me in the fucking ground."

They stood there staring at each other for a beat before, with a burst of laughter, Marietta exclaimed, "No wonder Felix went to all this trouble! Dora would've *loved* you."

Not sure whether she was being laughed at or not, Dahlia put her hands on her hips and demanded, "Take me to his office. I'm clearing this up right now."

The other woman wiped a tear from her eye, her shoulders still shaking with mirth. "Oh, absolutely. I wouldn't miss it for the world."

MY GIRL

do you have any friends?

I have a lot of cousins

they don't count

Then no

why not? Too busy cutting hands off and
generally terrorizing the populace?

The general consensus is that I'm a bit of a shit

wow that's incredibly validating

SEVENTEEN

"YOU'RE GOING TO DELIVER MY DAUGHTER TO ME TONIGHT."

Felix picked at his claws, his swivel chair turned toward the windows behind his desk. Outside, he could just make out some little Amauris running around in the dark, squabbling over a ball and tackling each other into the soft grass. It was damn good to see. He and the cousins never had the chance to run around like that, squealing like little piglets in the moonlight.

They'd had guns put in their hands too early and had been taught to compete with each other, not play. It was a miracle they'd managed to scrape together the camaraderie they had. Certainly none of the elders or their parents' generation cared if there was loyalty between them.

Only Dora learned to value it. Too bad that revelation came too late. By the time she realized she'd made a mistake, she'd cultivated a generation of monsters.

It was Felix's job to set that shit right. When his eyes tracked the progress of Will, one of the littlest children, pelting across the grass with a ball tucked against his chest, a tension he always seemed to carry eased. It was like releasing a held breath after a little too long. Good, but painful.

One day soon, his and Dahlia's kid would join the rambunctious crew chasing after Will. They'd have a better life than the one he and the cousins had been given. Felix would make sure of it.

But whatever softness existed in him didn't extend to Alastair fucking Bowan.

"Took you long enough to find her," he replied, sniffing disdainfully. He could feel Milo's exasperated frown from across the room, but he didn't care about antagonizing the old prick. "Some father you are. I know you're new to the job, but you really should keep a closer eye on your kids, or else folks might start to think you're careless."

Alastair wasn't a yeller. He was too classy for that sort of thing. Instead, his voice came through the line with cool, crisp fury. "Tell me what it'll take."

Ransoms, tribute, exchanges of favors — these were all normal things in their world. Between syndicate families, kidnappings happened all the time. Generally, they were fairly civilized affairs, and one could expect to be treated well until the ransom was paid, since there was a chance the captor's family members might meet the same fate someday.

To avoid a cycle of retribution, it was generally agreed that it was best to hold any torture or mistreatment until after ransom talks fell through.

So it was a perfectly reasonable request for Alastair to make. The problem was that when it came to Dahlia, Felix wasn't anywhere close to reasonable.

Claws sinking into the armrest of his chair, Felix calmly informed him, "There is no amount of money that would make me give her to you."

Milo made a sound from his place on the leather couch. It was a cross between a sigh and a groan.

Felix shot him a glare. He had no idea what his cousin thought he'd do. They both knew there wasn't a chance he'd actually let Alastair buy Dahlia back. *Maybe* if she'd been someone else they could've reached a deal, but she wasn't. She was his. She'd been his a lot longer than she'd been a Bowan, and he hadn't been bluffing when he told her that the only way he'd step aside was if someone shot him.

Alastair could pry her from his cold, dead claws.

"I always knew you were impulsive and reckless," Alastair bit out. "But I had no idea you were so eager to start another war when you just finished one."

"Doesn't have to be a war. I've known Dahlia for years. We met the night Bounds and his anchor killed Julius. That makes my claim older than yours. Acknowledge it and we can come to an agreement."

"Whatever claim you might've had became moot the instant my blood took. She's a Bowan. She needs to be with Bowans, not with the wild animals you call family."

His blood pressure rose. "So you can sell her off to the highest bidder? That's why you met with Yvanna, isn't it? She wanted your grandnephew to be her groom."

"And I'll tell you the same thing I told your aunt: I don't sell my family. And I certainly wouldn't sell them to *you*. No daughter of mine is joining a family who kills each other for fun. You can't care for her. You're incapable of it."

The insult hit its mark. Felix sat up in his chair, the phone's weak metal body creaking under his brutal grip. "Listen here, fucker—"

There was no respectful knock on his door. It swung open and hit the wall with a bang, rattling art and photographs.

Felix swiveled his chair around to face the doorway. Milo was already on his feet, one hand straying to the gun on his hip, and he could just make out the top of Marietta's hair, but all he really noticed was Dahlia.

His focus honed in on her with laser-like precision, blocking out everything besides the figure she cut in the doorway.

Dressed in a mid-length dress of shiny, clingy material and black stilettos, with her hair damp and her cheeks flushed, she looked like she'd just stepped out of one of his fantasies. Especially when her nipples tightened beneath the draped neckline of the dress.

A raw pulse of hunger nearly distracted him from the way she stormed across the office, her expression a mask of outrage. She didn't even spare a glance for Milo who watched her with a bemused sort of fascination.

"You're going to tell me right here, right now, that I can leave," she announced.

Felix frowned. "We discussed this. You aren't—"

Alastair's voice snapped through the phone's speaker. "Is that Dahlia?"

"Of course it's fucking Dahlia," he growled.

She narrowed her eyes. "Who is that?"

Felix pinched his nose and sighed, "It's Alastair Bowan."

Nearly simultaneously, Dahlia held out her hand for the phone and Alastair demanded, "Put her on, boy."

"I am not putting her on," he replied, glaring at Dahlia's outstretched hand. "You don't need to talk to her. She's fine."

"I'll hear that from her own damn mouth or I'll burn that gaudy mansion down tonight, whelp."

"Keep threatening me, prick. See what— Damn it, Dahlia!"

Felix lunged across the desk, trying to snatch the phone back, but she was faster. Dahlia stood a few feet away from the desk, ignoring Milo and Marietta who watched everything unfold like it was the championship round of the UTA shifter games.

Pressing the phone to her ear, she propped a hand on her hip and said, "Hello?"

"Dahlia," he snarled, pushing up from his chair. He flattened his palms on the mahogany desktop between them. "Give me the phone."

She eyed him with open disdain. He could just make out the

sound of Alastair's voice coming through the speaker, but not what he said.

"Uh-huh. That's what I was told. And I can't imagine it would've happened any other way." There was a pause. She held his glare as Alastair said something else. "No offense, Mr. Bowan, but that really doesn't mean anything to me."

Felix's heart raced. There was no real threat, but his instincts screamed at the thought of her talking to someone who wanted to take her away from him. All he wanted to do was grab the phone and smash it, ending the conversation.

Gathering the flimsy threads of his control, he ordered, "Speakerphone. Now."

She didn't obey right away. Frankly, he was surprised she listened at all. Maybe she saw how close he was to ending the call completely. Whatever the reason, Dahlia lowered the phone and tapped the screen.

Placing it on the desk, she said, "You're on speaker, Mr. Bowan."

All business now, Alastair asked, "Have you been harmed?"

Felix watched Dahlia's expression closely. It was gratifying to see she looked a little offended on his behalf when she answered, "No, I haven't."

"It's good to know Felix has some manners after all." Alastair's tone was scathing.

"Let's not get ahead of ourselves," Dahlia replied, rolling her eyes.

Felix made a face. He couldn't very well deny it, but that didn't mean he wanted Dahlia and Alastair getting all chummy about it.

"Listen, Mr. Bowan," she continued, ignoring him. "There seems to be some cultural misunderstanding happening here, so I'd appreciate it if you could explain what you want with me."

There was a slight pause. "You're my daughter." The answer was brusque, utterly self-assured. "You belong with the Bowans. You should be here, living with us and under our protection."

He had no idea what answer Dahlia expected. Felix had told her that Alastair would claim her as his daughter, so he really didn't feel like the shocked look on her face was warranted.

"You don't even know me," she protested.

"I don't need to. Most people don't get to choose their children. We accept what we're given, whatever and whoever they are."

Dahlia seemed taken aback by that for a moment. Gathering herself, she muttered, "That's lovely, I guess. But I'm a grown woman, Mr. Bowan. You can't just decide where I should live and who I should be with."

Alastair brushed her point off as easily as one might swat a fly. "I'm your father. Of course I can."

"How do we know for sure that it was your blood, anyway?" Felix arched a brow at her sudden backtracking on the fact she'd been so very sure about just an hour ago. "I mean, *really*, it could've been anyone—"

"Dahlia," Alastair sighed, "we both know that isn't likely."

She swallowed. "So what happens now?"

"Felix sends you to my home unharmed, avoiding any bloodshed, and you move into the house with myself and my anchor — who hasn't slept in my bed since this happened, by the way. He's furious I let you be taken. For the sake of my relationship, Dahlia, you need to come home."

Felix reached for the phone. "Not happening, prick."

Slapping his hand away from the screen before he could end the call, Dahlia said, "Okay, that's a very nice offer, but I'm going to have to pass. I am not moving in with you, Mr. Bowan, and I'm not going to be Felix's prisoner, either. I have a life. I'm not just going to leave it because my biology is a little different."

The men protested at the same time. Felix scoffed, his eyes rolling at the idea that Dahlia was his prisoner, of all things, while Alastair made a firm noise of dissent.

"That's not going to be possible. It's unsafe for a blood bride to wander around without protection, and it's even less safe for a

Bowan to do so. There's no other option. You'll move in with us."

"You are *not* going to the Bowans," Felix argued, snagging the phone off the desk at last. "You're staying here because you're mine. You've been mine for years, Dahlia. You're not a *prisoner.* I'm doing everything I can to keep you safe."

When Alastair began making derisive sounds through the speaker, Felix finally had enough. He ended the call and stuffed the phone in his pocket. Without taking his eyes off his girl's increasingly livid expression, he pointed over her shoulder to the door.

"Hey, voyeurs — fuck off. I need to talk to my bride."

Milo and Marietta shared a look before they turned and exited the office. The door closed with a soft click only a second before Dahlia hissed, "You can't keep me here, Felix. I came with you because you told me I was in danger, *not* because I agreed to live with you."

"I can keep you here because I *am* protecting you," he argued, headache beginning to throb in his temples. Skipping sleep had been a bad idea. So had letting her anywhere near a phone. "Dahlia, you don't seem to understand that the life you had is gone. It isn't something you could go back to even if I wanted to let you, which I don't."

"Why not? Explain it to me, Felix!"

He sliced a hand through the air. "You aren't Dahlia McKnight anymore! You're Dahlia fucking Bowan! And you're a blood bride. I wish that didn't mean anything, but it does. It means you're a syndicate pawn just like the rest of us. It means that you'll be hunted to the ends of the fucking earth by vampires who want what your new family has. You'll never be free of it, Dahlia. You'll never be able to change their minds or make them see reason. You're just a venom type to them. A fucking name brand *womb.*"

"Oh, I see. And it's not like that for you, is it? You're not influenced by this newfound importance of mine." She leaned over the desk, palms planted on the wood, and snarled, "Then tell me why you waited three years, Felix, but the moment you got the news, you showed up at my front door."

"I told you why I waited three years." Matching her posture, Felix hunched his shoulders to bring them nose to nose. "But fine. You want the full truth? You'll get it. When it was safe, I was going to keep you for a little while. Enjoy my life and get a little taste of actual love before I resigned myself to a soulless fucking existence with a blood bride. I was going to let you go, Dahlia, because I care about you too much to make you live that life with me."

Dahlia's eyes widened. Her mouth worked but no sound escaped. When she did finally speak, it was with a disturbingly quiet voice. "You... You were going to marry another woman?"

Marry? Felix had to think for a second, weighing what the word meant.

Vampires didn't traditionally do marriage. They shared blood, after all. What were pretty promises spoken in front of an altar compared to a bite? But it was a very human thing to make a claim through marriage. It was roughly equivalent to the bond a vampire formed with their anchor, he supposed, if comparatively shallow.

Curious to see how she'd react, Felix nodded, his attention keenly focused on the way her pupils contracted into tight little points. A scratching sound briefly drew his gaze to where her nails had scraped the desk as her fingers curled into fists.

Measuring his words carefully, he said, "A blood bride is necessary for me to get the elders completely on my side. I didn't want to do it, but I haven't worked this hard and come this far to lose their support—"

"So you were going to throw me aside the moment you found a better fit? After *three years* of— of making me actually—" Her lip curled, revealing those darling little fangs again. "Who was it, Felix?"

Anger bled into something hotter. Felix's breathing picked up as he took in her defensive stance, the bared fangs, and the color in her cheeks. Dahlia wasn't just pissed. She was territorial in a way he recognized intimately.

His girl was *jealous*.

A slow, pleased smile spread across his mouth at the same time that his cock went rock hard beneath the desk. In a husky voice, he taunted, "Why, pet? I thought you didn't want me. Shouldn't you be happy that someone else was gonna take me off your hands?"

He didn't think her face could get any redder, but it did. "You do *not* get to waste three years of my life hounding me and making me actually care about you, only to throw me away for some bullshit political marriage, Felix!"

"Well, if you don't want to be my blood bride, what choice do I have?"

He knew he was pushing it. Felix toyed with instincts she probably didn't even understand, plucking at them with reckless abandon just to see what she'd do. But he couldn't stop. He needed her to understand, to want him as badly as he wanted her, and he'd never cared about fighting fair before.

Leaning backward, he lied, "If you don't want it, I could let another woman bite me."

In hindsight, he should've known to stop there, but he'd always been one to go a little bit too far.

Felix barely had a second to register the fact that Dahlia had crawled over the desk before his back hit his chair. She was on him just as quickly, their momentum sending the chair swiveling as she tore the lapels of his shirt aside.

Pain exploded in the juncture between his neck and shoulder. "Fuck!" he wheezed, grabbing her waist to steady her. He planted his feet on the floor, stopping their dizzying spin, and groaned.

The bite was clumsy, too deep, and almost certainly at the wrong angle, but it didn't matter. Triumph roared inside him as her venom released. It was warm, a little ticklish, and within a few heartbeats, he could taste it bleeding through the thin membrane of his cheeks.

It was sweet. So sinfully sweet. Like ambrosia sweeping through his veins and coating his tongue, a gift from Grim herself.

EIGHTEEN

His mind went blissfully fuzzy as the pain numbed. Felix dropped his head back, exposing more of his neck to her.

When she began to rock her hips into his, seeking friction, he made quick work of freeing his cock and pushing aside her soaked panties. They both shuddered as he lined them up. Dahlia sank down on him in one hard movement, sucking him into the hot well of her body like it was her due.

She clamped down hard enough that he swore he could feel the throb of her heartbeat all around him. Careful not to dislodge her, he grabbed her hips and began to rock her up and down, just a little, just enough.

"That's it, pet," he encouraged her thickly. "That's my girl. Ease up a little. Just— just bite with your top teeth. There you go."

He groaned again as her fangs slid free. Dahlia's lips sealed over the wounds to pull directly from his veins. Each suck was greedier than the last, and each one made her cunt spasm around the hot bar of his cock like she was trying to milk him dry in every way. It was the most painfully erotic thing he'd ever experienced.

Felix hadn't been entirely certain he'd let his blood bride feed from him. His reluctance wasn't out of some macho bullshit like some, but rather a practical thing. If he intended to be away from her as often as possible, it wasn't feasible to have them so reliant on each other.

To conceive a child it would be necessary for her to take his venom regularly, but after the fact it was less so. He intended to feed only enough to keep her from experiencing venom withdrawal, but he wasn't about to introduce that weakness into his own life.

But, as always, everything was different with Dahlia.

The joy of feeling her messy, painful bite was exquisite. It even eclipsed the satisfaction of his own bite. He discovered that it was one thing to claim Dahlia, but it was another to be claimed *by* her.

To be possessed by her, to sustain her, to have *her* venom flowing through *his* veins, and to be her first...

Thumbing her tight little clitoris, he came with a pathetic little cry, his hips jerking. She rippled around him, her back stiffening with her own orgasm, but she didn't stop drinking. He filled her up as she took from him, drop by glorious drop.

Felix stroked her hair out of her face as she drank her fill, savoring every pull of her lips and the silk of her half-dried hair under his fingers. Her weight in his lap was perfect. The heat of her silky, dripping cunt around his softening cock was bliss. Everything from her scent to her little hungry noises made him want to keep her there for as long as she'd let him.

But vampire stomachs could only take so much. Blood brides had a larger appetite than most, since they were designed to feed on their fellow vampires — who themselves had razor thin margins for nutrition — but even they couldn't take more than a pint at a time.

Dahlia pulled back with a shudder, her breathing heavy. She rested her temple on his shoulder as her body lost all its tension.

"You did great, pet," he sighed, cuddling her close to his chest. "I'm fucking honored to be your first bite. And your last."

She said nothing.

He hummed, riding the pleasant high of her venom as it made its lazy way through his system. He'd always wondered what it'd be like to experience venom. Now he understood a little of what a vampire brought to the table. It didn't completely negate the bite, of course, but it was a nice perk. The closest thing he could equate it to was drinking a smooth alcoholic synth. It was just enough of a buzz to feel loose and warm.

That was probably why it took him a second to notice she was shaking.

Suddenly on high alert, Felix sat up a little and tried to get a good look at her. Dahlia had gone sickly pale. Her eyes were squeezed shut and her lips were clamped between her teeth as silent tears tracked down her cheeks.

Salt bloomed in the air, souring the sweet scent of her and the musk of sex.

"Dahlia," he whispered, stroking her cheek. Worry cut through him. "Baby, what's wrong? Talk to me. Did you hurt yourself? Did *I* hurt you? Should I call Alvin back?"

Seeing his proud Dahlia reduced to tears was gutting. Felix floundered, helpless and increasingly alarmed, when she pressed her face into his ravaged neck and let out a plaintive cry.

"What's *wrong* with me?"

Holding her closer, he answered, "Nothing. Nothing's wrong with you. You're perfect."

"I don't want to be a vampire," she cried, shoulders shaking in earnest as she fought back sobs. "I don't want to drink blood. I don't want to— to— feed on you or bite you when you make me so mad I could spit. I've become an animal. I just want to go back to how I was before."

Regret wasn't something he felt often, but when he did, it was excruciating.

Felix silently cursed himself as he stroked and kissed her hair. "Oh, pet. No. You didn't bite me because you were mad. You bit me because you were *possessive*. That's just being a vampire,

Dahlia. It's instinct. I knew it and I pushed anyway to see what you'd do. I'm sorry. I forget that this is new for you. I should've... I should've been gentler with your first bite. I didn't think and fucked up."

She sniffled. "Did the boogeyman just say sorry?"

"He's been known to do it every now and again." Felix pressed another kiss to her hair, a little bit of his worry easing. Hearing a little of her spark come back didn't help the regret, though. If anything, it made it worse.

I have to be careful with her, he thought, unpleasantly reminded of Alastair's cutting remark.

In a more serious voice, he added, "I can't imagine how hard this is for you, but I also need to be honest with you, Dahlia: you being turned is the best fucking thing to ever happen to me. Even if that does mean I'll have to deal with the prick Alastair Bowan forever."

"Because you needed a blood bride."

"Because I need you," he corrected her. "It would've killed me to give you up."

"But you would've." There was an understandable note of accusation in her tone, but it was overshadowed by her curiosity. "Why? I never clocked you as the type to give up the things you want. No one tells Felix Amauri what to do, right?"

Resting his cheek against her hair, he let out a heavy breath. "No one except you."

"I'm being serious."

"So am I. You don't seem to understand how much control you have over me, pet. Someday soon you're going to figure it out. I honestly can't wait." He was quiet for a moment, trying to sort through his thoughts so he could explain himself to her in the way she deserved.

They both knew he wasn't good at this feelings shit, but he owed it to her to try. She'd given him her trust — conditional and perhaps ill-informed as it was — and that meant he had to return the favor.

Clearing his throat, he said, "But there are some things that even I can't fuck around with. My family is one of them. If it was just me and you, I would've made you mine the night we met. But it's not and never has been. I owe my cousins my loyalty. They're my responsibility. Not just them, but their kids, too. Keeping them safe sometimes means I don't get what I want."

He wasn't sure what to make of the surprise in her voice when she replied, "Your family means a lot to you."

"Why so shocked? Don't most people care about their families?"

Dahlia sat up a little, dislodging his head. She still looked pale and shaken, but there was some life in her eyes when she deadpanned, "Felix, you blew up your aunt."

"It's complicated," he replied, smoothing his hands up and down her bare arms. He couldn't tell if the touch was meant to soothe her or himself. Not that it mattered. He'd always be greedy for her, and he'd never take it for granted that she belonged to him.

Never.

"If Yvanna had backed down and let me take over the family like my grandmother intended, we never would've had an issue. The problem was that she and my uncle Julius — the man who died the night we met — belonged to a generation of Amauris that…" He drifted off, struggling to find the right words to describe how absolutely monstrous his father's generation had been.

"They were bad people. All of them in their own special ways. My grandmother was the generation that rebuilt the city after the dragons razed it in the Great War, and she felt like her children needed to be just as tough and ruthless as she was."

"But they didn't have to survive the same way she did during the war," Dahlia astutely pointed out. "Those things weren't as necessary."

He nodded. "Exactly. What she got was a generation of monsters, each of them special in their own ways and not one of them loyal to each other. When I was born, she vowed to do things differently. For me, family comes first. Real family. My cousins. Their kids. The people who've pledged their lives to our name whether they share it or not. They're my responsibility."

"You once told me that your grandma raised you." Big blue eyes, so soft compared to how they normally appeared when they gazed at him, looked even brighter with the sheen of tears in her eyes.

Felix rubbed his thumb over her bottom lip, a kick of arousal hitting him hard as he smeared his blood across the cushion. Answering her unasked question, he muttered, "My father was a piece of shit who lived too long. Dora had him killed a few years before she passed. She didn't want me to have to do it."

Dahlia grabbed his hand and held it, their fingers twining against her steadily beating heart. "And what about your mom?"

"She's around. Not my biggest fan, as you can imagine. She hated my dad, but they had some sort of fucked up bond between them. I don't think she'll ever stop blaming me for his death."

"But you didn't kill him. Your grandma did."

He shrugged. "I would've, though. To fix this fucked up family, I would've."

Dahlia gave him a long, considering look. "What do you want to do with it? Get out of the syndicate?"

A laugh exploded out of him. "Fuck no!"

"It was a valid question," she snapped, releasing his hand to smack his shoulder.

He shook his head. "I want the family to stop eating itself alive. I want the kids to have time to grow up without being put to work before they can even drive. I want my own to not worry that someday their siblings will take them out. So no, we're not getting out of the syndicate. I doubt we'd ever do that. The syndicate built this city, Dahlia. It built this family."

"What if I don't want to be part of that?"

The moment hung taut between them, heavy with the weight

of expectation. Felix tried to relax his fingers on her waist, but it took more effort than he liked.

Trying to keep his voice level, he answered, "I wish I could give you a choice, Dahlia. I really do. But I can't."

She turned her head sharply, her gaze locked on some distant point across the room. The softness between them, sweetened by the sharing of blood and sex and secrets, evaporated. Its sudden absence left a cold vacuum somewhere in his chest.

"So I really am a prisoner," she said, flat and bitter.

Felix swallowed a sour taste in his mouth. "You're my bride. I'll do anything for you — except let you go."

I'm serious, Dahlia. Next time someone gives you shit, I'm handling it

MY GIRL

have you ever considered the fact that maybe just talking to me for a few hours is better than threatening to kill people when they upset me

A. That was more than a few hours. You have no idea how much paperwork I got done while we talked. We should do that every night. I might actually get shit done around here.

B. No.

C. You don't have to deal with everything yourself.

you can't fix everything for me. Sometimes I've got to be a big girl and take things into my own hands, Felix. Independence is important

(now is not the time for a joke about what that thing should be fyi)

I respect your independence. It's sexy as fuck. You should independently tell your man when someone's fucking with you so he can handle the problem. Respectfully

(you get one free pass)

I'm going to bed, boogeyman. Independently

Damn right you are

NINETEEN

AT A CERTAIN POINT, THE BRAIN COULD ONLY TAKE SO MUCH.

Dahlia firmly believed that she'd reached her limit forty-eight hours ago. She'd officially passed it when Felix handed her the gun, and then she'd left it in the rearview mirror when she sank her fangs into his neck.

To have it confirmed under no uncertain terms that she wasn't allowed to leave sent her so far beyond what she could handle that she simply retreated inside herself like a turtle into its shell. There was no dealing with it. There was no negotiation or problem-solving. There was only survival, and that meant pretending her problems didn't exist.

After Felix walked her back to his room — *their room?* — she could do nothing except crash for a few hours of blissful, dreamless sleep. There was no Alastair Bowan or blood brides or sharp teeth in her dreams. Just a blessed blackness that wiped all that away.

She woke up groggy and disoriented sometime later to the feeling of Felix's fingers in her hair. The strokes were gentle, almost like he wasn't actually trying to wake her.

Between coming out of a deep sleep and true wakefulness

there was a perfect stillness where she didn't care about where she was or why he was touching her — only that he didn't stop.

Dahlia let out a long, pleased sigh and tilted her head into his hand. The rhythm briefly faltered before it picked up again, this time with a little more pressure.

Felix's low, amused voice filled the quiet. "If you sleep much longer, you won't be able to catch Cecilia before she goes to bed."

Her eyes snapped open. "Cecilia? What—" She sat up, dislodging his hand, and looked around like her best friend might pop out of the shopping bags she'd tossed on the floor or from behind a thick curtain. "Where is she?"

"Back at her apartment, I imagine." He withdrew her phone from his pocket and placed it in her lap. "Give her a call, pet. She's probably worried about you. And it'll make you feel better."

It felt like a calculated move to reinforce his assertion that she wasn't actually a prisoner, but she didn't care. Dahlia snatched the phone out of her lap.

Chuckling, Felix stood up from the bed, but he didn't leave. Instead, he bent low to press a kiss to her forehead. "You don't have to hide anything from her," he whispered, rubbing the pad of his thumb over the corner of her jaw. "But if she offers to stage a rescue mission, I'd try to put her off. Or don't. There are a lot of single Amauris roaming around who'd love to meet her, I'm sure."

She could tell he was only half-joking. No doubt Felix would find it absolutely hilarious — and suit his nefarious purposes — to hook her best friend up with one of his cousins. Then she'd *really* never be able to leave, because there wasn't a chance she'd abandon Cecilia to fend for herself among the Amauris.

Giving him a wide-eyed look of indignation, she said, "No, no, no. None of you go anywhere near Cece. She couldn't handle your bullshit. She's way too nice."

Felix tapped the end of her nose. "Then no rescue operations, hm?"

Stepping away from the bed, he cast a look at the bags scattered hither and yon across the floor. A dark brow arched. "Are you not gonna use your closet?"

"If I can wrap my head around the idea of having a closet in your house, I'll consider it."

He tilted his head back to give the elaborately molded ceiling a long-suffering look. "Fine. I'll just buy you more until you *have* to put stuff in the closet or risk breaking an ankle on a ten thousand dollar purse."

His ability to dodge the things she threw at him was deeply aggravating. The silver dish she could understand. The pillow he could've given her, for her pride's sake. But he didn't.

Felix stepped to the side in one fluid motion, dodging the silk tasseled monstrosity she'd chucked his way, and continued laughing as he left the bedroom. She waited until she couldn't hear his footsteps anymore before she frantically pulled up Cecilia's contact page, cursing his name all the while.

"Have you considered jumping out a window?"

Dahlia pawed through the bags on the floor. Marietta had pulled out all the fancy stuff, but there were heaps more she hadn't touched. White tissue paper piled up around her like snowdrifts as she sorted through silky pajamas, high end loungewear, the fancy kind of jeans that could be passed down to her children, and several fashionable coats strong enough to withstand a New Zone winter.

Before escaping reality via a blackout nap, she'd changed into a soft pair of pants and loose shirt, which allowed her to sit comfortably on the floor as she explained to her best friend all the ways her life had gone to shit.

"I haven't even looked outside," she admitted, pinching the phone between her ear and shoulder as she briskly folded a cashmere sweater. It must've cost him an egregious sum of money, so she made a mental note to take it with her when she left.

"Dahlia, that's Kidnappee Rule number one! Survey your surroundings for possible escape routes!"

"All right, all right, I'm getting up." Dahlia levered herself off the floor.

All things considered, Cecilia had taken things well. After railing at her hysterically for several minutes over her disappearance, she'd calmed down enough to listen to the whole story. The worst part was having to explain Felix — who he was, what he did, and what *they* were. Had been. Might be.

Dahlia stood by her reasons for hiding him, but it didn't quite soothe the guilt that pierced her when Cecilia exclaimed, *"You've had a secret syndicate boyfriend for three fucking years?"*

She tried explaining that Felix wasn't her boyfriend several times. It didn't do much good. Cecilia had only been convinced to give up the argument when Dahlia told her that, boyfriend or not, she was technically being held prisoner.

Padding over to one of the towering windows, Dahlia nudged a heavy curtain aside and peered out into the darkness.

"Huh."

"What do you see?"

"We're in the city," she answered, surveying the sprawling yard and the intimidating walls that separated it from what looked like an exclusive gated neighborhood. Not far off were what could only be apartment buildings and the dull glow of the city. When she turned to her left, a dark swath of water glimmered with the house's lights.

"I think Felix lives on the Potomac."

He'd once told her that he lived in the United Washington, but she'd always assumed he lived in some modern monstrosity of a penthouse in the heart of the city. She couldn't have been more wrong. The waterfront house was huge and the yard was carefully landscaped. Play structures for children dotted the grass, and she was pretty sure she spied the edge of a pool.

"Do you see a way to get out?"

Dahlia cupped her eyes to block out the glare from the low bedroom lights and squinted. She wondered if she'd ever get that superior vampiric night vision to go along with all the other horrific side-effects she'd been saddled with — like ravaging the neck of someone she cared about the second they started talking about other women.

Shuttling that thought out of her mind as quickly as it came, she eyed what looked like a sturdy pergola beneath the window. It didn't look like *too* high of a drop.

"There's an awning or something below one of the windows," she explained, "but Marietta said that the place is super guarded. Even if I could make it out and down without killing myself, my choices are the walls or the river. Both of which are probably monitored, right?"

Cecilia made a skeptical noise in the back of her throat. "That doesn't sound like a woman with a can-do attitude. Are you sure you really want to leave? It's okay if you like him, you know."

Dahlia straightened. "Of course I want to leave!"

"I'm just saying, it doesn't sound *so* bad, and you've been dating this guy for three years. I get that the situation's fucked, but—"

"I'm being held against my will, Cece. I can't just *stay.*"

It didn't matter that she was living in luxury, or that she was safe from what sounded like a new overbearing father figure, or that Felix was turning out to be a lot more complex than she thought he was. Just because it turned out he'd do anything for his family, for *her*, didn't mean she could allow herself to be held prisoner.

At least, that's what she kept telling herself.

"Then stop dawdling and get your head in the game. How

do you escape your hot vampire captor who wants to pamper you and give you unlimited orgasms?"

"You are *really* making me regret telling you things."

"Look, I'm not saying it's right, but also it doesn't sound so bad. You need help learning to be a vampire, and he seems like he's head over heels for you. He's *been* head over heels for you. Some of us keep getting stood up, Dahlia. Maybe count your blessings a little."

"Cece, that can't be my life. I can't be a kept pet here. I have a list. I have *goals.*" She eyed the yard, her throat oddly tight. Dahlia hated that a part of her really didn't want to leave. It looked at that stretch of dark water and asked her why they couldn't just stay with him.

But the other half of her rebelled at being... whatever it was he expected of her now. It couldn't just let him or anyone else bulldoze her. She was still Dahlia, even if she was a vampire now. Staying true to that had become more vital than ever.

If she let her entire identity go, she'd be giving up everything she'd fought for. It wasn't about her feelings for Felix, which she could privately admit were distressingly considerable. It was about her. She'd just be a thing to these people. A blood bride. A daughter. Not Dahlia.

She refused to let that happen.

"All right. I hear you. Let's get you out of there," Cecilia said, all notes of teasing evaporated from her voice. "Let me just ask: Did Marietta say that the house was guarded against people *leaving* or people *intruding?*"

TWENTY

I<small>T HONESTLY DIDN'T OCCUR TO HER THAT SHE'D GET AWAY WITH IT.</small>
She wasn't sure what divine blessing carried her down that pergola
without breaking her neck, or how she managed to avoid the
guards that walked the perimeter of the property. When she
slipped between a painfully narrow gap between the fencing by the
private dock behind the house, she braced herself for alarms, for
the ripple of wards being breached, for barking dogs, for anything.

But there was nothing but the faint sounds of people enjoying
what appeared to be a laidback party and the rhythmic thud of
boots as the guards did their patrols. Like always, Cecilia was
right: Felix really didn't expect her to run, so he hadn't thought
to increase the security for people exiting the grounds.

Her heart hammered in her ears as she kept low and
followed a long dock that connected all the fancy homes to their
even fancier boats. The paranoia that someone would catch her
at any minute and tackle her to the ground increased her pace
until she was jogging down the dock, toward another gate.
Cecilia remained on the line, just in case, tucked safely in the
pocket of Dahlia's lounge pants.

She cursed her choice of clothing when they snagged on the

sharpened ends of the fence that poked from the top of the locked gate. She yanked hard, tearing the fabric, and sent herself careening over the other side with a muffled yelp.

Dahlia landed hard, forcing the air from her lungs. There was some squawking from the vicinity of her pocket, but she didn't have the breath to acknowledge it for several seconds.

When she got a bit of her wind back, she forced herself into a sitting position with considerable effort. Every part of her back and shoulder hurt, but nothing felt broken.

Retrieving her phone, she spared a second to mutter, "I'm fine. Just fell over a gate. Please shut up."

"Don't scare me like that, then!" Cecilia snapped.

Dahlia only grunted before shoving the phone back into her pocket. Her pace was considerably slower with her newfound limp, but she made it into some sort of small, ritzy park on the edge of the neighborhood before eventually navigating her way out into the city.

She hadn't grown up in a city. Her formative years were spent in a small, nothing sort of town on the edge of the Sacramento basin. The first few months in San Francisco had been a continuous culture shock that forced her to adjust almost immediately. United Washington wasn't exactly the same, but the indifference of the people was. No one looked twice at her torn pants or the leaves in her hair as she blended in with the nocturnal crowd.

Despite the late hour, the streets were packed with people doing shopping, pushing strollers, or going out for drinks. No one spared her a glance as she attempted to find her way to a public transit stop.

It turned out that the Metro wasn't too dissimilar from San Francisco's Muni. An m-lev train was an m-lev train, no matter what side of the continent it was on.

Dahlia had no idea where she was going, only that she needed to leave — no matter what the feeling in her gut was screaming at her. It seemed that the more distance she put between herself and Felix, the louder that screaming became.

It wasn't just a new animal instinct to stay close to her food source. It was a deep, clawing yearning to go back to someone who, against all odds, made her feel special. The certainty that she was leaving something important behind was almost unbearable.

Settling back on her hard plastic seat, she put her phone to her ear again. "Okay, I'm on a train. What should I do now?"

"Come home?"

Dahlia winced. "I can't do that. That's the first place people would look. Which reminds me — whatever happens, do *not* talk to any strangers or vampires who come sniffing around my apartment, Cece. If someone asks about me, tell them you have no idea where I went. I won't let you be involved in any of this."

Cecilia choked. "What? You're gonna just go on the run without me? Fuck you! That's not allowed!"

Pinching her nose, Dahlia replied, "I'm not going on the run. I'm— I'm figuring shit out. I have to get my head right, and I can't do that with everyone around me telling me what I should be doing or how I should feel about it. And I sure as shit can't put you in danger. You're the only family I have."

"I don't care about danger," she stubbornly insisted. "We're a duo. We *do* everything together. We put the *do* in *duo*, Dahlia. I'm not letting you run across the UTA and have a crisis about being a vampire while I sit on my ass and do nothing. You're my best friend. Nothing about that has changed."

Dahlia covered her face with her free hand and hunched her shoulders, letting her wavy blonde hair shadow her expression. Her voice was thick when she replied, "I love you, Cece. It's going to be okay. I'll call really soon, I promise."

"Dahlia Francine McKnight, don't you fucking hang up on—"

She pocketed her phone and stood up from her seat. The

slight swaying motion of the m-lev train forced her to keep her grip on the hand rails as she slipped around bored passengers to peer at the digital map on the wall. Her eyes were a little blurry, but she forced the tears away.

Everything's going to be fine. I'll call her when I get where I'm going.

The problem was that she had no idea where that should be. She'd never traveled farther than San Francisco. There were no friends to crash with in the Draakonriik or a farm to hide out on in the Shifter Alliance, the two closest territories to the Neutral Zone.

But she clearly couldn't stay in United Washington. It was Vampire Central and, as far as she'd put together, the main hub of the syndicate. If she wanted space to figure out what she was going to do with the bullshit she'd been handed and whether she wanted what Felix was offering, then she had to at the very least leave the city.

Weighing her options, she decided that the best one was an interterritory m-lev train. Taking a plane would require identification, and she didn't know how far Felix's or Alastair's reaches were. A train could get her out the territory quickly enough and a ticket could be bought with the ID chip all citizens of the UTA had implanted into the meat of their right thumbs.

It took two line switches, but she eventually made it to Union Station. The bored teller behind the glossy window barely spared her a glance when she requested a ticket to Grand Central Station in New York. Another place she'd never been, but she figured a big city had to be easier to get lost in.

"Nocturnal car or diurnal car?"

"I'm sorry?"

The teller looked up from their computer screen, brows arched. Speaking slowly, they repeated, "Nocturnal car or diurnal car?"

"Oh, I—" Dahlia blinked rapidly, disoriented by the question and by the fact that she suddenly had a preference. Speaking low like it was some sort of secret, she answered, "Nocturnal, please."

They rolled their eyes, their fingers already tapping at their keyboard. All around them, the sounds of shoes on the polished floor and tinny announcements echoed off the high ceilings. Dahlia hunched a little, unable to shake the feeling of exposure in such a big, crowded place.

"The next train leaves in thirty minutes." The teller slid the thin paper ticket through the slot. They eyed her balefully when they added, "You're cutting it close to dawn. I wouldn't sit too close to any windows while you wait."

It took her a second to process that she'd been recognized as a vampire.

Dahlia reeled. It was harder to catch her breath from that than it was after she fell. It was one thing to have Felix or one of his ilk know, but to be *recognized* as anything other than human for the first time was terrifying.

Snatching the ticket, she clutched it to her chest and blindly sought a place to sit. She didn't notice the windows or think about what time it was. Sinking onto a wide wooden bench, she fought the urge to put her head between her legs.

Dahlia thought she'd come to terms with being a vampire. Not completely, but in a way that meant it didn't quite feel like the world was falling down on her head.

Whatever tentative peace she'd found died when she allowed Felix to take her home, and it'd been buried six feet under when she sank her teeth into his neck like an animal. Her mouth still watered at the memory of how his blood gushed into her mouth — hot and tangy and perfect. Synth couldn't compare.

And the way it *felt*…

Not just to drink real, actual blood not from a can, but to release her venom into his veins and mark him so everyone knew he belonged to her. It was the most exquisite pleasure she'd ever experienced. Never in all her life had she felt more connected to another being than when his blood poured down her throat.

And Felix had gone down on her once already that day, so the bar was high.

But afterward, when the bliss wore off and his blood sloshed in her stomach, Dahlia came to her senses and discovered an unrecognizable version of herself sitting in his lap.

She didn't *bite* people. She certainly didn't lose her mind over the idea of her boyfriend leaving her for another woman. Yeah, it would've pissed her off, but she didn't strike out with violence.

If she just sipped from synth bottles and didn't look too hard in the mirror when she brushed her teeth, she could've pretended like not much had changed. There was no running from the truth when she had her fangs in Felix's neck.

Especially not when she *liked* it.

She couldn't even hide it from strangers. Dahlia was a vampire — and she had no idea what that meant. Not really.

A sense of overwhelming loneliness crushed her — an unmooring that left her aching for home, for the scent of caramel and smoke and soft fingers in her hair. Shoulders rounding, she clutched her ticket in one clammy fist and wrapped her arms around her middle like it could help keep her together.

What am I even doing?

She didn't know how to survive as a vampire. There hadn't even been a thought about whether she'd be out after sunrise. She didn't know what synth to buy or how to sunproof windows or *anything*.

And worst of all was the fact that everything in her screamed to go back to Felix. He wouldn't just know what to do. He'd teach her how to fend for herself. He'd tell her she *could* handle it, and then he'd hold her close anyway, not because she was fragile, but because he liked having her near.

All she had to do was trade her freedom for comfort.

What kind of thinking is that? I can't willingly go back to a cage just because I'm scared. I'm tougher than that.

Dahlia didn't feel tough, though. Her body ached. She was cold. Her stomach was beginning to rumble again, despite the full meal Felix had given her, and a future full of unknowns yawned before her.

New York was as foreign to her as United Washington. There was nothing for her there except distance. Gods knew how long that would last, though. It occurred to her that Felix and Alastair might not be the only threats on the horizon. New York could've been full of vampires like Devon. She had no idea how far the syndicate's tentacles really spread.

Hopelessness threatened to squeeze the life out of her. It was a lucky thing that someone chose that moment to settle down beside her on the bench, not quite touching but close enough to draw her attention.

A smooth bass voice said, "Next time you decide to run, you should take a cab out of the city, *then* a train. And pay with cash."

Dahlia's head snapped up. Sitting beside her was a beautiful man with deep gold skin. He was dressed in a half untucked black button down and dark pants. His sleeves were rolled up, revealing muscular forearms — one of which was splashed with a distinctive tattoo of a bloody wave. His hair and matching beard were dark except for a streak of white that passed through both.

Amauri.

The man's eyes creased with a knowing smile as she recoiled. At any other time she would've found him disarmingly attractive, but now the twinkle in his eyes seemed more menacing than friendly.

He held out one great, callused mitt. "I'm Luis. You must be the famous Dahlia. My brother had a lot to say about you."

Her first instinct was to run, but even as her eyes scanned the crowd, looking for an escape route, she knew it was pointless. He'd catch her in a second.

That didn't mean she had to shake his hand, though. Staring straight ahead, she bit out, "I don't know who your brother is."

He dropped his hand, but nothing in his tone suggested he'd taken offense to her snub. "That'd be Milo. He was in Felix's office earlier when you came in like a demon on the warpath. We don't look too much alike, so it makes sense you wouldn't see the resemblance. I'm way more handsome."

Dahlia grunted. The truth was that she'd barely noticed there was another person in the room when she barged into Felix's office. The world had a way of narrowing to a pinpoint when he was around. Sometimes it was because he made her so mad she couldn't focus on anything else, but mostly it was because he was just... him.

"So..." Luis leaned his elbows onto his knees and looked around the terminal. "What was the plan here, sugar?"

"Does it matter? You're just gonna drag me back to Felix anyway." She wanted to be angrier about that. Some part of her *was*, but an even louder part was shamefully relieved.

I get to go home, that pitiful part of her sighed. *Thank the gods.*

"It matters. I've got to know why you ran so we can make sure that doesn't happen again."

"You going to put bars on the windows?"

Luis snorted. "I *knew* it was a window. There was no way you could've gotten out of a door unseen." He didn't sound annoyed. Instead, he appeared more amused than anything. "Ballsy. But if you hurt yourself, don't come crying to me when Felix is a terror. Speaking of — you realize how dangerous it is for you to be out at this time, right? You're freshly turned, sugar. Sun sickness could actually kill you."

She wasn't sure what compelled her to admit the truth to him. Maybe it was because they weren't looking at each other. Maybe it was because they were strangers. Or maybe it was because he reminded her of Felix.

Whatever the reason, she found herself whispering, "I didn't think about it. I didn't even remember. I… I don't know how to be a vampire. I don't *want* to be. I can't take all of this at once."

Luis was quiet for a beat. She watched his hands move between his splayed knees, one clawed thumb brushing over a scarred knuckle as he considered his answer.

"And you thought that hoofing it to New York on your own would help you figure things out?"

Dahlia stiffened. "How'd you know I was—"

"You paid digitally," he answered, not unkindly. "Next time, use cash."

She bent at the waist to press her forehead to her knees and groan. "I hate all of you. I shouldn't have to think about shit like that."

A heavy hand patted her between the shoulder blades. "Running away to someplace where you'll have no help, no allies, and no resources isn't going to make the adjustment any easier on you. I bet it's scary as fuck, so I don't blame you for acting out, but you've got to be smart. We could help you. We *want* to help you."

"And all I need to exchange for that is my future, my freedom, and all my goals," she replied, bitterness bubbling up like acid.

"Who the fuck said that? I know for a fact Felix wouldn't."

Dahlia reared back up and gestured sharply to the room at large. "Everyone! Felix wants me to be his blood bride and lock me away in his house, and Alastair wants some weird fatherly version of the same thing, with the possibility that he might sell me off to the highest bidder for some fucked up syndicate alliance *very* high.

"And even if neither of those things were true," she continued, really on a roll now, "I'm a vampire! My entire future has been rearranged because of one awful night. I won't ever be the normal me again. I— I never wanted to be more than I was. I just wanted to be happy."

Luis was quiet for a beat. Leaning his broad shoulder closer to hers, he lowered his voice and murmured, "How about you take a look around?"

Dahlia sniffled. "Why?"

"Because you might see something that interests you." He nudged her shoulder, urging her to look at the people rushing around the terminal. "We aren't the only vampires cutting it close to dawn. Look, sugar."

She didn't want to, but she did. "What am I looking at?"

"Did you know that the New Zone has the highest population of vampires in the UTA?" He nodded toward a cluster of people hustling toward a doorway. They all looked normal enough. A little pale, maybe, but normal. "Vampires. And over there, that mom pushing her stroller as quick as she can to get on the train — vampire. There's dozens of them in here. Did you even notice?"

Dahlia looked more closely. It took her a second, but eventually she spotted a flash of fang, a bottle of synth peeking out from a bag, the telltale flash of green in the backs of eyes as someone glanced quickly in their direction.

They *were* vampires. Not all of them. But a lot of them.

In a slightly gentler voice, Luis continued, "They look normal enough to me. They probably have goals. They have lives. I don't see any reason you can't be the same."

He was right, to some degree, but that didn't change several key facts.

Dahlia shook her head. "That's the difference, though. They're *normal*. They're not whatever freak shit I am."

"I'll grant you that your circumstances aren't exactly typical." He gave her a sympathetic look, but she wasn't naive enough to trust it. Luis had the kind of charm that oozed out of his pores. She was pretty sure he could get whatever he wanted from anyone without having to lift a finger. Especially not with *those* lashes.

"I'm not gonna say that what you're going through is fair or something you should suck up and deal with. It's not and you should be mad. But what I *am* saying is that there's a flipside to everything."

He lifted his left hand. "On this scale, you've got all the bullshit that comes with being a Bowan and also my cousin's bride — so sorry about that, by the way." He lifted his right, putting them about equal in the air for a moment before he began edging it a little higher. "On the other side, you've become an heir to one of the most powerful syndicate families on the continent *and* an Amauri overnight. So yeah, your goals might look different. But have you considered that they might be *better?*"

"How is that possible?"

"Listen, Felix is a vampire. It's hardwired in all of us to provide for our anchor's needs — blood bride or not. Their happiness, their safety, their health… it's all wrapped up in our DNA. So what I'm saying is that if you told Felix what you need to be happy, there's a good chance he'd skin himself alive to make it happen."

Dahlia stared at him for what felt like a long time. The tinny announcement of the final boarding call for her train eventually snapped her out of her surprise.

Shaking her head, she muttered, "You can't be this well adjusted and reasonable. You're secretly the biggest freak of all, aren't you?"

A toe-curling laugh rumbled out of him. Standing up from the bench, he said, "Look at that! You're catching on already. You're going to fit in great, sugar." Shoving his hand under her nose, he wiggled his fingers. "Now come on. We've got to get you home before sunrise — and before your man blows another gasket."

Dahlia eyed his hand with growing resignation. "I'm surprised he didn't come down here himself."

"I was closer." His fingers wiggled again, more insistently this time.

Letting out a breath, she asked, "Do you really think Felix would listen to me?"

When she put her hand in his, his grip was firm but gentle as he levered her up from the bench. He made no comment on her torn pants or what she suspected were several leaves in her hair.

All he said was, "I think he'd give anything in this world to make you happy, sugar. If it were me, I'd do the same."

LUIS

got ur girl. No injuries that I can see but she
might be limping idk

headed home now

or not. Might fuck around and keep her since
you seem to be having some trouble

I really hope Milo enjoys being an only child

TWENTY-ONE

IT WAS THE LONGEST THREE HOURS OF HIS LIFE. HE MADE DAMN SURE it was the longest three hours of his mens' lives, too.

They'd been celebrating the end of the war for too long. That was the only reasonable explanation he could come up with for how Dahlia managed to waltz out of the house completely unchallenged. His girl was a lot of things, but trained in stealth techniques and exfiltration she was *not*. For her to have so easily escaped spoke of a dire lack of discipline among his men.

His wrath rippled outward through the ranks, promising retribution against everyone who failed one of the most basic and important jobs in their organization. If *Dahlia* could walk right out, there was every chance someone could walk right *in*, and they had way too much to lose to allow a breach like that.

Tracking her down was easy enough. She had no cash on her, so all they had to do was wait her out before her payment ID pinged somewhere in the city.

He couldn't sit still, though, so he'd gone out with the search parties, hitting all the nearest transit hubs in the hope that someone would find her as soon as possible. Every man knew exactly how important it was for their health that she be returned unharmed.

Of course, it was Luis who got to her first.

Felix and Milo got to the house a few moments before his cousin did. He swaggered into the foyer like he expected trumpets and a herald to announce his victory. Dahlia walked stiffly beside him, looking considerably worse for wear.

The relief of seeing her whole and healthy, if disheveled and a little dirty, was a punch to the gut.

"Milo, you owe me fifty bucks," Luis crowed, clapping his hands together with delight. "She jumped out of the window and onto the pergola!"

Milo, who was somehow more upset than Felix at the breach in their security, scowled at his jubilant older brother. He then leveled that look at Dahlia. If he thought it would intimidate her, he was sadly mistaken. That look had made hardened soldiers shrink in their boots, but Dahlia was made of stronger stuff.

She glared back at him, arms crossing in front of her chest, and tapped her foot.

Cutting right to the heart of Felix's second in command with deadly precision, she sniffed, "Your security could use some work. The window wasn't even locked."

Luis found that hilarious, but the man in charge of said security markedly less so. Milo sucked in a deep, calming breath. In his usual tightly controlled voice, he said, "I'm glad you made it home safely."

Still not looking at Felix, she scoffed. "Barely. Your brother drives like a maniac. Do they not have speed restrictions on the grid here?"

Luis rolled his eyes. Like they were best buddies all of a sudden, he wagged a finger in Dahlia's face and explained, "Vampires built this city, sugar. No way any of us were going to let some m-grid tell our cars how fast they should go."

"Then what is the point of having one in the first place?"

"Well, everyone else—"

Felix's voice cut through the air in one clean, vicious stroke. "All of you — *out.*"

There was no argument, though Luis did give Dahlia a sympathetic pat on the shoulder before sauntering away. From over her shoulder, he raised his eyebrows at Felix and went *bzzt bzzt* while miming pressing a button with his thumb. When Felix scowled, he shrugged and walked out of the foyer.

After gesturing sharply for the men to follow him, Milo went in another direction. It would be his job to see everyone who'd fucked up punished appropriately and retrained.

That left Felix and Dahlia alone.

She eyed him warily, clearly bracing herself for his wrath. "Look, Felix, I know you're—"

He didn't let her finish. In two long strides he had her face between his hands and their lips crushed together in a hungry, devouring kiss. The tension that had seized his muscles the moment he discovered she was missing finally dissipated, leaving all of his nerve endings buzzing with a sudden influx of energy.

He kissed her again and again and again, until his lips were sore and the urgency gradually bled out of him. "A *window?*" he growled, tangling his claws into her hair. "You could've broken your fucking neck."

"Honestly, getting over the dock's gate was more danger-ous," she muttered.

"Do you have any idea what could've happened to you out there? Alastair could've snatched you out of that train station as easily as we did." His heart squeezed at just the thought. Getting Dahlia back would've been much harder than keeping her under his roof. A siege on the Bowan house really *would* start a war.

He'd do it, though. In a heartbeat.

"Yeah, well, your annoying cousin got there first."

"Most people find him charming."

Dahlia pinched his side. "When have I ever been *most people?*"

"You're right. Most people wouldn't have jumped out of a

third story window." Pulling back to really look at her face, he snapped, "What the fuck, Dahlia?"

"You tell me I'm a prisoner and I'm *going* to try to escape, Felix. What is so hard to understand about that?"

Speaking through gritted teeth, he demanded, "Tell me you didn't hurt yourself."

She made a face. "Jumping from the window or over the gate?"

"Dahlia."

"I'm fine," she sighed. "A little bruised. Some scrapes here and there. Definitely tired and hungry. But *fine.*"

His pulse jumped at the mention of her hunger. Even pissed at her, the instinct to provide for her melded with the erotic pleasure of her bite to make him crave it.

Clasping the back of her neck, he steered her around and up the stairs. He marched them through the labyrinthine hallways until they reached their wing. "You need to drink more than other vampires," he grated. "You need more care now, Dahlia. And to run so close to sunrise— Are you trying to give me a heart attack?"

"I know it can be hard to process, but not everything is about you," she shot back.

"Then what is it about, hm?"

Felix pushed the door to their suite open and nudged her inside. Instinct compelled him to get her somewhere safe and dark as the sun rose outside. Though the light was blocked by their vampire-safe windows, which cost a fortune, age-old instinct wasn't so easily swayed.

He frog-marched her into their bedroom and deposited her on the edge of the bed before he went around the room. Agitation made his movements jerky and quick as he secured the heavy drapes over the windows.

Her eyes tracked him as he worked. He could feel her gaze like soft hands raking their nails down his back.

Felix gripped the heavy velvet curtains tightly, unable to

release them. He couldn't turn to look at her. Some small, weak part of him was afraid of what he'd find there.

He wasn't an insecure man, but doubt could sink its teeth into anyone. It whispered possibilities to him, each one more gutting than the last: that she might be telling the truth when she said she didn't want to be with him; that she didn't feel the same visceral connection he did; that she really, truly couldn't see herself making a life with him.

Staring at the drapery until his eyes burned, he croaked, "Tell me. Tell me why you ran. The *real* reason."

Dahlia didn't answer right away. Just when he was beginning to think she never would, she murmured, "I'm scared, Felix."

He whirled around. Something sharp pierced him — not a blade, but a deadly sort of feeling. "Scared of *me?*"

Dahlia sat on their bed, framed by the four-poster's curtains. Her toes barely brushed the floor and her fingers were curled into the blankets on either side of her thighs. She looked small. Breakable.

"No," she answered, gaze on the floor. "I'm not scared of you, Felix. I should be. A sane person would've run screaming from you years ago. I pretended like I tried but I think we both know I didn't. Not really. I always liked you more than was healthy."

Dahlia shifted to one side. Patting the spot next to her, she said, "C'mere."

Eyeing her warily, like this sudden shift in attitude was some con to get him to let her go, Felix crossed the room to sink down on the mattress. Their thighs and shoulders pressed together.

Looking up at him with those big blue eyes, she asked, "If I tell you what I need to be happy, will you help me get it?"

Felix tilted his head toward her. A muscle ticced on his jaw. "As long as it isn't letting you go, yes. Anything."

"Yeah, I think we established that." She bumped his shoulder with her own, a sardonic smile tilting the corners of her mouth. But whatever lightness buoyed her was brief. It was there and gone in a moment as she leaned her weight into his side.

In a hushed voice, she admitted, "I'm scared, Felix. Of all of this. Of me. Of being this— this new thing with instincts and urges I don't even understand. And I'm afraid that everything I've cared about or worked for is being taken from me now that I'm whatever *this* is."

She spread her arms in front of her, gesturing to some unseen expanse. "In a couple days, I've lost my identity, my home, and all the things I'd imagined for my future. It's more than the fact that I drink blood now. It's the fact that I can't even imagine what my life will look like a few weeks from now — which is really scary for someone who built their entire adult life around hard goals."

He wanted to argue. Gods, he wanted *argue*.

She hadn't lost anything. She'd gained a new life, a new family, a whole new strata of influence and power. But Felix managed to curb his natural inclination to push. This wasn't an argument or a challenge he could win. It just *was*.

Instead, he rasped, "How do I fix it? Tell me what you need."

How do I make you happy?

Dahlia sat up a little straighter. Folding her hands in her lap, she took a deep breath before answering, "First on the list is I need to keep the things that make me Dahlia. I can't just be a pet you keep locked away in your house. I'm not cut out for the cushy pampered housewife stuff. I need to work."

Lists, Felix thought, indescribably relieved. *She's giving me a list. I can work with that.*

"You could work with me," he offered immediately.

When Dahlia gave him a shocked look, he explained, "C'mon. Did you really think I wanted you to stay in the house all day? That'd be a waste. When I let myself imagine what I really wanted, I always pictured us as partners. You've got a wicked business mind, pet. And selfishly, I'd like to have you doing a job that keeps us together."

"You really think *I* could be in the syndicate?"

Felix snorted. "You're more vicious than most of the vampires born into it. So yeah, I think you could."

There would need to be safeguards in place, and it wouldn't be like she'd be out running guns or doing hits, but the business side of things was safe enough. Dahlia was sharp and ruthless. He had no doubt that once she got the hang of things, she'd be a tougher boss than him.

Looking a little dazed, she said, "I... Okay, I'll think about it."

He nudged her shoulder. "What's next on the list?"

"I need freedom," she answered immediately. Before he could protest, she clarified, "Not to *leave,* but to have a life. I want to be able to leave the house. Go shopping. See Cecilia. Actually, that's a must. I *have* to see Cecilia."

Felix blew out a breath. "Pet..."

"That's non-negotiable," she stressed, twisting at the waist to meet his gaze. "I have to have a life, Felix. I *have* to."

Scraping his claws through his hair, he muttered, "You know what I find most upsetting about that?"

"What?"

"That you thought this whole time that I actually *wanted* to keep you prisoner. For fuck's sake, Dahlia — of course not. This isn't forever. I wouldn't do that to you. I'm not going to make you sit at home all day for the rest of our lives or force you to ask permission every time you want to go to one of your vintage swap meets."

"Ugh!" Dahlia threw up her hands. "What— Then why were you talking like—"

"Because," he dragged out, pointing to her bitten thigh, "venom takes a while to settle in. It takes way more than one bite for you to become fully saturated with it and officially off-limits to any other vampires. Until then, you're not safe. Once it settles, not even Alastair would risk taking you from me because you'd go through the worst kind of withdrawal."

"So I'm not going to be locked away in the house like some vampire Stepford wife?"

Cupping her cheeks, he leaned in close to make sure she didn't miss a single word. "Pet, you are *not* a prisoner. You're my *bride.* You're my whole fuckin' world. As soon as it's safe, I want you to run wild and tear United Washington up. Spend our money. Fuck with the other families. Break all the speed limits with your new car. Be vicious and beautiful and so damn smart. All I ask is that you be *mine.*"

He didn't think he'd ever be used to Dahlia's tears. They shined in her eyes, making them seem painfully blue. She curled her fingers around his wrists, holding tight. "You're not just saying that because you need a blood bride? *Any* blood bride?"

"No," he rasped, "I'm not. I'm saying that as the luckiest vampire on this godsforsaken planet. There is no one I've ever wanted to share my life with other than you, Dahlia. Anything or anyone else would've been nothing but sacrifice. But you— How did I get so fucking lucky? My girl is my *bride.*"

She nodded, blinking hard. "There's one more thing on my list."

Smoothing his thumbs over her cheeks, he said, "Anything."

"I want to have kids. Not, like, *this* second, but soon. I want to have kids who grow up in a home where they're loved and cared for and they don't feel like they have to run away to survive and..." She sucked in a deep breath, cutting off the torrent. "I want them to have the home I always dreamed of when I was a kid, Felix."

Instead of that sharp pain in his chest, a dull, bone-deep ache settled in. It wasn't a bad feeling, necessarily, but more like the stretch of an untried muscle.

In a thick voice, he replied, "And this is why we're perfect for each other, pet. We want all the same things. It just takes us a second to fight it out."

"So... I get to have a job, I get my freedom, and... a couple of kids soonish," she summarized, sounding more skeptical than he liked.

Felix dipped his head to press a quick, fierce kiss to her lips. "Yes to all of that. A job running the family business, your freedom as soon as my venom settles, and kids whenever you want them. Anything else?"

For the first time since he brought her home, Felix had the privilege of witnessing a real megawatt smile burst across her face.

Dahlia laid a smacking kiss on his lips before she answered, "Currently, the only other thing I need is a shower. That pergola was *not* very clean."

"All right." Setting her a little bit away from him, Felix stood up from the bed and began to shrug out of his suit jacket. A satisfied smile kicked up the corner of his mouth as Dahlia went very still, her wide eyes tracking his progress as he slowly unbuttoned his shirt.

"What are you doing?" she breathed.

He slowly peeled his shirt over his shoulders before he moved onto his belt. Whipping it through the loops, he replied, "You need a shower, and your man is nothing if not accommodating."

TWENTY-TWO

DAHLIA WASN'T ENTIRELY SURE HOW THINGS ENDED UP THE WAY they had. A large part of her had braced for Felix's fury when she returned to the house. She never could've predicted he'd show her a glimpse of the raw turmoil beneath the mask she'd become so used to.

And then the baffling man went and agreed to everything she asked for.

She was still trying to wrap her head around that as Felix fiddled with the ludicrously complex shower panel. Steam hissed from jets in the wall, and a massive rain showerhead came on, filling the luxurious bathroom with the sound of a captive waterfall.

The shower itself was made of some sort of fancy green marble that probably cost more than all the money she'd ever made. It was big enough to fit four people his size, and a wide bench stretched across one side. Nooks built into the walls contained the high end bath products of her dreams.

It was as close to a spa experience as she'd ever come, and it got infinitely better when Felix stripped down to nothing and stepped inside with her. She'd imagined what he'd look like a

199

thousand times over the years, but her imagination didn't do him justice.

Felix was all pale skin, bloody tattoos, and lean muscle. A heavy, half-hard cock hung between toned thighs, and when he leaned his head back into the water to wet his wavy hair, the livid wound of her bite stood out like an erotic beacon on his pale throat.

A heady pulse of arousal moved through her as she watched him run his claws through his hair, scraping it back from his high cheekbones with quick, practiced movements that made the muscles of his biceps bunch and release.

Trying to distract herself from the unsettling mix of sexual arousal and hunger that seemed to come with being a vampire, Dahlia turned away and tipped her head back as well. Hot water ran down her body, soothing the minor bruising and scrapes she'd picked up on her outing.

"Do all of you have those tattoos?" she asked, voice echoing off the marble walls. "I noticed Luis has a similar one on his arm. Milo and Marietta, too. Though I think hers is on her ankle."

Big hands settled on her hips, drawing her back into him. Felix dipped his head to skim his lips over her shoulder. His fangs scraped her skin, sending a shiver down her spine.

"Mm," he hummed, running his hands over her stomach and up to cradle her breasts. His thumbs traced the outline of her nipples, teasing them into tight points. "Just the cousins."

It wasn't easy to think clearly when he touched her like that. It was gentle but possessive, like he wanted to map every part of her that belonged to him.

His skin was slippery where it met hers, and the scents of steamy fresh water and the natural musk of him made her core clench with need. Dahlia's eyes fluttered as she swayed into him, feeling the hard bar of his cock against the small of her back.

"Why... why just the cousins?" Gods only knew how she managed to get the words out.

"We wanted something that bound us all together that wasn't

just our names or our hair. Something we chose." Felix slowly rolled her nipples between his fingers, punctuating each soft word with pleasure. "It wasn't enough that we were related. We wanted something that'd show we'd chosen to be family — unlike our parents and grandparents, who all hated each other."

The more he spoke about his family, the less she felt like she understood Felix. Dahlia couldn't quite wrap her head around the fact that he seemed so... caring. Not in any traditional or healthy way, maybe, but in a way that was true to him and his world.

Felix seemed to speak another language, almost. How he expressed his love wasn't the way she expected, but it was there. It was real. And it made her question a lot of the assumptions she'd made not just in the past few weeks, but throughout their entire relationship.

Hooking a hand behind his neck, Dahlia tilted her head to one side, allowing him greater access to gently nibble at her throat and shoulder. The gentle fall of hot water over their heads nearly drowned out her voice when she summoned the bravery to ask, "Felix, do you love me?"

Another man might've tensed up, the blunt question killing the mood as he scrambled to come up with some evasive answer. Not Felix.

He let out a low, sensual laugh against her skin. One hand abandoned her breast to snake down, following the trail of water to slip between her legs. He stroked her slowly, stoking the building heat, as he drawled, "Obviously."

Dahlia's breath sawed in and out of her. Her legs widened, feet sliding on the shimmering tile to accommodate his talented hand working its magic on her cunt. Still, she somehow managed to gasp, "Obviously? What does that even mean?"

"Did you think I *didn't?*"

"Not really, no—"

Felix whirled her around so fast, her feet threatened to go out from under her on the slippery tile. Luckily he held her firmly as he loomed over her. Eyes narrowed dangerously, he pressed, "What do you mean *not really?*"

"Well, I…" Dahlia tried to gather her thoughts as her mind went from arousal to defensiveness in a few heartbeats. "I always thought you were more interested in a conquest than anything else. You hated talking about feelings, Felix. We were never lovey-dovey, were we? And you got so mad that I didn't tell you I was hurt at the bar, but you also didn't *ask* if I was okay. Forgive me for wondering if you didn't actually care that much."

She expected an argument, not to be hoisted up against the wall. Jets of steam pumped from little holes in the marble on either side of her as Felix pinned her there, his hands clutching her ass like he owned it. She instinctively wrapped her legs around his waist as she grabbed his wet shoulders, steadying herself.

Water sloped down his forehead to run in rivulets down his sharp nose, high cheekbones, and beautifully carved lips. It clung in sparkling droplets to his long, spiked eyelashes, which gave his glare an unfairly pretty quality.

"I don't see the point in talking about my feelings when they're obvious," he coolly informed her. "I didn't ask if you were okay because I assumed my girl, who knows how much her safety means to me, would *tell me* if she were hurt. And I didn't do lovey-dovey shit because I thought you liked our games, pet."

Words escaped her when he brushed his lips against hers. In a low, husky voice, he asked, "Isn't that true? You liked being chased. You liked teasing me. You liked when I showed you how far I'd go to get your attention."

Her nails dug into the meat of his broad shoulders. Heat rolled through her in a slow, inexorable wave, stealing what little fight she still possessed. Dahlia's thighs tightened around his lean hips.

There was no pride left in her when she'd been hollowed out, left aching for the one thing and the one man who could fill her up.

"Yes," she whispered, "but I want both."

"Both of what?"

"The games and the lovey-dovey stuff."

His smile brushed against her lips. "I can do that, pet. All you ever have to do is ask."

Dahlia had no idea what to expect. He wasn't exactly a soft man, and she doubted he had much experience going slow or being tender with a lover. But as she was coming to learn, Felix Amauri was full of surprises.

He took his time with her there against the shower's cool stone wall. Pinning her weight with his hips and one braced knee, he freed his hands to tease her nipples, the sensitive skin of her inner thighs, and higher. He touched her with featherlight strokes of his fingers, never staying too long in one place or providing enough pressure to get her off.

His kisses were deep and hungry. Their tongues met in a languid glide, the prick of fang adding a sharp note of pleasure-pain irregularly enough that she never quite knew when it'd come.

By the time he finally lined himself up and sank into her, one agonizing inch at a time, Dahlia was a needy, whining mess. Her fingers had moved to his hair, twining themselves in the wet strands, and her heels dug into his back to spur him on.

"That's my beautiful bride," he breathed, thrusting shallowly — a cruel tease that made her core flutter around him in a desperate attempt to pull him deeper. "You were born for this. You were always meant to be mine. To take me just like this."

Dahlia nodded mindlessly, her lips tracing the hard tendons of his neck to find his thrumming pulse. The sharp ache in the roof of her mouth was familiar now, but something stopped her from sinking her fangs into him just yet. It wasn't the fear that had hit her like a truck after her first bite, but a clear instinct that it wasn't quite the right time. If she held out just a little longer, it'd be sweeter.

Their bodies came together again and again, filling the shower with the sounds and scents of sex. Felix unlocked her legs from around his waist and in one smooth step moved them over to the bench. A deep sound of discontent escaped her as he pulled out

He chuckled as he arranged her on her knees, placing her on top of the bench with her hands flat against the wall. Digging his fingers into the crease where her hips met the tops of her thighs, he yanked her ass up and back. His slick cock bobbed between her legs, taunting her.

In that sexy, amused voice, he said, "There are two things that drive vampires. Can you guess what they are?"

Dahlia's nails scraped the marble. Her hips rolled back, desperate to find him again, but he held himself just out of reach. "Blood and fucking," she growled, the need to be filled again narrowing her focus until she couldn't concentrate on anything other than what he denied her.

"Close, but no." Releasing one hip, he began to rub his cock-head up and down her slit, making sure to use extra pressure when he reached the swollen nerves at the apex before skimming back up to push inside just a little. Not nearly enough.

"*Felix,*" she gasped, slapping the shower wall. Her back arched, sending water down between her shoulder blades and the curve of her spine.

His breath tickled the curve of her ear when he whispered, "Feeding and breeding, pet. That's what we're after. A full belly, a well-bred anchor—" He thrust in to the hilt, bottoming out with enough force to make the breath explode out of her lungs. "—there's nothing better in the fuckin' world."

Gripping the underside of her jaw, he pried her head back as he set a punishing pace. The change in angle made every stroke a punishment and a reward all in one. His voice wormed its way inside of her, keeping time with the battering of her poor cervix, stirring instincts she didn't even know she had.

Felix nipped the corner of her jaw, his breath ragged. "Wanted to fuck you this way from the moment I saw you," he panted. "Like you're *mine.* Like you're gonna take my venom and my come so fucking good. Is that what you wanted too, pet? To be fucked by your man until you're his forever?"

Her senses spun. Dahlia could hardly tell where she ended and he began as an orgasm hovered just beyond her reach. The pain in her mouth doubled, making her whine and clench hard on his shuttling cock.

He slammed deep and held himself there. Breathing hard against her cheek, he growled, "Use your words, pet."

A full-body shudder shook her. "Yes," she gasped, hips moving in desperate, clumsy rolls in a vain attempt to regain that delicious friction. "Yes, *yes.* Felix, I want it!"

He pressed an incongruously gentle kiss to her cheek before his hips reared back, only to ram forward. Dahlia's locked arms were the only things keeping her from sliding clear off the bench as he thrust hard and fast. Her heartbeat became a blur — a hummingbird's rhythm as her body turned into something built solely for this purpose.

For *him.*

Felix dropped his head to the juncture between her neck and shoulder. One sturdy forearm pressed against her lips in a silent command as his hips began to move erratically, pumping with more urgency than finesse. Electricity raced up her spine, tightening all of her muscles in a wave that broke when he plunged his fangs in her neck.

Now.

She didn't remember biting him. It was pure instinct as his release splashed inside her, his cock buried deep as it could go. The pain of his bite was drowned out by pleasure and the syrupy warmth of his venom. His blood painted her throat and dripped from the corners of her mouth as she took everything he had to give her.

Felix grunted when her cunt clenched hard around him. The fingers of his free hand moved to where they were joined, rubbing in quick circles that made her thighs twitch.

They groaned together as she pulled just a little more from him — blood and seed both.

A long time later, they sat on the bench together, loose-limbed and sated. Dahlia curled up in his lap as he played with the ends of her hair, listening to the steady sound of his heart inside his tattooed chest.

"You love me," he said, breaking the drowsy silence. It wasn't a question, and she supposed it didn't need to be.

Dahlia sighed. "Obviously."

The *"against my better judgment"* went unsaid, but going by the smug chuckle that rumbled his chest, he heard it anyway.

TWENTY-THREE

"So... what's it like?"

Dahlia eyed the racks of clothing that lined the spacious closet. Standing in only her newly purchased lingerie and a pair of pointed-toe heels, she held the phone to her ear as she tried to decide on what outfit to wear to meet the Amauri family. Formally, anyway.

Rifling through the hanging garments that had mysteriously showed up from her apartment along with all the new things that Marietta continued to gleefully deliver, she surveyed her choices.

"What's what like?"

"Being, like, married or whatever," Cecilia clarified. The volume of her voice changed as she moved around what sounded like her bathroom, no doubt getting ready for work.

Married. She guessed that's what they were. Felix did love calling her his bride.

Dahlia pulled a vintage blazer dress off the rack. Determining that it was too *boss bitch* for a family meeting, even a syndicate one, she put it back. "It's only been a few days. I can't say my opinion is fully formed yet."

"Okay, but it's formed enough for you to agree to stay with

him — after giving your best friend in the whole world a heart attack and not calling me back for *three days,* by the way."

"You did say you were the one who'd die first," Dahlia dryly replied. "Hey, what outfit should I wear to this meeting? It's not business, but it feels weirdly like an interview with a board or something. I don't want to look like I'm trying too hard, but…"

"You kind of have to try too hard," Cecilia finished. The familiar sound of a makeup brush tapping the side of the sink came through the line. "Go for the slouchy green top and the fitted black slacks. It's dressy but not formal. It says, *I'm a sexy new vampire with better taste than you.*"

Dahlia hurried to find the parts of the outfit. Stepping out of her heels, she tugged the pants on and then slipped the top over her head. Shoving her feet back into her heels, she walked over to the towering mirror at the far end of what no normal person would actually consider a closet.

Cecilia was right, of course. It was the perfect outfit.

What neither of them considered, however, was the way the slouchy, off-the-shoulder top revealed the patchwork of lovebites and *actual* bites that decorated her throat and shoulders. Dahlia's cheeks turned bright pink as she traced them with her gaze.

And those were just the ones above her neckline.

She wasn't sure why they took her by surprise every time she saw them. Working in a vampire bar for as long as she had, she'd seen so many bites — old, new, and in-progress — that she'd stopped noticing them. But there was something very different about seeing them on her own skin.

Each one was a reminder of Felix. They were bright neon signs declaring his ownership, telling the world what they'd done and how often they'd done it.

Dahlia hadn't allowed a man to so much as leave a hickey on her neck since she was a teenager. She found them unnecessary and more than a little embarrassing. Felix's bite was different, though.

Probably because he sported nearly twice as many as she did.

"How's it look?"

Cecilia's tinny voice shook her from her lusty observations. Coughing into her fist to clear her throat, Dahlia retrieved her phone from where she'd left it on the massive circular cushion in the center of the closet.

"Needs some jewelry," she said, trying to sound normal.

"Oh, has he bought you anything outrageous yet? He seems like the type."

Dahlia snorted. "You have no idea."

The click of her heels softened by the plush carpet, she made her way over to the wall of cabinets that contained everything from her silk scarf collection to all the jewelry she'd ever sent back to him over the years. It took barely a touch for the narrow drawer to glide soundlessly out. Carefully displayed on dark blue velvet were an array of diamonds, pearls, emeralds, rubies, and jet.

Some pieces she recognized, others appeared to materialize out of thin air whenever she wasn't looking.

Selecting a simple strand of alternating jet beads and small, perfect diamonds, she clasped it around her marked neck before she went hunting through the other drawers. One was entirely dedicated to watches. From there she selected a slim silver time-piece, then moved on to rings.

She'd never gotten to wear them at work, since they could tear gloves, so she took great pleasure in sliding a handful of light-as-air silver bands on several fingers. There was no telling what was Felix and what was Marietta getting a kick out of spending his money on her behalf, but either way, Dahlia wasn't too proud to say no to any of it.

Assessing herself in the mirror one more time, she fluffed her hair with one hand as she asked, "Do you have work tonight?"

"Yup." Cecilia took extra care to pop the *p*. "Not all of us get to skip off to the land of hot vampire men desperate to shower a woman in jewelry."

"How's the vibe been? You know, what with..." Dahlia

trailed off, not wanting to say the words *"Devon's mysterious disappearance into a barrel of lye"* if she didn't have to. She'd given enough hints to Cecilia about what had happened for her to get the drift.

"Better, for the most part. But I heard from Beau that Duke is coming back into town tonight to look for his brother. Can't imagine that's going to be pretty." Cecilia paused. The sound of something — setting spray, probably — being spritzed came through the line before she spoke again. "Other than that, it's the same old stuff. A lot less fun with you gone, though."

Dahlia turned away from the mirror, her senses sharpening with concern. "You're gonna steer clear of Duke, right?"

"Well, I'd *planned* on climbing him like a cat tree, but if you're worried..." Cecilia blew a raspberry into the phone. "Of course I'm not going anywhere near him! I mean, it's not like I had anything to do with Devon taking an unplanned hiatus from life as a scumbag, but I'm not a buffoon. Head down, tray up — just like always."

Letting out a relieved breath, Dahlia replied, "Just be careful, okay? If he starts asking you questions or bothers you or— *whatever.* Tell me. Felix and I will handle it."

"You and Felix, huh?" Her friend sounded a little too smug. "Look who's gotten *real* comfortable!"

Dahlia rolled her eyes. "If I was there, I'd throw something at you. Please react appropriately."

"Oh *no,* you just chucked a blush palette at my head! How dare you? It's *shattered* on the *floor* and I'm *bleeding*—"

"I'm hanging up!"

Cecilia blew another raspberry. Somehow, Dahlia was almost certain she could hear a smile in it. "Love you! Knock 'em dead, tiger."

Rolling her shoulders to loosen her tense muscles, she replied, "They won't know what hit 'em."

Marietta was the one to fetch her from her room. Dahlia had been assured several times that she could wander the house at will now that they'd come to an understanding, but she still found the place too confusing to confidently navigate on her own.

And it wasn't like she'd had much incentive to leave. For the past three nights, they'd been holed up in their bedroom, making up for lost time. And of course, she'd been practicing the surprisingly difficult art of the bite.

With their little honeymoon period drawing to a close, Felix had been busy for most of the night, so it was up to Marietta to be her guide.

Dressed in a white skirt and bustier top, Marietta could've been mistaken for a vampiric pin-up model. She looked like the kind of woman who could drop a glove on railroad tracks and still have a man rush to retrieve it for her.

Linking their arms together with a large, red-lipped smile, she led Dahlia down the hallway.

"Nervous to meet the in-laws?"

Dahlia shook her head. "Not really. It feels more like I'm going to a job interview."

"That's not a bad way to look at it," Marietta replied. "I mean, you've met almost everyone whose opinion really matters to him, so it's more of a formality at this point. Meet the elders, kiss some baby cheeks, let them see what a badass you are. Easy-peasy."

Looking sidelong at her guide, she probed, "Felix is really close to the cousins, huh?"

"Very close. I mean, he's never been the warmest guy around, but we're all pretty fucked up, so who are we to judge?"

Dahlia tipped her head in a nod. It was hard to argue with that. "I'm curious about why you threw your lot in with him over Yvanna. I know that his grandmother named him the heir, but didn't Yvanna have more experience and the approval of the older generation?"

"There was never a question that we'd stand behind Felix," Marietta answered, a little bit of her normal levity hardening into something fierce. "Yvanna and Julius — they saw people as tools. The family was just a means to an end for them, and everyone else could be stepped on. Felix and Grandma Dora decided there was a better way. We would've been out of our minds to go against him."

Dahlia mulled her words over as they made their way downstairs. Getting to know this side of Felix had been enlightening, to say the least. It wasn't that she hadn't known him before, but since being strong-armed into his family life, her understanding of him had expanded in ways she didn't expect.

He was never going to be touchy-feely. Felix had been forged by the syndicate, and it made him sharp in ways that the average person would probably never be able to handle.

But he wasn't heartless.

She got a peek at that heart when she stepped into what she could only describe as a lounge. In another mansion, it probably would've been the main dining room. Seeing as vampires didn't sit down to eat together in the same way, the space was dedicated to sprawling couches, coffee tables, loveseats, and break-off areas where people could play chess or read.

Dozens of people were scattered around — young families with children playing on the floor, elders with their white heads bent together, and what could only be described as a battalion of young men standing in loose clumps around the perimeter of the room. Not all of them had a visible white stripe in their hair, but many did.

Before she drew too much attention, Dahlia leaned toward Marietta to whisper, "Are all of those guys Amauris?"

"Some are sworn into the family, so not blood related, but most of them are second or third cousins," she answered.

Dahlia did a rough headcount. "Not a lot of women in the family, huh?"

"Oh, don't bring it up around Alvin if you don't want to sit through a three hour lecture." Marietta nodded toward where a familiar blond doctor stood by a towering window, apparently deep in discussion with someone. The fact that he was present for an all-family meeting was telling. "Vampires tend to have more boys than girls. I don't know if anyone really understands why yet, but Alvin sure likes to theorize."

The hair rose on the back of her neck a moment before the weight of a familiar hand settled on the small of her back.

The smell of smoke drifted over her when Felix bent his neck to press a lingering kiss to her nape. "Hello, pet," he whispered. "Ready to face the family?"

Suppressing a shiver, she half-turned to look at him. "As ready as I'll ever be. Why do you smell like a bonfire?"

Felix stepped smoothly beside her, one arm curled possessively around her waist. "Your father lit one of my clubs on fire."

"What?" Alarmed, she grabbed a fistful of his shirt and demanded, "Was anyone hurt?"

Of course she'd heard a little bit of what had been going on outside the walls of the Amauri home as Felix fielded phone calls and the occasional stop-in from Milo or Nash, but she had no idea the animosity between them had escalated that far.

"Nah. It was around dusk, way before anyone was due for work. He was sending a message, not declaring war. Yet." His thumb drew soothing circles on her waist. "Don't worry. He'll either do something that gives us an excuse to take him out or he'll give up soon. Either way, we'll be fine."

Marietta cleared her throat. Giving Dahlia's exposed neck and shoulders a significant look, she dryly suggested, "Well, seeing as you two have been putting in the work, it might speed up the process a bit if Dahlia was seen in public."

Ignoring Felix's rumbling growl, Dahlia gave her a considering look. "Felix said I need to wait for the venom to settle before I go out."

"Yeah, and you two have been working overtime to make that happen."

"It's only been a week," Felix broke in, his tone hard. "I'm not going to rush it and risk them thinking there's still an opportunity to take her back. End of discussion."

It wasn't often that Felix appeared to pull the boss card with his cousins, but when it happened, they backed down immediately. Marietta put up her hands. "Just a thought."

But *she* wasn't held by the same rules. For all of Felix's many, many flaws, he'd never discouraged her from arguing with him. If anything, she felt like it was her obligation now that she had a stake in the family.

Dahlia frowned at him. Thinking of all the people in the lounge and what could happen to them if Alastair decided to crank up the heat — literally and figuratively — she said, "It's worth considering, Felix. I don't want anyone getting hurt because of me. What if the club had been set on fire during work hours? What if one of the cousins got shot? Shouldn't we do everything we can to minimize the chances of Mr. Bowan escalating things?"

Felix propelled her forward, into the lounge. Muttering under his breath, he said, "Later."

TWENTY-FOUR

She wanted to argue with him more, but it wasn't the time. Marietta walked in ahead of them and perched on the armrest of a couch, one shapely leg draped over the other. A little crystal charm dangling from the clasp of her heel sparkled in the light as her foot bobbed with an expectant rhythm.

The hum of conversation died away as all eyes turned to them. Dahlia pulled her shoulders back, her expression smoothing. It was a reflex from spending so many years in The Lush.

In a lot of ways, walking into the lounge was similar to a shift at the bar. Facing the Amauri family was a lot like walking into work every day, not knowing if the vampires she'd face would try to take a bite out of her or not.

Even the children stopped playing to look up at her, their big eyes watchful and serious as they weighed her worth.

Her stomach somersaulted as she caught the little streaks of white in their hair and the tiny fangs that peeked out from behind their lips. They were a vivid image of the future she'd signed up for, and made her even more determined to have it out with Felix in the privacy of their bedroom.

If she was going to be his partner, that meant that she was

responsible for the safety of everyone in this room — and that included the kids sitting cross-legged on the rug.

Giving her waist a squeeze, Felix waved a hand at the room at large. "All right," he began, as casually as one might address their family at a Sunday barbecue. "Everyone, meet my bride, Dahlia Bowan. As you probably know, she was formerly Dahlia McKnight but has been officially claimed by Alastair Bowan as his heir."

A round of chuckles and huffs went through the room. Felix waited for the commotion to die down a bit before continuing, "Dahlia is my blood bride and going forward, my partner. You'll answer to her the same way you answer to me. Understood?"

An elder eyed her up and down from where he sat in a wing-back chair. His blue eyes were a little rheumy, but they had a keen look when he noted, "Alastair never seemed the type to risk making an heir. What makes you so special?"

Felix had explained to her that it was the elders who were the most against his authority, and it was their ideals that made taking a blood bride necessary. Neither facts made her particularly inclined to like them, let alone cater to them. Still, she didn't intend to make enemies right off the bat.

Dahlia pursed her lips. Aware that everyone in the room was judging her not just for what she said but what she didn't say, she answered, "Nothing besides being in the right place at the right time. Alastair turned me accidentally when someone decided the best way to accomplish a hit was to throw a *grenade* at a rooftop."

Giving the men who were clearly soldiers a long, narrow-eyed look, she coolly added, "I suppose I have one of you to thank for all this."

There were several winces and even more muffled laughs around the room. The old man wasn't laughing, though.

Making a clicking sound with his tongue, he demanded, "So you have no loyalty to the Bowans?"

"I don't know them," she answered honestly. "But I've

known Felix for three years. If I have loyalty to anyone, it's to him."

"Why?"

"Because he's mine. I'm his bride. He's my husband," she answered. There was zero hesitation and no thought. Just a truth that had been building in the shadows for years and recently burst into the light.

Felix squeezed her waist. A peek at his expression showed him looking as smug as she'd ever seen him, which was saying something. His lips twisted to one side as he fought a big, shit-eating grin, and the self-satisfaction in his eyes was unmistakable.

From across the room, Luis clapped his hands together, breaking the tension. "That settles that, then," he laughed. "I guess I really don't have a chance anymore."

"To be clear, you *never* had a chance," Felix replied, rolling his eyes. "Now, does anyone have any other questions?"

Hands went up all around the room. Soon enough she was peppered with inquiries about herself: where she'd been born, what her education was, how close she was to her human family, and more. She didn't have much to offer on that front. Her hometown was a speck. Her education was slow and not particularly glamorous. Her family was full of deadbeats and criminals. She didn't match up with any of the pedigreed blood brides they'd had in mind for Felix, but she held her head high anyway.

What mattered was that she knew she belonged there. If they didn't like that, they could suck it down with their synth.

By far her favorite questions were the ones that came from the children, which Felix seemed to take as seriously as those that came from the elders.

Dahlia looked down to find a little vampire tugging at her pant leg, her eyes huge and curious in her face. A lock of tight white curls dangled against her cheek, while the rest were pulled back into pigtails. She couldn't have been older than five, and aside from what looked like a fresh baby swaddled in her dad's arms in the corner, appeared to be one of the youngest children in the room.

Crouching down to be at eye level with her, Dahlia murmured, "Yes?"

"How long have you been a vampire?"

The timeline was squishy, but since she didn't feel the need to explain all the gory medical details to a child, Dahlia chose the simplest route. "About three weeks, give or take."

"Oh." The little girl drew out the sound with great solemnity. "That makes me older than you. I've been a vampire for *five* years."

Dahlia nodded, biting the inside of her cheek to fight a smile. "You must know a lot, then. What's your name?"

"Sonia," she answered. "And I *do* know a lot."

"Well, Sonia, maybe you could give me some advice sometime."

The little girl nodded. "I can help you. You're gonna need it."

Felix placed a hand on top of Sonia's head. "Sonia gives great advice. A couple weeks ago she told me it'd improve morale to install a slide and swing set in the yard."

Dahlia stood up. She didn't bother hiding her smile this time. "And did it work?"

"For the youngest Amauris," he dryly replied. Meeting Sonia's satisfied smile with an arched brow, he said, "I suspect that we didn't go far enough. Maybe a treehouse will get us there. What do you think?"

Sonia widened her eyes and sucked in a huge, dramatic breath. "A *treehouse?*"

"A treehouse. You should go ask Luis to build it for you. Tell him I said it's not optional."

They watched Sonia scamper off, her head bobbing with agreement. The smart girl stopped to gather her cousins, who exploded in breathless excitement before they all rushed to corner Luis. He watched them come at him like a tidal wave with obvious alarm.

"That was cruel," she muttered, leaning into Felix. He swayed her back into his chest as they watched the spectacle unfold.

"He likes to press my buttons. This is what he gets." Felix shrugged. "It's fine. He'll just pay to have someone build it and then take all the credit when the kids worship him like a god for a couple weeks."

Tucking her under his arm, he began to guide her around the room, introducing her to everyone individually. It was hopeless to actually attempt to memorize everyone's names and where they fit into the family tree, so she didn't try. Dahlia devoted her energy to picking up other important details, like how they reacted to her, whether they had children or not, and what generation they seemed to fall under.

That last one quickly became the most important to her. There was a clear demarcation between the generations that went beyond who wore the bloody tattoo or not. The way the elders held themselves, how they spoke to them — they were just *different*.

Colder. Hardened. Hawkish. When they looked at her, they were assessing where the tenderest bits to pick off were.

Not all of them were outright unfriendly, but none of them were warm. Dahlia wasn't offended, but it did make her wonder how much of their opinion really could be swayed by the fact that she was a blood bride.

Looking into their flinty eyes, an upswell of protectiveness rose from deep within her. *These* were the people who would've happily sided with Yvanna against Felix. They would've taken his death completely in stride. They might've even helped make it possible.

They were sharks in the otherwise clear, welcoming waters of the family, and Dahlia wouldn't let them out of her sight for a second.

It was a relief when they finally made it over to the corner where Nash, Alvin, and Milo were gathered. She was a little surprised to see another non-vampire or Amauri spouse there as well.

Genevieve, the tattooed witch who'd torn open space and time like it was as easy as sneezing, sat in a chair with her feet propped up on Nash's thick thigh. He sat caddy-corner to her, his huge, muscular arms spread over the back of his chair. A bottle of synth was clutched loosely in one hand, but he didn't appear to be drinking from it as he listened intently to something the witch was telling him.

His posture looked a little stiff, too. She couldn't quite put her finger on what was strange about it until she saw the fingers of his left hand twitch and curl into a fist, like he was actively trying to resist grabbing something — the slim ankles in his lap, maybe.

Before they got close enough to be overheard, Dahlia whispered in Felix's ear, "Are they together?"

"No." He paused, eyebrows arching in a look she recognized as his shit-stirring face. "But there's a bet going around over when Nash will work up the courage to take a bite. I've got a hundred bucks on six weeks. Luis doesn't think he'll ever make a move, and Marietta is betting on less than a month."

Going by the moon-eyed way Nash was looking at her, Dahlia didn't think Felix was far off. Six weeks seemed like a solid estimate, considering Felix himself had waited three years to act on *her*. "I'm surprised to see her and Alvin here, though. I thought this was a family only thing."

Felix shrugged. "Things used to be stricter, but I don't think that's fair. Alvin and Genevieve have proven their family loyalty more than half the old fucks in this room. They deserve to be here."

Dahlia squeezed his arm. "Good call. Blood doesn't mean anything if you don't act on it."

"I'm glad you approve."

Normally she would've brushed off the praise as mocking, but Dahlia was starting to understand Felix's nuances better. A glance at his pleased expression proved he wasn't making fun of her. He really meant it.

A warm fluttering took up residence in her belly as they closed in on the corner. Knowing Felix didn't just want to own her but *valued* her was a heady feeling unlike any other.

She was powerful not because he gave her power, but because he'd always respected what she already had.

Instead of greeting them like a normal person, Milo swept his mismatched gaze around the room and grunted, "Survive the vultures?"

Felix waved a hand. "Better question is whether they survived her. They're really not going to know how to handle Dahlia when they piss her off."

"I'm sure they'll figure it out soon enough," she said, casting a cool look over her shoulder, where several elders were bunched together.

Alvin cleared his throat. "How are you feeling? Have you been taking the supplements I sent over?" He paused to cast Felix a look. "Both of you?"

"Yes," Felix answered immediately. "You think I'd let her get sick?"

All the assembled vampires looked away quickly, the corners of their mouths twitching as Alvin took the full heat of Felix's glare.

To his credit, the doctor who looked like he'd be more comfortable playing polo on the weekends than standing in a room full of vampires didn't even flinch. He met Felix's gaze with an unperturbed look, his pretty face smooth.

Alvin had sent over a small drugstore's worth of supplements and a binder explaining what each of them did. Apparently while two vampires feeding exclusively on each other *was* possible, it could greatly diminish their fat and calcium reserves over time, so modern medicine recommended they both take regular vitamins and minerals.

The hassle of it annoyed her, but Felix was relentless about it.

He stood over her like a drill sergeant until she swallowed the last of the gel packs, and she was pretty sure he'd read the binder front to back three times.

Knowing how touchy he was about her health, Dahlia decided it'd be best to defuse the situation before Alvin implied a worse insult than he already had.

"Felix makes me take them at dusk every night," she said, patting his arm. "Even though they taste disgusting."

"That's because they're fruit flavored. The artificial flavoring is non-toxic to you, but doesn't taste great. I keep sending them emails asking for them to make vampire-friendly versions, but I haven't had any luck," Alvin replied.

Dahlia sighed. "I used to love fruit. And burgers. And tacos. And hotpot. And sponge cake. I think I can learn to like a lot about being a vampire, but I'll never get over that."

Genevieve spoke up. "If it makes you feel better, you can watch me eat all that stuff. I *love* food. The last date I went on, we did a buffet crawl. I thought I might actually die from the amount of crab legs I ate. The sexiest date idea I've ever had? No, but worth it."

Every vampire's eyes flicked to Nash's face, which had gone remarkably still. If he noticed that everyone's attention was on his reaction, it wasn't because he looked at any of them. His focus was solely on the witch.

Speaking in a stiff, formal sort of way, he asked, "When was this?"

"A couple weeks ago," she answered, shrugging. One side of her oversized sweater slid down, revealing a tattooed shoulder.

"And you didn't tell me?"

Genevieve made a face. "Since when do I have to tell you when I go on dates? It's not work related."

Dahlia watched in fascination as a flush settled into Nash's broad cheekbones. "Your safety is my job," he protested. "I need to know where you are at all times. We talked about this, Ginny."

"Your job is to keep me safe when I'm *working,* which I definitely wasn't doing with Blake. We were way too busy eating crab legs and tiramisu by the pound."

"Blake?"

Giving Felix an exasperated look, Genevieve implored, "Can you please tell him that I am allowed to do whatever I want in my off time? Including Blake?"

Extremely curious to see how Felix would handle the situation, Dahlia's gaze bounced between the trio. She honestly couldn't say whether Felix would do his cousin a solid or not. After seeing so many nascent vampire courtships go wrong in her line of work, Dahlia wasn't sure what she'd do in this situation other than wash her hands of it as quickly as possible.

Felix did neither of those things.

Tucking his free hand into his pocket, he rocked back on his heels and made a show of considering his words. "Well… you *are* supposed to be on call 24/7, so the argument could be made that Nash, as your bodyguard, should know where you are at all times."

Just when the powerful line of Nash's shoulders began to relax, Felix continued, "However, your contract does state that you are under no obligation to report your personal life to the family as long as it doesn't interfere with our business interests. So you're free to date who and when you please without telling anyone if it doesn't cause any issues for the family."

"Ha!" Genevieve wagged a finger in Nash's direction. "See? I win."

Nash looked like he'd swallowed a whole lemon, but he didn't argue. Dahlia half-expected him to take the card Felix had handed him — the one that said it *was* an issue for the family, mainly him. But he didn't.

Nodding to the group, Felix laid a hand on Dahlia's back and began to guide her away. When they were more or less out of ear-shot, she leaned in close and whispered, "I want in on the bet."

"Yeah?"

"Yeah. And we're going to discuss ending this bullshit with my father."

Felix breathed deeply. "Dahlia—"

She smiled down at the children who scrambled by her, all squeals and laughter and safety. Without dropping her smile, she hissed, "Partners, Felix. Remember?"

His fingers slid down to the curve of her waist. "I remember, pet. I could never forget."

TWENTY-FIVE

THE LAST THREADS OF HER PATIENCE SNAPPED WHEN SHE WALKED into the little clinic on the first floor of the mansion. She hadn't even known it was there until Milo told her where Alvin would be setting up. The fact that they had a use for a private medical space in their home didn't surprise her, but walking in to find her husband sitting on one of the exam tables made its existence almost intolerable.

Dahlia practically vibrated as she stalked across the room, her heels tapping on the sterile white tile. A cluster of men stood off to one side, Milo among them, and appeared to be debriefing. A few more sat on chairs or perched on beds, their faces streaked with dust and blood.

Felix was by far the worse off.

Alvin bent over his naked torso, painstakingly gluing together the torn skin on his shoulder and side. Blood streaked across his chest and splattered his stiff jaw as he held his right arm up at an angle to allow the doctor to work.

A buzzing noise took up residence in her ears. It blocked out the sounds of conversation and the whir of an air purifier. Even her own breathing was muffled.

In an instant, she understood a little bit of how he must've felt when he found out she'd been impaled. Seeing him injured, knowing that he could've *died*, was so wrong it felt incompatible with reality.

She had no way of knowing what was new vampire instinct and what was the natural result of loving him. Whatever it was, Dahlia had never been so angry and so happy to see someone in her life.

The men leaned back as she passed them, their gazes hastily averting as if they feared getting caught in the cross-fire of her temper.

Felix watched her storm in with a look of trepidation. "I'm fine," he assured her, glancing quickly at Alvin. "Tell her I'm fine."

Alvin dutifully repeated, "He's fine."

Dahlia jammed a finger into Felix's undamaged shoulder. "Are you fucking kidding me with this?"

"What? I didn't do anything!"

"Felix, you could've died!"

Wincing as Alvin applied a rubbery bandage to his side, he replied, "Alastair wasn't trying to kill us. He was getting us back for torching his yacht last week."

Dahlia propped her hands on her hips. The tit-for-tat fighting between the Bowans and the Amauris had been going on for nearly two weeks. She wasn't even sure how much of it was about getting her back anymore and how much was pure, masculine bullshit.

In a more normal world, she would've brushed it off and put her attention somewhere more important. But this wasn't normal. Sooner rather than later, someone was going to get killed — and then it wouldn't just be burned yachts and exploded warehouses. It'd be war.

It'd taken a minute, but Dahlia had come to like seeing Felix whole and undamaged. The rest of his family could stay that way, too.

In the two weeks since she'd begun to really settle into syndicate life, she'd accompanied Felix during meetings, negotiations, and deals all within the walls of the mansion. She'd gotten a crash course in navigating Amauri business interests alongside a taste of the internal workings of the family.

She'd always tried her best to not learn too much during her time at The Lush, but she had. And all that knowledge gave her a surprisingly solid foundation as she found her footing beside him.

The elders couldn't intimidate her. They had nothing on a drunk vampire mercenary *"just looking for a sip"* at the end of her shift.

The soldiers looked at how she handled Felix and quickly fell in line. They were used to Dora, Marietta explained, and overall seemed relieved to have a strong woman at the helm again.

And when it came to Felix himself... Well, he wasn't bluffing when he said he wanted a partner. He included her in everything, even if she felt like it was above her pay grade or outright unnecessary. A new desk had been purchased so they could sit beside each other to work. He looped her into text threads and suspiciously squeaky clean accounts. Nearly every decision he made, he ran it by her first. Not because he *needed* the help, but because he wanted it.

Just about the only thing they couldn't seem to collaborate on was the damn foolish pissing contest he was determined to win against Alastair.

"This has to stop," she announced, trying to sound calm when all she wanted to do was throttle *and* kiss him. "Soon enough one of ours or one of his is going to actually get hurt, and then this will stop being a game. I won't have anyone dying for me, Felix. This is my family, too."

Like always, it appeared he was about to put her off, but Dahlia wasn't having it this time. "You aren't keeping me locked in the house any longer. I am going to go outside. I am going to show Mr. Bowan that he should stop fighting this. And *you* are not going to stop me."

She knew it'd be a good night. Felix begged to differ.

"This is a terrible fucking idea."

"No, it's not," she breezily replied, pressing her foot down on the gas pedal of her shiny new sports car. It zipped down the strange, narrow streets of United Washington at something slightly less than a breakneck speed.

They were headed for Old Blood, the premier vampire establishment in United Washington. Mere steps from Congress, where the representatives of all the territories and their factions met to vote on laws, it was apparently one of the few buildings to survive the century of war that saw the city burned to the ground. Milo, who turned out to be something of a history buff, had explained to her that it was where the first members of the syndicate had agreed to rebuild the city themselves.

Dahlia and Felix weren't going to make history. They were going to make a statement.

When they pulled up to Old Blood, Felix didn't let the valet open her door for her. Standing in his black on black suit, he swept the door of her silver sports car open and held out his hand. Dahlia's red nails gleamed against the pale skin of his palm as she placed one heel on the street.

Her heels and tights were a matching crimson, creating one streamlined swath of bloody red beneath her short blazer dress. The neckline plunged nearly to her bellybutton, exposing bare skin — and a tapestry of healing bites and hickies.

She figured Felix would've been a lot more smug about the sight of them if she hadn't forced him into this position. But some things had to be done.

Tossing her keys to the valet, he pressed close to her. A warm hand settled on the small of her back. "Half an hour," he whispered, escorting her around the front of the car and onto the curb.

Two Amauri soldiers slipped into place behind them as they approached the antique glass doors of the social club. Bringing some security had been the only way to get Felix to agree to the outing. While Old Blood was supposed to be neutral ground, the likelihood of violence was low but not impossible.

They had to take their own car, though, because her new baby could only fit the two of them.

Felix's mouth pressed into a hard line as he opened the door for her. Dahlia swept inside, her eyes quickly adjusting to the dim lighting of the social club. In some ways, it was just like The Lush: a long bar dominated one side of the room, semi-private booths dotted the other half, and one corner was dedicated to music.

Except it couldn't have been more different.

The bar wasn't acrylic and lit by LEDs to show off the rows and rows of expensive synth below and behind it. There was no chrome and no cheap red vinyl. Everything, from the walls to the bar to the booths, was made of richly polished wood accented with brass.

Instead of a DJ booth, there was a small stage with a grand piano, where a heavy-lidded man played a sultry tune. Golden light spilled from globe lamps and twinkled in the antique mirror behind the bar. Oil paintings in heavy gold frames covered the walls. When she glanced up, she found the ceiling painted with a scene featuring the goddess Grim by her riverbank, surrounded by adoring vampires. By her feet, sinful souls reached up from the muddy bank, their mouths open and tears streaming.

Perched on stools and lounging around tables with white tablecloths were vampires of every stripe. The only things they seemed to have in common were the reek of wealth and the bottles of luxury alcoholic synth in their hands.

Dahlia had never really considered The Lush to be low class. If anything, she'd always thought it was pretty trendy. The design was sophisticated, the service good, and the music passable.

But compared to Old Blood, the nicest thing she could call it was *tacky*.

The hair on her arms stood up as attention swung their way. She didn't need to recognize any of the faces in the room to know that every single one of them hid a powerful predator.

Only the elite of the syndicate were welcome in Old Blood, and only the most dangerous vampires could earn the title.

Am I one of them now?

It was a bizarre realization to have as Felix guided her to a table in the center of the room. Their security found a table slightly off to the side as she slipped into her seat.

A tuxedo-clad waiter materialized by their table almost instantly. Not a crease out of place, sterile gloves fitted perfectly, and expression one of carefully calibrated professional warmth, he took their orders like serving them a couple bottles of hundred dollar synth was the highlight of his night.

When he stepped away, Dahlia leaned over to Felix and muttered, "This is *so* weird."

He slung an arm around her shoulders and drew her into his side. Gaze moving around the bar, Felix affected a casual but proprietary air as he leaned back in his seat. "In what way?"

"Like a month ago I was working in a vampire bar," she answered. "Now I'm a customer at the most exclusive one on the continent. Just feels…"

Dahlia trailed off, unable to explain the nuance of it to him. Felix had grown up in this life. He'd never worked a service job or been looked down upon in the same way she had. It wasn't just about having suddenly swapped places with the waiter. It was about the fact that she had *power*.

It hadn't really hit her until that moment, when they walked through doors that never would've been opened to her in her old life.

She was so used to being prey that suddenly being seen as one of the predators was jarring.

Felix rubbed her shoulder with his thumb. It was a deceptively lazy touch that stood in stark contrast to the tension she could feel radiating off him in waves. "If you're uncomfortable, we could go home," he offered far too eagerly.

Dahlia rolled her eyes. "You promised me a half hour."

"Did I? Doesn't sound like me." He ran his tongue along the length of one fang, his gaze still roving the room like he thought someone was going to jump out of the paneling and snatch her. "We could go home right now, tell everyone to fuck off, and you could let me eat you out on my desk again. That sounds like a way better night."

Trying to look relaxed, like she belonged, Dahlia replied, "Let's not pretend like you aren't going to do that anyway. If there's a man who likes to eat pussy more than you, Felix, I haven't met him — and wouldn't survive him if I did."

A bark of laughter erupted out of him. Quickly covering his mouth with a fist, he chuckled as the waiter returned with their synth.

He cracked the seals on the fancy black glass bottles, activating the heat and ensuring it was fresh, before he set their bottles down in front of them. The waiter vanished as quickly as he arrived, leaving them to their drinks.

Eyeing her bottle with interest, she whispered, "I only ever sold a couple of these bottles to VIPs at The Lush. I always wondered what made them special enough to be worth the price."

Felix looped his fingers around the neck of his bottle but didn't drink. Giving her an indulgent look, he said, "Try a sip and tell me if it's worth it."

Careful with her lipstick, Dahlia brought the bottle to her mouth for a taste — and promptly choked.

Turning her face toward his shoulder to hide her coughing fit, her eyes watered as she forced the mouthful of rancid alcoholic piss water down her throat. Felix's laughter was more like a maniacal giggle as he rubbed her back. "What? Don't like it?"

"What *is* that?" she hissed, staring in horror into the opening.

It didn't taste like any of the synth she'd had before. Admittedly, she'd only ever tried two brands before drinking from Felix replaced any bottled nutrients, but none of them had tasted like hot bottled *ass.*

"That's top-shelf alcoholic synth," he answered, lifting his own bottle to peer thoughtfully at the label. "Used to be my favorite. Now it probably tastes like sewer water."

Grimacing, she set her bottle well away from her. "What changed?"

Felix tilted his head to press a lingering kiss to the freshest bite on her throat. "You."

Pressing her thighs together, Dahlia tried to rein in the surge of lust that shot through her whenever he put his lips anywhere on her body. Over the last few weeks she hadn't just begun to adapt to her new life. She'd also been trained to crave his lips on skin and the sweet pain of his bite.

Feeding him and being fed by him were the two greatest pleasures she'd ever known. It was impossible for her to imagine a life without them now.

"Feeding on me makes synth taste awful?" she asked, voice a little huskier than before.

Felix hummed. "For those of us lucky enough to feed from the vein, synth will never compare. We're primed to prefer the taste of our own venom mixing with our anchor's blood. It makes them taste so much sweeter."

That made sense. Still, Dahlia couldn't help but mutter, "If you knew it'd be undrinkable, why did you order two hundred dollars worth of synth?"

"We're in a bar," he answered, shrugging. "It'd be rude not to order something."

"You didn't have to encourage me to drink it, though, did you?"

Whatever levity Felix managed to scrounge up evaporated as his attention snagged on a man striding toward their table. "Let's call it my toll for letting you talk me into this."

TWENTY-SIX

IT WAS INSTINCT TO FALL BACK ON HER COOL CUSTOMER SERVICE expression as the man neared their table. She tried not to tense. *I belong here*, she reminded herself. *I get to sit at this table. I'm not prey anymore.*

The man was slightly shorter than Felix but built a lot sturdier. His shoulders were broad and his chest deep. The man was pale, with auburn curls shaved close on the sides and left a little long on top. A red beard had begun to grow in thickly on his cheeks and even though the light was too dim to be sure, she thought his eyes were a soft, warm brown. Dressed in dark pants, a white t-shirt, flannel, and shit-kicker boots, he looked far more out of place than she did. In fact, he looked like he'd just gotten back from a hike.

Flashing a blinding smile full of fang, the man rumbled, "Well, I didn't want to believe the rumors, but congrats must be in order."

"Byrn," Felix greeted. His tone wasn't unfriendly, but it wasn't exactly warm, either.

"Amauri. You gonna introduce me to your new bride?"

Looking like he'd rather pull his own fangs out, Felix said,

"Dahlia, meet Robert Byrn, head of the Byrn family. Byrn, meet my bride, Dahlia Bowan."

Smile widening into something that might've devastated her before she met Felix, Robert winked and said, "Call me Robbie. It's a pleasure to meet you, Dahlia. Damn shame we didn't get a chance to be properly introduced before you took a shine to Felix here."

It took everything in her not to blush when he gave her throat a significant look. Wearing bites proudly — and owning exactly how one got them — was normal in the vampire world. She'd known that for years. But it was a whole new ball game when strangers started ogling them.

"The pleasure's mine," she replied, lifting her chin. "Sorry you didn't get a chance, but my husband doesn't play fair. Can't say I mind."

Robert arched a heavy ginger brow. Sliding an inquiring look toward Felix, he parroted, "Husband?"

Felix shrugged. "Anchor. Mate. Husband. All the same shit. As long as it means forever, I don't care what word she uses."

A flurry of butterflies exploded in her stomach. Dahlia had to quickly suck her lips between her teeth to stop herself from breaking out into a big, soppy grin. Felix wasn't even trying to be sweet. He just meant it, plain and simple.

Robert crossed his burly arms over his chest. "Can't fault that. You're a lucky bastard, Amauri. Though I can't say you won the lottery on in-laws. I heard Alastair torched one of your clubs recently."

"And I sank his yacht, *Atlas*," Felix replied mildly. "It's a game we play, him and I."

"Can't say I expected Alastair to be a gracious father-in-law. Or for you to be an easy son-in-law, for that matter." Robert gave Dahlia an impressed look. "You must have the patience of a saint."

She snorted. "I really don't. That's why we're here."

Nodding, he took a look around the bar. Following his gaze,

she noticed several other people watching them, apparently waiting for their chance to approach the table. "Well, if you came to get the rumor mill going, then you'll accomplish that."

"We don't want there to be any doubts," Felix replied, his smile all sharp teeth and menace.

Robert tipped his head. "There won't be any of those after tonight. You both look like pin cushions."

It was impossible to maintain her aloof veneer. Dahlia felt herself go a little pink, and knew for fact that she had when a deep laugh rumbled out of Robert's chest. "That's cute as fuck. You got a sister or something, Dahlia? I'd love to find a girl who blushes like that."

"No sisters, I'm afraid," she muttered, trying to regain her composure. The closest she had was Cecilia, and while Robert was certainly her type — minus the criminal affiliations — Dahlia had no intention of introducing the two. Her friend was busy, after all.

Robert let out a dramatic sigh and took a step away from the table. "Damn. Well, I've got business to handle, so I'll leave you to your rumor mill. Dahlia, let me know if any long lost cousins appear, all right?"

Felix tapped his claws on the cloth table top. "Stop trying to charm my bride."

"Can't help it. The charm comes natural to all Byrns," Robert shot back, his grin wide and lethal. If she hadn't spied the gun strapped to his side, she would've said he had the boy next door charm down to a deadly science.

Spinning on the heel of his boot, he gave them a casual wave over his shoulder before he made his way out of the bar.

They didn't have to wait long before they were approached again. For the entire half hour they sat at the table, they entertained a steady trickle of United Washington's most dangerous vampires. They couldn't seem to help themselves. Everyone wanted to see if the rumors were true — not just about Felix snagging a blood bride, but about her.

They seemed far more interested in her side of the story than she could've anticipated.

Dahlia was used to being seen and not heard. *Head down, tray up.* That was the motto. Not being noticed was a survival strategy. But that wasn't how it worked in the syndicate. To be someone, to have power in her own right, she had to be seen *and* heard by everyone in the room.

Nothing about it felt natural, but it began to come easier to her as person after person drifted their way. It still felt strange to say, *"Yes, I'm Alastair's daughter,"* but seeing how seriously they took it, she stopped feeling outright silly every time the words left her mouth.

And when Felix tightened his arm around her shoulder and introduced her as his bride? That felt *right.*

Her half hour of allotted time flew by. Before she knew it, Felix was standing up and ushering her out of her seat, hardly sparing a glance for the young brother and sister — the Enamorado siblings — she'd been talking to.

Offering them a hasty goodbye, she let him guide her out of Old Blood with a mix of relief and disappointment. It was heady being taken seriously by so many powerful people, but it was exhausting, too. It felt a bit like she'd crammed an entire eight hour shift into her half hour of socializing. It was invigorating, but she also couldn't wait to get home.

Watching the valet drive her car up to the curb, she asked in a low voice, "Do you think Mr. Bowan will get the message?"

"He'd have to be completely delusional not to," Felix answered. Opening the passenger door, he nudged her in.

Dahlia frowned. "It's my car. I want to drive."

"And I want to live to eat out my bride, which means I'm not letting you drive again tonight. You're worse than Luis."

"Don't be rude. I'm nothing like that speed demon. He told me the other day that he's broken *every* traffic law in the UTA." Despite her huffing, she did slide into the passenger's seat. Her brain felt too full to drive, anyway.

Felix closed her door with a snap, and after a quick adjustment of the driver's seat to accommodate his long legs, they peeled away from the curb to head back to the Amauri mansion.

Laying his hand on her thigh, he confirmed, "That's actually true. You wouldn't believe how many traffic violations Milo has had to bribe Luis out of."

"Why doesn't Luis do it himself?"

"Because he doesn't care. He thinks it'd be fun to go to jail for a little while. Pretty sure he believes he could break out." Felix slowed to a stop at a red light. The streets near their exclusive neighborhood were understandably less busy than those closer to downtown. There was hardly anyone else on the road — just them and the black car driven by their security.

Dahlia began to tick off points on her fingers. "So Luis thinks it'd be fun to break out of jail. Marietta collects swords. Alvin has some weird blood fetish. And I'm pretty sure Nash has a secret shrine to Genevieve somewhere in the house. We need to get the Amauris some better hobbies, Felix. Seriously."

Felix made an indignant sound. "You forgot Milo."

"I thought Milo was normal." As normal as a man as intimidating as him could be, at any rate.

They didn't speak much, but that didn't seem to be unusual. Milo was the strong and silent type. When he spoke, it was only because he actually had something to say. Otherwise he was content to stand off to the side, his gaze ever-watchful and his scarred face impassive. He couldn't have been more different from his brother or cousin Marietta, who both had personalities bigger and gaudier than the Amauri mansion.

Almost afraid to ask but way too curious not to, she said, "Tell me he doesn't collect, like, severed heads or something."

"Who do you think we are?" Felix gave her an offended look as he took a turn. "We don't keep heads. We dispose of all body parts properly like the professionals we are."

"Very reassuring."

"I'm glad you think so."

Dahlia waited for a beat. When she couldn't take it anymore, she exclaimed, "Are you gonna tell me or not?"

Lips twitching, Felix answered, "Milo likes to—"

The hit came out of nowhere.

One moment they were taking the last turn on the narrow private road before entering their gated neighborhood, the next a large black SUV side-swiped them, sending the car careening into the guardrail that protected the park.

Felix hissed a curse and attempted to maintain control of the wheel, but there was nowhere to go. The back end of their car bounced off the railing, sending their front skidding back toward the road. Dahlia yelped as she was yanked hard against the seatbelt.

Felix attempted to reverse, but the SUV had been joined by another that swept in behind them. Within seconds, the vehicles had blocked any escape routes and the line of sight of their security.

"Felix," Dahlia rasped, watching with wide eyes as he unsnapped the buckle of his seatbelt and reached for his gun.

"Stay in the car," he commanded. She barely had time to open her mouth before he was throwing the driver's door open, gun raised.

Her heart jumped into her throat as men poured out of the vehicles. They had more men and far more guns — all of which were aimed directly at Felix.

Fear hit her harder than the SUVs did. It was worse than when she woke up impaled. It was worse than getting the news in the hospital. It was worse than Devon barging into her apartment.

It was fear for *Felix,* and it seeped into every crevice of her being like bitterly cold ice water.

I can't watch him die.

Through the open driver's door, she heard him say, "You know, that was a fucking stupid thing to do, Tomas. I actually liked you, but now I have to kill you."

"We don't want anyone to die, Felix." The voice that replied was smooth and lilting. A singer's voice, maybe, in another life. "We just want my cousin."

"So you ran her off the fucking road? You could've killed her!" Felix had sounded cool and composed before, but now his fury whipped out like a lightning strike.

Tomas didn't seem to care. "Unlikely. I'm a very good driver."

It was hard to tell what was going on or how many men there were when Felix blocked most of her view. She didn't need to see, though, when he growled, "Take another step and I shoot."

"Kill me and my uncle will take out every Amauri in that ugly house." Tomas sounded more exasperated than concerned, but the threat didn't feel forced. It had real weight to it.

Her heart stopped as the faces of Sonia and Will and all of the other children snapped to the forefront of her mind. It wasn't just them they had to protect, either. They were responsible for Nash and Genevieve. Marietta. Luis and Milo. Even freaky doctor Alvin.

If something happened to them, it was because *they* failed.

And Dahlia couldn't imagine existing in a world without Felix. He'd become more than just her boogeyman. He was her *everything* — as annoying as that was.

"Do you really want that, Felix? Just hand Dahlia over and we can end this bullshit before it gets any worse."

Dahlia's breath shortened as the sound of tires squealing around the corner reached them. It had to be their security, but she knew instantly that they'd only make it worse. There was no way Felix would back down, and if it devolved into a shootout, everything she'd hoped to avoid would happen in the worst possible way.

She'd started the night with the intention of ending the conflict. Now she really had no choice.

Unbuckling her seatbelt with trembling fingers, Dahlia called out, "Felix, stop! Just stop!"

"Dahlia? This is your cousin Tomas. I'm going to bring you to your father. Can you get out of the car or do you need help?"

"You stay in the fucking car, Dahlia," Felix snarled. "Put your head down and cover your ears."

"No, no. I'm not doing any of that. Both of you, just *listen* to me." She had to jam her shoulder into the door to get it open. There would be time to be pissed about her beautiful new car getting totaled, but it would have to come when she wasn't trying to save her husband's life.

He bellowed something else at her. She ignored it as she stumbled out of the car and onto the grassy shoulder. Her heels sank into the dirt, but it didn't stop her from rounding the front of the severely damaged car.

The scene that greeted her was nightmarish.

Felix stood facing off with a dozen armed men. Their two security guards had their own guns aimed at the group, but were hopelessly outgunned and in a terrible position. Between them was a lithe, golden-skinned man with neatly styled black hair and a model's face. His features were almost too refined, his nose too straight and his mouth too full. He looked like he belonged on the cover of a magazine, not aiming a rifle at Felix's head like it was just another chore.

When they locked eyes, Dahlia instantly recognized something of Alastair in him.

"Dahlia," Tomas greeted. "It's great to finally meet you. Please get in the car."

"She's not going anywhere." Felix moved to step in front of her. A series of high whines filled the air as all the Bowan men released the safety on their bolt guns.

"Felix, stop!" Cursing the rough terrain more than her footwear, Dahlia hurried onto the road. Dodging his swipe at her arm, she stepped between the men. A cold sweat broke out over her body as she held her hands out — one to him and one to Tomas.

"Everyone just *stop*. No one is going to die tonight. For Grim's sake, put the guns *down*."

Tomas looked genuinely regretful when he said, "Can't do that, cousin. I've got orders. And he's kept you from your family long enough."

Trying not to sound as pissed off as she was, she demanded, "What are your orders?"

"To kill him if he won't let you go."

Dahlia turned her head to look at Felix. He stood rigidly behind her, his face pale and his eyes bright with the kind of fury she knew could tear Tomas apart. But he was only one man, and even if the full force of the Amauris came down on them, a blood bath was inevitable.

The universe moved in predictable patterns and so too did vampires. All the signs were there. If she didn't stop this, someone she loved would die.

I'm not prey anymore, she thought, sucking in a deep breath of the muggy summer air. *I'm one of the predators, and I'll be damned before I let someone take what's mine.*

Meeting his eye, she murmured, "Don't be mad, okay? I love you."

The skin pulled tight over Felix's skull as her intent registered. "Do *not* — "

Turning back to Tomas, she took a step toward him. "I'll go with you."

Tomas's dark eyes flicked over her shoulder, no doubt taking in the rage painting Felix's expression. "Will he shoot?"

"Not if I'm with you," she answered, passing him stiffly. "He loves me too much to risk it."

—MISSED CALL FRIDAY 2:08 AM
—MISSED CALL FRIDAY 2:15 AM
—MISSED CALL FRIDAY 2:20 AM
—MISSED CALL FRIDAY 2:22 AM
—MISSED CALL FRIDAY 2:35 AM

TWENTY-SEVEN

THE BOWANS LIVED IN A GRAND FOUR STORY HOUSE IN THE HEART OF the oldest neighborhood of United Washington. Built of gray stone with a copper roof that had long since oxidized to a rich blue-green, it was exactly as classy and sophisticated as Dahlia expected it to be.

Nerves tightened her stomach as she stared out the SUV's window at the ornate stonework surrounding the dark blue front door. She wasn't worried about the meeting. After everything, Dahlia was confident she could hold her own with Alastair and Tomas. What she couldn't stand was the thought of Felix losing his mind back home.

He wouldn't risk her safety, but he would do just about anything to get her back. That meant that she had a very limited window in which to resolve this mess before he did something reckless.

Just barely resisting the urge to slap the hand Tomas held out to her after opening her door, she thrust her shoulders back to stride toward the elegant front steps. A massive gold lion's head knocker glared at her from the center of the door.

Her whole body ached from the crash and she was pretty sure the protective base of one heel had come off at some point, but she ignored it all. It wasn't like this was the first time she went to work with a broken heel.

Tomas used his long legs to overtake her. Giving her a slight smile, he opened the front door and ushered her inside a gleaming white foyer. A grand, domed ceiling soared above a sweeping black marble staircase, and towering pieces of modern art hung on the white walls. On either side of the base of the staircase were two black tables absolutely overflowing with massive flower arrangements.

Dahlias, she realized with a start. The obviously handmade crystal vases were bursting with her namesake. The sight made an involuntary twinge of warmth take root in her chest.

It didn't make the way her family had been threatened okay, but she wasn't heartless. Someone had clearly gone out of their way to put *those* flowers there. It was sweet, if a little misguided under the circumstances.

Hardly a minute passed before movement at the top of the stairs drew her eye.

A burly older man wearing a pair of glasses leaned over the banister to peer down out at them. His salt and pepper hair was cut short and his eyebrows were thick enough to touch the rims of his glasses when he frowned.

"Tomas, who have you—" The man blanched. "Good gods, is that our Dahlia?"

She glanced over her shoulder at Tomas, who'd lifted a hand in a wave. "It's her."

"Ah!" The man threw himself away from the railing. He hustled down the curved staircase with surprising agility. By the time he got down to the bottom, his face was flushed and his glasses had nearly fallen off the tip of his nose. She noticed instantly that he wasn't a vampire, but whether he was arrant or not, she had no way of knowing.

A little alarmed by his sudden approach, Dahlia took half a step back. It didn't do her much good. The man lunged for her.

In an instant she was swept into a bone-crushing hug and lifted off her feet.

"Oh, thank the gods. I don't have to punish Alastair anymore!" He swung her around, nearly dislodging one of her heels. A cloud of expensive cologne and the scent of fresh oranges washed over her — not bad, but unmistakably unappealing compared to caramel and smoke and *Felix*. Dahlia had to bite back the instinctive urge to claw herself free.

Perhaps seeing her discomfort, Tomas stepped in. He laid a hand on the man's shoulder and muttered, "Uncle Colin, you haven't even introduced yourself yet. Maybe the hugs can wait a minute."

"Oh, you're right. I'm so sorry!" Colin didn't sound the least bit sorry.

Her release wasn't quite immediate, but he did eventually put her down. Stumbling back a step, she smoothed her hands down the front of her dress and eyed the pair of men warily.

Tomas stepped up to introduce them. "Colin, meet Dahlia. Dahlia, this is Uncle Alastair's anchor, Colin. They've been together over a hundred and fifty years."

"Just celebrated our one hundredth and seventy-second, but who's counting." Colin grabbed Tomas's arm like he needed to hold onto something if he wasn't allowed to manhandle her anymore. "Gods, I just can't believe it. Look at you! I saw your pictures but they don't do you justice. And you're smart, too. Tomas, did I tell you? She's gotten 4.0s her whole academic career!"

"Yes, you told me," he muttered.

Dahlia made a face. "How do you know that?"

Alastair's dry, cultured voice came down from the top of the stairs. "Because knowing things is what we do."

She looked up to find the man descending the stairs at a much more sedate pace than his anchor had. There was no ornate cane or expensive coat this time, but Alastair Bowan didn't need either to be intimidating. His gaze pierced her from across the foyer.

"Dahlia," he greeted, reaching the bottom of the stairs.

"Mr. Bowan," she coolly replied.

"Oh, please, you can't call him that." Colin blew out an exasperated huff. "We're family now. You can call him Alastair, but I'm sure he'd be happy with papa."

Dahlia narrowed her eyes at Alastair. The humor of calling *that* man anything other than his name, let alone *papa*, would have to be examined later.

Clearing her throat, she said, "Please forgive me if I'm not feeling particularly warm and cuddly right now. Seeing as you just ran me and my husband off the road, then held him at gunpoint."

Colin whirled on Alastair. *"What?"*

For his part, Alastair looked utterly unrepentant. "Tomas is competent. I knew you'd be fine."

Dahlia put her hands on her hips and demanded, "You complain about the Amauris being reckless with their family, but you don't think twice about letting your nephew ram your daughter's car into a guardrail?"

It was Tomas's turn to receive Colin's horrified glare. "You did *what?"*

Tomas put up his hands. "They were spotted at Old Blood and I was told to take the opportunity!"

"Alastair!" Colin jammed a finger in Dahlia's direction. His low voice became a hiss of disapproval. "That is our *daughter."*

"My love, you told me to bring her home. That's exactly why I did everything in my power to get her back." A shade of exasperation had finally entered Alastair's expression. "It worked, didn't it? I don't see what you're complaining about."

Wrapping an arm around her shoulders, Colin cast a venomous glare toward his partner and began to lead her through the foyer. "One hundred and seventy-two years," he muttered, "and that man still finds new ways to be an idiot. Sweetheart, I'm so sorry. Please don't lump me in with him."

Allowing him to lead her into a modern sitting room, Dahlia replied, "This wasn't completely against my will. I decided that since neither him or Felix could be reasonable about the situation, I had to take things into my own hands. I want to talk this out."

"I've been saying the same thing for weeks," he confessed. "All of this fighting could've been resolved with a few phone calls."

"He sank *Atlas.*" Alastair's acerbic voice came from the doorway as Colin settled her on a charcoal gray couch. Wisely, Tomas appeared to have made himself scarce.

"And you burned his club to the ground," she shot back, crossing her arms.

"He kidnapped my daughter." Alastair strode into the sitting room. The slightest hitch in his step belied the need for the cane, but it didn't diminish the raw power he exuded as he joined his anchor on the couch across from her.

Sick to death of masculine pride, Dahlia rolled her eyes. "Let's not pretend like this has anything to do with me, please. You don't know me. This is about your family legacy and your ego. You don't like that Felix made you look weak, and Felix doesn't like that you're trying to separate us. Both of you need to get *the fuck* over it."

"You've gotten bold since we last saw each other," he dryly noted.

Dahlia gave him a tight, close-lipped smile. "I'm a Bowan now."

Alastair draped an arm behind Colin and crossed one ankle over his knee. "You're also wrong. This isn't just about our name and ego. This is about the fact that my daughter was kidnapped by a family that is notoriously unstable and generally agreed upon as intolerable. Even if I *liked* Felix, I wouldn't have allowed it."

"Why? Because you want to be able to sell me off to someone of your choosing?"

Colin laid a hand on Alastair's thigh. In a firm voice, he answered, "No. We don't believe in that. Never have. When Tomas was born, we all agreed as a family that he would get to choose his partner. You do, too." There was a pause, then, with a significant look at her throat, "And it seems you have."

Dahlia smoothed her hair back behind her ear. "If you think this is bad, you should see the other guy."

Alastair looked like he'd swallowed a mouthful of sour blood, but he didn't comment on the state of her neck. Instead, he asked, "Can you blame us for wanting to keep you safe?"

"No," she replied, "but I can call you hypocritical for vilifying Felix when you didn't think twice about risking my life tonight. Say what you want about him, Mr. Bowan, but he would *never* intentionally put me in harm's way."

"I seem to remember the night we met going differently than you do."

Dahlia winced. She couldn't exactly fault him for bringing that up. "I wasn't supposed to work that night. He had no idea I switched shifts with another employee. If he had, he wouldn't have let that happen."

But as she sat there in the sparkling sitting room, locked in a staring contest with her new father and desperate to get back to her husband, Dahlia couldn't say she would've changed things. Getting impaled and turned wasn't exactly on her bucket list, but Luis was right.

Sometimes change sucked. And sometimes it made things a whole lot better.

Becoming a vampire had taken a lot from her, but it'd given her even more in return. A month ago she would've gritted her teeth and taken these men steamrolling her, believing she had no other choice, but not now. The Dahlia who lived by the motto *head down, tray up* was dead.

The new Dahlia wouldn't just stand up for herself. She'd bite back.

Colin leaned forward, interest splashed across his expression. "Wait, you knew Felix before you were turned?"

"We dated for three years," she answered, only fudging the truth a little.

Clearly trying to align that with the facts he had at hand, Colin gave her a puzzled look. "How did that work? You were in San Francisco, and Felix has been busy fighting Yvanna over here for years."

Dahlia gave him a quick and sanitized version of the story, starting with the night Felix's uncle was murdered in The Lush and ending with Yvanna's death. If she left out the parts where she wanted to throw her phone in the ocean or throttle him, the story actually sounded a little romantic.

Felix wanted her right away and pursued her, but couldn't risk her safety, so he'd forced himself to keep his distance until the Amauri civil war ended. It was an honest version, she supposed, even if the story lacked a few critical pieces of context.

But even that didn't change the fundamental truth that Felix cared. He'd always cared. He'd loved her since day one and showed it the only way he knew how. Always, he'd been trying to do his best by her — even when he planned to let her go.

Her chest tightened painfully as she thought of how worried he must've been at that moment. The urgency to get back to him clawed at her.

Turning to Alastair, she said, "I don't want to be at odds with you. I don't want any of the Bowans or the Amauris to be hurt because of me. But I'm not leaving Felix. So you either need to pull your head out of your ass, or you need to leave me alone — because if you take one more shot at my husband, I'll kill you myself."

Each word landed hard. She spoke them calmly and with the full force of her chest. They came from a deep well of certainty in her, the same place where her feelings for Felix had always lived, even when she didn't want to acknowledge them.

It was a place of power. One that not even a vampire like Alastair Bowan could rattle.

A taut silence lasted several tense seconds before Colin leaned back with a long exhale. Rubbing his eyes beneath his glasses, he chuckled, "Good gods, she really is your daughter."

Alastair's lips pursed beneath his snowy mustache. "I told you."

Dahlia's gaze bounced back and forth between them. Colin appeared to relax, and if she wasn't mistaken, Alastair did, too. It was harder to tell with him, though. Whatever softening he underwent was marginal at best. Like the sheen of water on the outermost edge of an ice sculpture, maybe.

Still, she sensed a shift when he dropped both feet onto the floor and leaned forward, putting his elbows on his knees. Steepling his fingers, he gave her a keen-eyed look. "What will it take to get you to be part of this family?"

Confused, she narrowed her eyes and sat back in her seat. "I told you I'm not leaving Felix."

"That's not what I asked."

Oh. Dahlia blinked, suddenly wrong-footed. She'd expected a lot more resistance, but with her neck being covered in bites, she supposed there was no point in Alastair trying to separate them now. What she couldn't understand was what he actually wanted from her.

"What do you mean by being part of the family, exactly?" She gestured to herself and Alastair with a finger. "I'm still not totally clear on how this blood-adoption thing works."

"To them — and us — it's considered the same as if we discovered Alastair had fathered you and just not known," Colin explained. "We never had children. Things always got in the way, and then we felt like we were too old. So having a brilliant, beautiful daughter dropped in our laps..." He smiled, and there was an aching amount of hope in that expression.

Alastair wasn't nearly as warm or open as his anchor, but when he grabbed Colin's hand and cast him a long look out of the corner of his eye, it was obvious how much he cared.

"I want to retain my rights as your father," Alastair announced, as clipped and brusque as a businessman declaring his terms. "You'd keep the Bowan name and be given a share of the family wealth, as well as a say in all major family decisions. In exchange, you'll visit us here regularly — monthly at minimum — and stay in regular contact with at least one of us. Should you choose to procreate with the whelp, we request visitation rights with our grandchild as well."

It took her a second to translate what he was saying into what it'd mean coming from a normal, emotionally available person.

Dahlia curled her fingers into the hem of her dress. A gooey sort of warmth took up residence in her chest, even if a part of her still couldn't quite believe what she was hearing.

She'd never known her father. He'd taken off long before she was born, and if she were honest, she was a little iffy on whether the name on her birth certificate was even correct. To suddenly be given not one but *two* fathers felt a bit like she'd won the lottery and then used the winnings to hit the jackpot on a slot machine.

"You want to get to know me," she said, her wonder unhidden. "You actually want me to be your daughter. Like, *really* be your daughter."

Alastair sniffed. "Yes, obviously. Now tell me your terms."

She opened her mouth to say she had none but stopped herself just in time.

The new Dahlia didn't get to have no demands. She lived in a world of predators who'd happily eat her and the people she loved at the first sign of weakness. That meant she had to take advantage of any and all opportunities that arose.

And she was pretty sure Alastair *wanted* her to bargain. He probably wouldn't know what to do with her if she didn't have demands of her own.

So she took a deep breath and said, "I can agree to monthly visitation and regular contact, but I can't take decision-making power within the Bowan family. That'd be a conflict of interest between my loyalty to you and to my husband's family. On that score, I'd like your assurances that there will no longer be any hostilities between you."

Alastair let out a long sigh. "I can't promise I won't want to kill him."

"I didn't say you had to. Only that you won't."

After a beat of what looked like intense internal debate, he growled, "I want him to replace my yacht."

Dahlia raised her eyebrows. "Are you going to replace his club?"

"Why would—"

"Then you're both going to take it on the chin," she interrupted. "I'm not going to ask Felix to do something when you won't meet him halfway."

"Fine," Alastair bit out. "But how do you know he'll agree to set hostilities aside? Amauris are unpredictable and disloyal. They'll stab their own kin in the back to get ahead."

"Not my husband and not his cousins," she firmly answered.

"How do you *know?*"

Dahlia lifted her chin. "Because he loves me, and I'd bet you anything that he's on his way here right now — even if showing up at your door means being shot on sight. If that's not loyalty, I don't know what is."

The words came out naturally, utterly unforced. Maybe it wasn't the kind of love she expected, and it took her a long time to recognize it for what it was, but that didn't make it any less real. Felix would do anything to make her happy. He'd given her complete power over him from the start. All she had to do was take it.

But with that came a responsibility — not just to him, but to all the Amauris. What was in their best interest had become hers. If Alastair and Colin could be believed, that meant fitting them in there somewhere, too. She wasn't entirely sure how that was going to work, but she had an idea of where to start.

"Now," she began, mirroring Alastair's keen look, "do you remember what we talked about the night we met?"

TWENTY-EIGHT

MILO DIDN'T BOTHER TO LECTURE HIM ON WHY HIS PLAN WAS A terrible idea. Not because Felix was right, but because they both knew it was no use.

He still couldn't seem to help himself, though, when he muttered, "They could kill you. They probably *will* kill you."

Felix unclipped his gun from its holster and shoved it into the glove box of Milo's muscle car. They were parked a few blocks away from the Bowan house. There was no back-up and no exit strategy. He would go in unarmed and alone.

"If they do, you're the head of the family," he grunted, reaching for the knife strapped to his ankle. "And it's your responsibility to make sure Dahlia doesn't destroy herself trying to kill every last Bowan when I'm gone."

Milo accepted the knife with a bemused grimace. "You really think she'd do that?"

Felix shrugged out of his torn suit jacket and tossed it in the back. "Tonight, she climbed out of a wrecked car and willingly stood in front of a dozen guns without fucking blinking just to make sure I didn't get shot. Yeah, Milo, I do think she'd do that."

And he'd go to his grave haunted by the sight of her in that position, with flecks of shattered glass glittering in her hair and her back so straight as she walked right up to Tomas.

He'd never been so in love or so angry with her.

He intended to *never* put her in that position again, but to make sure of that, he had to get her back — which got a lot fucking harder with her behind enemy lines.

A siege wouldn't work, and attempting to wait them out wouldn't either. One put her at risk and the other meant she would start to experience withdrawal. They both would, but he couldn't care less about what happened to him.

That was precisely why this plan was the only one that could work.

Felix shoved the door open and set one foot on the street. A hand on his shoulder stopped him from throwing himself completely out of the car.

Turning to look back at his cousin, he found Milo's normally serious expression much more severe. The lights of the dashboard gleamed blue and green in his one pale eye when he growled, "Don't fucking die. I don't want your job, and I *really* don't want to deal with Dahlia if something happens to you."

Felix offered him a sharp smile. "Tough shit."

Shaking off his cousin's hand, he climbed out of the car and slammed the door. Taking a deep breath of the muggy air, he started walking.

They'd see him coming long before he actually got near the house. The entire block was surveilled and patrols circled in slow-moving cars like great mechanical vultures. So Felix put his hands up and walked slowly, giving them plenty of time to decide to shoot him or not.

There was no fear. No hesitation. No worry that maybe he wasn't doing the right thing or that he ought to let her go.

If they shot him, they shot him.

They'd have to get him in the head to keep him from reaching the gate, and they'd have to put him down completely to stop him from finding Dahlia, one way or another.

He supposed there should've been some worry or reluctance on his part. After all, he'd worked damn hard to get to where he was. He'd killed and he'd sacrificed and he'd spilled his own blood to build up the Amauris into something new and better. He'd even been prepared to give up the woman he loved for the sake of his family.

But he saw how short-sighted that was now. *I never would've been able to do it,* he realized.

Like always, Milo had been right all along.

Felix couldn't have given her up. He couldn't now. It wasn't because she was a blood bride. It was because she was *Dahlia.* The woman who'd taken one look at him and said, *"If you want me, be better."*

It turned out that when push came to shove, he would give everything up for her. His position. His wealth. His life. None of it mattered without her.

He didn't look down when the first red dot appeared on his chest. Nor when the second, third, or fourth did. Felix kept walking, his gaze locked in an unblinking stare on the tall black gate that blocked the entrance to the Bowan property.

Tomas stood on the other side, his arms crossed and his expression blank. By the time Felix reached him, a swarm of red dots crawled over his chest, neck, and head. Keeping his arms at his shoulders, he addressed the man coolly. "I'm here to see my bride."

"Really stupid to show your face, Amauri," Tomas replied.

Felix resisted the urge to reach through the bars and throttle the man. "Really fucking stupid of you to take my bride."

Tomas raised his perfect eyebrows. "She came willingly."

"Because you threatened her husband," he snarled, fingers curling into tight fists. "What was she supposed to do? Let you shoot me?"

The man shrugged. "If she didn't want to be with you, sure."

"You really thought I forced her to be with me?" Felix swallowed a bitter taste in his mouth. It didn't matter what anyone, let alone the Bowans, thought of him. All he cared about was his bride. "You don't know anything about me. And you know even less about Dahlia if you thought for a second she'd let that happen."

"Has she always been so..." Tomas made an all-encompassing sort of gesture.

Felix smirked. "Yeah, she has. Now are you going to let me in or am I going to have to start screaming her name?"

Tomas looked meaningfully down at the mass of glowing red dots on Felix's chest. "You're not exactly in a position to make demands, Amauri."

"Then take me as your prisoner," he offered. "I don't give a fuck. Just take me to my bride."

Tomas lost some of his aloofness. Brows furrowing, he said, "You've lost your mind. Just let her—"

"Go? Never." Felix took a step closer to the fence. His nose nearly touched the bars when he hissed, "I'll give you the same deal I gave her. If you really want me to leave her alone, then you're gonna have to shoot me. Aim for the head, fucker, because killing me is the only way to stop me."

"You can't seriously—"

Whatever inane question Tomas had been about to ask was cut off when the front door to the Bowan house swung open behind him.

Felix's attention snapped to Dahlia instantly. His heart stopped and restarted, its speed tripled as she sauntered down the steps and across the courtyard. The lights that ringed the high wall around the property gave her a golden halo as soft and perfect as the blonde curls on her head. Her broken heels tapped a quick rhythm on the pavement when she walked down the driveway. Holes had been torn in her tights and one shoulder of her blazer dress was torn, but she still somehow looked completely in control.

"Dahlia," he choked out, gripping the bars hard enough to make his knuckles bleach.

"Hi, boogeyman." Her voice was the sweetest thing he'd ever heard. And the smile she gave him as she got closer? He'd never forget it.

"Guns down. No one points a gun at my daughter. Ever," Alastair commanded from somewhere behind her. Felix barely spared the old man a glance as she strode up to the gate, her eyes locked with his.

Breathing harshly, he rasped, "Are you hurt?"

"I'm okay," she murmured just for him. "I promise, I'm okay. And I'm coming home."

Tomas made a sound of deep confusion. "Dahlia, you can't go with him. You just got here. You should stay and get to know your family."

Dahlia turned sharply to give her new cousin a vicious smile Felix was all too familiar with. "Tomas, I know we just met and you seem like a lovely guy, but if you try and tell me what to do one more time, we're going to have a fucking problem."

Alastair's voice carried across the courtyard again. "Let her go, Tomas. It's fine. We've reached a deal."

He looked like it was the last thing in the world he wanted to do, but Tomas waved at the guard station.

Felix's heart jumped into his throat as the gate vibrated under his hands and began to pull to one side. As it slowly opened, Dahlia turned to her new cousin and gestured for him to come closer.

He saw it coming long before Tomas did, but the poor guy really didn't know Dahlia, so he couldn't exactly blame him.

The punch was lightning fast, mean, and deadly in its accuracy. Blood gushed from Tomas's nose as his head snapped back. Felix grinned at the crunch of bone and cartilage, his cock twitching with keen interest behind his fly.

"Fuck!" The man wheezed, his hands immediately clutching his mangled nose as he stooped over in pain. Going by the way Dahlia flexed her fingers, it was a devastating suckerpunch.

In a terrifyingly calm voice, she told him, "Now we're even.

But if you *ever* point a gun at my husband again, I'll cut it off instead of breaking it. Clear?"

Tomas pressed his sleeve to his nose and nodded once, a gleam of respect making it through the pain in his eyes. In a nasally, muffled voice, he said, "Welcome to the family, I guess."

Dahlia patted his shoulder. "Thanks. You owe me a car. Make it red."

She waved at Alastair and his anchor standing in the doorway of their home before tossing her hair over her shoulder and waltzing through the gate, her long legs flashing in her crimson tights and sky-high stilettos.

If Felix thought she was devastating before, it was nothing compared to how she looked to him now.

Snatching her to his chest, he swooped down on her with a ferocious kiss. "I fucking love you," he gasped, reverent and needy against the welcoming warmth of her mouth.

Her smile curved against his lips. "I love you, too. Now can we go home? We've got work to do."

EPILOGUE

SEPTEMBER 2050 - SAN FRANCISCO, THE ELVISH PROTECTORATE

THE FLOWER MARKET WAS AN EXPLOSION OF COLOR, SCENTS, AND sound. The air was cool inside the massive warehouse building, saturated with water and all fresh green stems cut with small, sharp knives. Vendors and customers prowled the narrow paths between stalls, dodging massive white buckets full of chrysanthemums and baby's breath and calla lilies.

Even at midnight, the market was an oasis of life and movement. Day-dwellers weren't the only ones who needed beauty in their lives, after all.

Dahlia hooked her fingers into Colin's crooked elbow, a wide, satisfied smile on her face. He hadn't stopped gushing over the sights since they stepped into the market. Felix and Alastair trailed behind them. When she peeked over her shoulder, she found them deep in discussion — no doubt arguing over when to make their next move now that their legitimate businesses in the Protectorate had begun to turn a profit.

Those two loved to argue almost as much as she and Colin loved to ignore them. She wasn't sure when it happened, but at some point she noticed neither men appeared to loathe the existence of the other any longer. Instead, their arguments became something of a mutually enjoyable hobby. Kind of like putting on boxing gloves and stepping into the ring instead of starting a bare-knuckle brawl.

It was good for them. In their world, it wasn't often that they could be totally honest with each other, and finding someone who completely understood Felix's responsibilities and position was rare. They'd both vigorously deny it, but the men had become something akin to friends.

Felix still wasn't allowed on Alastair's new yacht, though.

It was fine. He just bought a bigger one and named it *The Bride*.

There was some debate, but she was ninety percent certain that the maiden voyage was when she got pregnant. Felix liked to think it was the week before, when they'd spent some quality time in the pool while the mansion was empty. Either way, they agreed water was involved.

Colin leaned in close to ask, "How are your feet doing?"

"They're fine," she answered, deciding not to mention the way her son was currently shoving his elbow into her bladder.

This was the last family business trip they would make before her son arrived. She intended to make the most of it, even if it felt a bit like the baby was doing constant diving elbow drops on her organs.

As annoying as his father, she thought fondly.

Unfortunately, Dahlia was not one of the lucky people for whom pregnancy was a joyous time of reverence for the miracle of what her body was capable of. It'd been miserable from the start.

She hadn't been able to wear heels in months, her son liked to kick her in the ribs whenever she began to fall asleep, and Felix had been glued to her side like a sexy, blood-sucking barnacle from the moment the test came back positive. The last several months had been an odyssey of raw physical discomfort and hormones — real nature documentary animal shit, as Luis liked to joke.

To say she was ready for her little Amauri parasite to evacuate his fleshy condo was an understatement.

That was half the reason she'd insisted on the trip to begin with. Not only did they need to check up on their interests in the EVP, but she hoped getting some walking in would help speed things along. Just a little.

"If you need a rest, just say the word. I don't want you tiring yourself out."

Dahlia squeezed his arm. "No, Dad. I'm not tired yet, I prom—"

"Do you need to sit?" Felix's voice rumbled directly into her ear as his hand settled on the small of her back, applying slight pressure.

"I do *not*," she answered, giving all three suddenly very attentive men a withering look. "Alvin said exercise is good, remember? I need to walk."

Felix muttered under his breath, "What does he know?"

"Hush."

Alastair sidled up beside Colin, the silver tip of his cane clicking against the concrete floor strewn with bits of bruised greenery. It was an old war injury, he'd confessed to her one night after dinner with the Bowans. He'd gotten it fighting along the border of what would become the Neutral Zone in the middle of the war, and it was that injury that brought Colin, a field medic, into his life.

The wound itself was long healed, but not even magic could completely erase nerve damage. It was a small price to pay, he told her, for meeting the love of his life.

The family joke was that Alastair didn't know how to acquire loved ones without a little bloodshed.

"Have you decided on a name yet?" Alastair asked.

She peered at him. "For The Lush or for the baby?"

He huffed — the Alastair version of a laugh. "Both. Either."

"We're still working on a name for the bar," Felix answered, guiding her around a table covered in buckets of fragrant rose bouquets. "But I think we've settled on a name for the baby."

She wasn't sure what it said about them as a couple that it was harder to agree on what to rename the bar they'd purchased than their first born child. Cecilia just shook her head when she found out they'd snatched up The Lush.

"I always knew you'd end up running this place," she'd laughed.

Dahlia was ecstatic that her friend had escaped the trenches serving drinks in a bar, but she would be lying if she said she didn't wish Cecilia could manage the bar for her. Too bad the damn woman was out enjoying her life and career, terrifying mate lurking in her shadow like the menace he was.

They were set to visit the couple after their trip to the market, but whether Cecilia's mate would show his face or not was always a toss-up. The man was more akin to a stray cat than anything else. If he wandered in through a window halfway through Cecilia's dinner, she wouldn't have been surprised. They were two perfectly matched weirdos.

"We're thinking something nautical, Papa," she blithely informed him. "You know, in honor of our shared love of boats. We've decided on Atlas."

Alastair choked. Colin, who'd been helping her brainstorm since her first missed period, let loose a bellow of laughter loud enough to draw the eye of several curious vendors. His mirth was so great, his glasses nearly sailed off his nose.

Whirling on Felix, Alastair hissed, "You are *not* naming my grandson after the yacht you sank!"

Felix slung his arm around her shoulders. Pressing his cheek against her hair, he smugly replied, "And here I thought you'd be honored, old man."

Snickering, Dahlia basked in the glow of their levity. Nothing mattered more to her than this. Them. The only thing that might've made it a perfect moment was if Cecilia was there. But she'd already taken a month off to stay in United Washington for the birth, so Dahlia couldn't fault her for needing time to wrap up her work at the school before then.

"I think Atlas Alastair Amauri has a lovely ring to it," she sing-songed.

Felix nodded sagely. "It really does. Very alliterative without being cheesy."

"And so regal. You'd never even know he was named after his grandpa's stupid boat."

"His cousins will make sure everyone knows," Felix assured her. "They're good at keeping each other humble."

Alastair stopped walking. After a few steps, the group came to a slow halt and turned to look at him.

The old man didn't show much emotion on a normal day. He hadn't even seemed worried when they were pinned together with a piece of jagged metal. He wore an aloof mask as much as possible, so it was rare to see more than a twinkle of humor in his eyes or a frown deepening the lines grooved into his face.

But in that moment, surrounded by a sea of vendors and flowers, Alastair looked truly stricken.

"You're naming him Atlas Alastair?"

Humor bleeding into tenderness, Dahlia broke away from Felix to reach for her father's hand. Giving it a squeeze, she said, "I wouldn't have any of this if we hadn't met that night. So yeah, that's what we've decided." A smile tugged at her lips. "And don't worry. Dad has already called dibs on the next one."

Alastair swallowed hard. He looked away quickly, but not before she spied the sheen of tears in his eyes. Clearly trying to regain his composure, he rasped, "I see. Well. That's fine, I suppose."

"Oh, look." Felix came up beside her and pointed to a stall just a few feet away.

Arrayed in baskets on the counter and around it were hundreds of dahlias. They burst from their containers in small floral explosions of reds, pinks, and creams. Each one was its own stunning creation, with every silken petal perfectly layered on top of its neighbor to create spirals of rich color.

Trailing his hand down her back to rest on her hip, Felix drew her into his side. "You know, I think I just thought of a great name for the bar."

Dahlia looked up at him. Whatever physical discomfort she felt was momentarily forgotten when she found him gazing down at her like that — as if she was the only thing in the universe that mattered.

"What is it?" she asked, a little breathless.

Mouth curved in that devastating fanged smile, he answered, "The Crimson Dahlia."

THE END

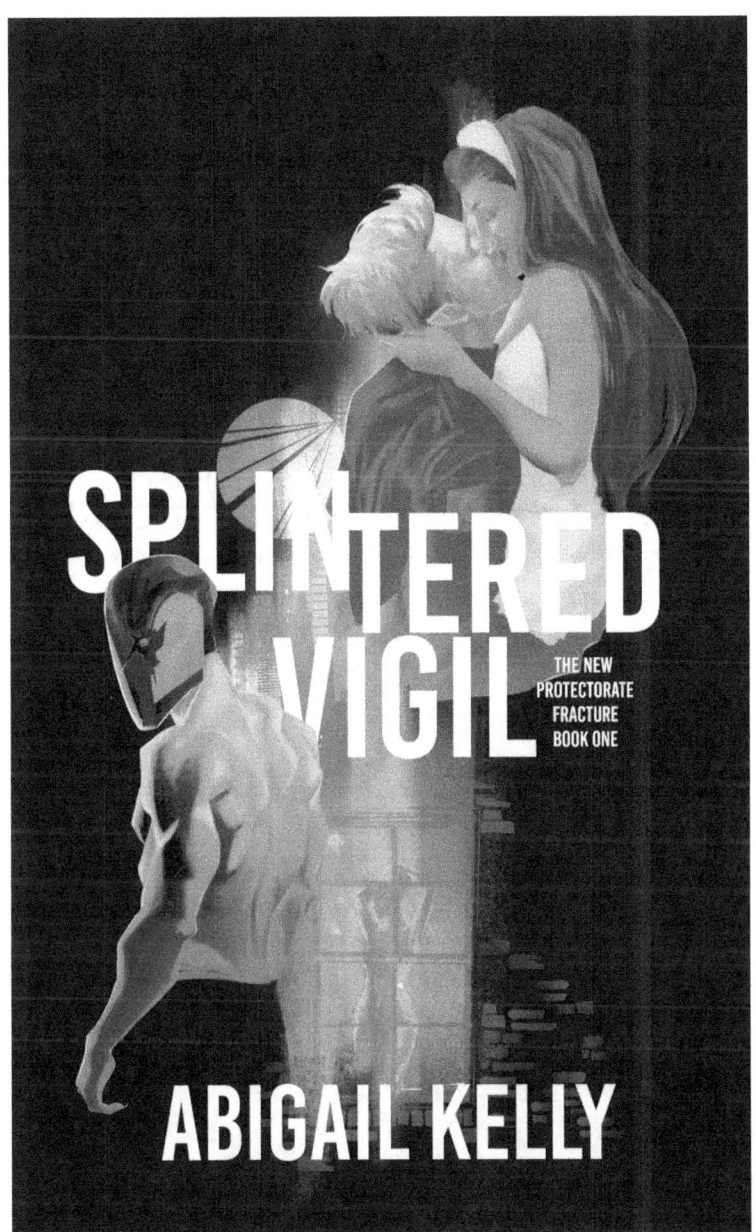

SPLINTERED VIGIL

THE NEW
PROTECTORATE
FRACTURE
BOOK ONE

ABIGAIL KELLY

SPLINTERED VIGIL: THE NEW PROTECTORATE FRACTURE: BOOK ONE

Finders keepers.

Sloane knows he shouldn't watch her. A predator trained from childhood to do what no one else will, his specialties are murder, mayhem, and torture. He's a danger to just about everyone, including the soft human woman he stalks day and night.

Losers get a bolt in the head.

Cecilia Warren is soft, sweet, and blessedly ignorant of the bloodshed he deals in — until the day she's attacked. The plan is to save her, not keep her. But everything goes awry when he finally gets her in his claws. Instincts blur loyalty. Desire makes letting her go impossible.

If they want to take her, they'll have to kill him first.

The mission objective shifts when he goes from protector to captor, secreting her away and going AWOL from the terrifying shadow unit known as Fracture. They have orders to hunt him down and free Cecilia against her wishes. Sloane won't give her up and he won't back down, even if that means destroying himself to protect the only good thing he's ever known.

ABOUT THE AUTHOR

Abigail Kelly is an author-illustrator of alternate histories, love stories, and women with drive. Her work is heavily influenced by both her modest family roots and her passion for history. After nearly a decade as a bookseller at independent bookshops, she still loves putting books in eager hands. Her favorite authors are Shirley Jackson, Yangsze Choo, Ursula K. Le Guin, Kresley Cole, Nalini Singh, and just about anyone who writes about the weird and wonderful. She lives in San Francisco with her dog, Babs, who remains stubbornly illiterate.

GLOSSARY

A full character directory and map can be found at Abigailkkelly.com

PLACES

United Territories and Allies: What we would consider the continental USA. A loose federation of sovereign states established after the Great War. The UTA capital is United Washington, in the Neutral Zone.

The Elvish Protectorate: Also known as the EVP. Stretches from Oregon to New Mexico. Capital city is San Francisco. Led by the elvish sovereign Theodore Thaddeus Solbourne and Margot Goode.

The Coven Collective: Also known as the Collective. Encompasses Washington state. Capital city is Seattle. Led by a large coalition of witch covens, with Sophie Goode acting as their leader.

The Orclind: Encompasses much of the Midwest. Led by the Iron Chain, a close-knit government made up of orcish clans and Queen Sigrid Seagrim. Capital city is Boulder.

Shifter Alliance: Takes up a section of the midwest and all of the south. (Unfortunately includes Florida.) Run by a very, very loose alliance of shifter packs from three capital cities — Minneapolis, Oklahoma City, and Atlanta. Unofficial leader is Lee Seymour.

The Draakonriik: Also known as the 'Riik. The second smallest territory, it takes up all of the Great Lakes region and stretches to New York. Led by Taevas Aždaja, the *Isand* (ee-zand) of the dragon clans. Pronounced: *dra-kon-reek*

The Neutral Zone: Also known as the New Zone. Technically it is held by a coalition government consisting of representatives from the UTA, but in reality it is run by a syndicate of feuding vampire families. It is a small strip of land squeezed between the Draakonriik and the Shifter Alliance.

GODS

Light & Darkness: The primordial gods who created all the others. Also known as The Lovers and First Union. Both are generally represented as female.

Loft: God of the sky and creator of flying beings. Twin sibling to Tempest. They know no gender. Also known as the Boundless One.

Tempest: God of the ocean and creator of all water beings. Also known as the Hungry God and the god of love.

Burden: God of the Earth, creator of all beings who live within it — most notably the orcs. Husband of Glory.

Glory: Goddess of sunlight, magic, and creator of elves. Worshipped by witches for giving the gift of magic to humanity.

Blight: God of forested places and disease. He works in partnership with his daughter Grim and shares her dominion over demons and all reviled creatures.

Grim: Goddess of death. Known as the Merciful One and the Brilliant Lady. She is widely beloved.

Craft: God of change, newness, and messengers. Creator of humanity and viewed warily by non-worshippers as the Chaos Maker. They change their gender frequently, but generally is referred to using he/him pronouns.

TERMS

Alpha: a broad term used by many communities generally associated with a leader — either of a small family group, a pack, or even a territory.

Anchor: a vampire's mate. Anchors are carefully chosen and usually longterm-to-permanent arrangements, as they take considerable energy to make/become. A vampire must inject their venom into a host many times before their blood chemistry adjusts such that they become unsuitable for consumption by another vampire and their sleep cycle switches to a nocturnal pattern. At this point, they can can also produce/carry to term a vampiric child. Temporary anchors do exist, although they are relatively rare due to the intense withdrawal symptoms associated with ending the regular venom intake.

Arrant: someone born without m-paths, or the ability to channel and use magic.

Burnout: the colloquial name for the degenerative medical condition caused by excessive magic in humans. Over time magic can damage nerves and brain tissue, which will inevitably result in death if not treated with with development of a witchbond.

Change: an elvish term for a sudden shift into adulthood. This is marked by 5-14 days of "madness", usually triggered by some stressful event around the age of 16-18. The elvish body is flushed with hormones to the point where sudden growth, over-whelming hunger, and aggression take over. Viewed as an incredibly vulnerable time, only immediate kin are charged with the care of their loved ones — which includes isolating them, preventing harm to themselves/others, and feeding them. The change marks the second phase of an elf's life, when they are no longer coddled children but young adults who can accept chal-lenges and family responsibilities. Formal adulthood is attained at 30.

Changeling: a term first used to refer to fey children fostered out to non-fey homes, now more widely used to mean any person raised by people who are not the same beings. *Ex:* A dragon couple raising a human child.

Chosen: the formal term for a dragon's mate. The act of finding a mate is called *Choosing,* and is considered sacred.

Consort: an elvish mate. A term used exclusively by elves to refer to someone they are biologically compelled to pair up with. This usually involves intense sexual attraction, but can vary from person to person.

Demon: a being with horns or antlers, pointed ears, and symbiotic shadows. They are generally considered to be some of, if not *the* toughest beings in the world, as their shadows can make them almost indestructible. They are also naturally extremely strong and durable. Demon clans tend to be extremely close-knit, partially due to the fact that the world at large is not wholly accepting of them and their mythological connection to the god Blight. Identifying mating features are utter devotion, heightened protectiveness, and the sharing of shadows. This is when a mate is "given" a piece of the demon's symbiotic shadow, which will then live on that person for the rest of their life.

Dragon: a person with a dual form. In their bipedal form, they have claw-tipped wings, horns, and a tail. In their quadrupedal form, they are roughly the size of a standard SUV and can fly at extremely high altitudes for weeks at a time. They come in a variety of extremely saturated colors that shift with the time of day (light to dark). They breathe cold blue fire and can see the Earth's magnetic field. Identifying mating feature is marked change in behavior, including the overwhelming urge to nest.

Elemental: a being created by a spontaneous magical eruption. They often take on the attributes of whatever weather they happen to be born into, *i.e.* a lightning storm might produce a lightning elemental, or a blizzard might make a snow elemental.

Empath: a person with the ability to feel and manipulate the emotions of others.

Elf: someone born with jewel-toned skin, claws, pointed ears, and four fangs. Very secretive and considered apex predators who require a strict hierarchy to function. Average height of 6-7ft. Identifying mating feature is the retraction of claws.

Fever: shifter mating imperative triggered by the "animal's" choosing of a mate. Marked by a perpetual near-shift — elevated body temperature, increased aggression, build-up of magic, and the compulsion to mark. A shifter displays their readiness to find a mate by creating a den.

Fey: a person with nearly vestigial, insect-like wings, small fangs, and claws. Usually live in large groups. Identifying mating feature is bioluminescence.

Foresight: the ability to see multiple possible futures. The average number is between 2-4, with the likelihood mental instability increasing with each subsequent possible future.

Great War: a conflict between the territories of the North American continent that began in 1817 and ended in 1917 with the signing of the Peace Charter, which established the United Territories and Allies of modern times.

Halfling: the elvish term for an elf with mixed heritage.

Healer: a person who possesses the ability to see into and heal bodies through touch.

Isand: the title of the leader of the Draakonriik. Pronounced *ee-zah-nd*

M- : M- is frequently used as shorthand to denote when something is infused or otherwise combined with a magical element.

Marriage Sigil: a custom symbol branded into the foreheads of spouses (pairs or multiples). Each one is unique and infused with a small amount of magic as a reminder of the power love holds. They are typically sought out by worshippers of Glory — mainly witches and arrants. Elves, though worshippers, don't usually take a marriage sigil when they find their consorts or form a unions with other elves.

Mate: a catchall term for a significant other. Used by many cultures, it has varying degrees of weight. To shifters, orcs, and demons, the word mate is synonymous with family, monogamy, and dependence. It is much more loosely used within arrant society, as well as amongst elves, who generally prefer the term *consort*.

Merfolk: a catch-all term referring to sentient beings who live in the ocean, lakes, or rivers. Due to the nature of the ocean and its inhabitants, classifying all beings individually is almost impossible, so a much broader term is used to refer to both mammalian and non-mammalian beings than would be used for those on land.

Met: acronym for *magically enhanced tech.* A branded home assistant that can do everything your Alexa can, as well as small, low-level magic to help around the house.

Metallurgic Inoculation: a vaccine given to all elves within hours of birth to make them immune to iron poisoning.

M-siphon: a containment device used to imprison a magical being and siphon off their magic. Highly illegal.

R-siphon: also known as *reverse siphon.* New technology that redistributes magic away from the siphon instead of into it.

M-lev: a play on *maglev,* meaning a high speed train that levitates using magnets. In this case, magnets *and* magic.

M-weather: magic weather. Very common, but can result in "clusters" or storms that wreak havoc if not properly contained. In rare circumstances, it can also produce a sapient being known as an *elemental.*

Orc: a person with green, gray, russet, or blue skin, two fangs, and claws. Widely renowned for their strength and beautiful voices. Identifying mating feature is "the kohl", or altered, dark pigmentation of the hands and feet developed after meeting their mate.

Pixie: a small, winged creature with compound eyes with about the same level of intelligence as a rat. In the wild they live in trees and in burrows, but have adapted to living in walls, pipes, mailboxes, etc.

Pull: elvish mating imperative. A sudden hormonal shift caused by exposure to a compatible partner's pheromones, marked by the retraction of claws and volatile mood shifts. The pull is only "satisfied" when hormone binding occurs — the term for long term exposure to a mate, resulting in permanent biological dependence on their pheromones. This process increases fertility and often results in the conception of multiples. Lack of exposure to a mate can cause severe physical reactions (lack of appetite, muscle pain, headaches, insomnia) as well as the deterioration of mental stability.

Shifter: a person who can shift into an animal form. They can partially shift (changing only parts of their bodies at will) and often take on characteristics of their other half. Famous for their strength and tenacity, as well as their dual-voiced "shifter purr" which many people find deeply attractive. Usually found in packs.

Sigil: a symbol used to channel magic. Western countries use the alchemical alphabet formally codified in the 1800's, though many, many variations are used all over the world.

Sovereign: the title of the ruler of the Elvish Protectorate. It is capitalized when used in place of a name.

Turbo Virgin (c): Theodore Thaddeus Solbourne, Sovereign of the Elvish Protectorate and Head of the Solbourne Family.

Union: an elvish marriage. Usually done for financial, political, or procreational benefit. The parties involved are not fated or biologically compelled to be with one another, and might have many lovers or even a consort outside of their union.

Vampire: a person who drinks blood to survive and cannot go out in sunlight. Vampirism can only be "caught" with the exchange of fresh blood, and as of 2045 is much more widely spread through procreation. Vampires can only breed with their *anchors.* Identifying mating feature is marked change in behavior, including overwhelming desire and need for total isolation.

Ward: a magical barrier with varying levels of protection. A ward can be something as simple as a proximity alert — "someone walked into my garden" — or as complex as full on defense — "someone crossed the threshold and has now burst into flames". The severity of the ward depends on the complexity of the sigils used to create them, and wards can have many layers, each one with a unique purpose. Personal wards can also be used, such as in clothing or embedded into jewelry, though they tend to be expensive and difficult to foolproof.

Were: a person infected with the were virus, a much mutated strain of the vampirism virus, resulting in altered physiology and magical ability. They can be identified by their heterochromia, or different colored eyes. They are the newest magical race and viewed warily by the general public for a variety of earned and unearned reasons. Identifying mating feature is marked change in behavior, including highly increased territorial instinct and the urge to nest. Pronounced *ware.*

Witch: Humans with the ability to use magic, which is passed down genetically. A person needs to be born with m-paths (a unique nervous system) to use it, however, humans were not initially adapted to use magic safely. Geneticists believe they acquired the ability through interbreeding with other beings. This interbreeding resulted in many unique qualities, such as the massive variety of abilities, power levels, and unique skills known to select families. However, it is also responsible for "burnout", which is the degenerative neurological condition a witch with mid-to-high level power will experience if they do not share their magical load with another being via witchbond. Witches are classified from least to most powerful — brightling, brilliant, and gloriana.

Witchbond: a magical bond formed between a witch and another being. Due to the nature of magic and humanity's much more recent adaptation to it, witches of *brilliant* and *gloriana* power must form a bond with another being usually beginning around 150-200 years old. This bond filters magic through the other being, neutralizing its damaging effects and reducing the chances of burnout to almost none. This bond also gives a power boost to the partner. A witchbond is permanent and can only be severed if one of the partners dies, at which point the surviving partner can form a new bond. Though commonly associated with a romantic partner, a witchbond is not inherently romantic and can be shared with a friend, sibling, or (ill-advised) an enemy.

Wraith: sentient shadow beings not dissimilar to elementals. They can affect the world around them in small ways, but can only speak to a very small number of demons. They lack physical forms but those that fully develop have complete sentience, personalities, and desires.

CONTENT WARNINGS

Stalking, blood, gratuitous violence, organized crime, unstable childhood, vomiting, elements of body horror, tooth-related horror, medical care, hospitals, explicitly described injuries, HIPAA violations, vampirism, murder, guns, imprisonment, pregnancy (epilogue), breeding, and explicit sexual content.

www.ingramcontent.com/pod-product-compliance
Lightning Source LLC
Chambersburg PA
CBHW070850260626
47170CB00007B/2566